SNAKES IN SUITS

Also by Hinemura Ellison & Ted Hughes:

Trinity Trilogy:

Book 1: Sharks with Lipstick

Book 2: Snakes in Suits

Book 3: Scorpions in Stilettos
(forthcoming)

SNAKES IN SUITS

Hinemura Ellison

&

Ted Hughes

BACH DOCTOR PRESS

This first edition 1.0 published in 2019 Bach Doctor Press

ISBN: 978-0-473-49442-1

ISBN 978-0-473-49443-8 Epub

ISBN: 978-0-473-49444-5 Kindle

Cover design by: Michelle Connor, EbookCoversOnline

*Many people spend too much time trying to be the
Captain of someone else's boat.
Learn to be a Lighthouse and the boats will find their way.*

Anonymous

Acknowledgements:

Thank you to our publisher, Darin and the team at Bach Doctor Press, our proofreader Belinda O'Keefe, our book cover designer Michelle Connor and our desk top publisher Mark Innes-Jones

Contents

Prologue

Two men wait impatiently outside the main door of the large three storied pale pink art deco building. Suddenly a large black Mercedes-AMG GT Coupe pulls up next to them. A tall thin man unfolds himself from the driver's seat and emerges, barking at the waiting men, "Well, what are you imbeciles standing there for? Get the doors open, I haven't got all night."

"Yes Sir, Mr Church Sir," the smaller of the two men replies, as he turns quickly and starts manipulating the lock.

The other man in the pinstripe suit and black backpack ventures, "You know, Sir, it would be much easier to wait until you own the place…"

"Shut up, idiot features! Damien, if you did what you were told on that last job instead of second guessing my instructions, we wouldn't be in this current financial mess," the thin man barks.

"Well how was I to know the old lady was going to make a miraculous recovery?" the pinstripe suited Damien replies. "Especially after the amount of Wolfsbane I administered."

"We're in, Boss," the smaller man hisses, as the lock suddenly clicks.

"About bloody time," Mr Church replies. "Well, come on you two, inside and let's have a look around. Thomas, you check the upstairs areas are empty, Damien, wait here with me, I want a word."

"Right Boss," the smaller man replies as he heads upstairs with his torch leading the way.

Once he is out of earshot, the thin man turns, demanding, "Damien, when are you going to learn to take responsibility for your actions?" But before Damien can reply, he barks, "It was a rhetorical question, you idiot. Come on, I want to see the basement."

Halfway down the stairwell, Damien suddenly stops and turns back to face his tormentor. "With all due respect, Mr Church, after diverting those insulation trucks to the Seaview warehouse and securing these explosives for you, I've just about had enough of your insults." Damien stares intensely at his boss, adjusting the heavy backpack before continuing, "I work damn hard for you and you know it!"

Coming to an abrupt stop, Mr Church puts his hand up and grabs an iron pipe above his head to steady his balance. "Just what are you saying, Damien? And be very careful how you reply…"

Chapter 1

Back in Town

Freya hops off the Interislander ferry, freshly back from her three-week stint on Outward Bound, a physically, spiritually and emotionally challenging yet rewarding course in the Pelorus Sounds in the South Island.

With her pack over her shoulder, feeling a huge sense of achievement and at long last direction, she and her overly familiar pack make their way outside the terminal. There waiting for her as usual is her old friend Zac, the ever reliable, trustworthy, honest and dependable Zachary Tyler MacLean-Smith. Zac has been around in Freya's life off and on since forever.

Tall, dark wavy hair with speckles of grey, like her, he is in his forties. Zac and Freya met back in the Bay when they were just kids, hanging out at the local Scout's Hall on Cheviot Road, he the big Cub and Freya the cute Brownie; but then they lost touch as she went away to boarding school at Nga Tawa in Marton and he to King's College up in Auckland. Maybe if he'd gone to a more local school like Whanganui Collegiate in nearby Whanganui their life could have been very different. Freya ended up falling in love with the local Marton vet while breaking bounds most nights (unbeknownst to her pesky set of matrons), but she'd stayed in touch with Zac over the years, as their parents lived in the same street in Lowry Bay.

"Hey Freya, look at you! Wow, don't you look the typical rough and ready backpacker? You would think you and your German friends had just finished backpacking all of the South Island and been freedom camping, escaping the luxury of showers," Zac says teasingly.

"Thanks for your vote of confidence, buddy. I am glad my *au naturel* looks are turning you on. I especially dressed up for you as you can see. I wanted to make a lasting impression as I bounced off the ferry," Freya replies quick-wittedly, posing and flicking her hair from side to side.

To be fair, the entire trip had been a series of physical pursuits from rock climbing, sailing a cutter, running a half marathon to navigating a waka over a series of lakes, and taking the biggest 'hīkoi' of her lifetime – a six-day hardcore walk up and down mountains, valleys and across rivers.

The weather had been poor and at one stage she had been sandwiched between a cyclone and a southerly front. The dress code had to be practical, warm, watertight and durable. Showers, and toilets for that matter, were a luxury, let alone sexy see-through camisoles and skimpy skirts. Besides, it was only Zac and what was the point of having a quick wash on the boat and scrubbing herself up? He was used to seeing her in all conditions.

They jump into his mum's classic red VW Beetle and head out on the motorway towards Eastbourne. Zac and Freya had long left Lowry Bay behind, but they still caught up when visiting their olds in the weekends. However, Freya's parents had recently left, although they still always managed to synch their visits with each other.

Tearing along the motorway, Zac strikes up his usual conversation – mainly questions. "So how did it go, Freya? What exciting stories have you got to share? Did you break any instructors' hearts? Did you fall for any of those cute Māori instructors?"

"Not a chance, Zac. No time for love; it was all about survival, kicking arse, trying to get as much sleep at night as possible, nursing my poor blistered feet and not wanting to let my team down by lagging at the back. You know how it is. Well, you did when you used to play little soldiers up at Linton and out at Trentham."

"Yeah, Freya, that was five lifetimes ago. I don't still have that burning urge to push myself to the max anymore – only you do that."

Freya interrupts, "Don't kill a girl for trying. It's not my fault I want to be fit and out there, better than sitting around like a couch potato, like your ex-missus."

"Ouch!!! Where did that come from? Did I deserve that? Here I am on a Tuesday morning fighting through rush hour traffic to come into town to pick you up on this blustery, windy Wellington day and this is the thanks I get? Anyhow, since when has my ex come into this?" Zac responds defensively.

Freya suddenly feels rather sheepish, wondering herself where that backhander came from. After all, it's not as if she and Zac are dating. She jumps in and apologises to Zac profusely. "Oh my god Zac, I am so, so sorry, I have no idea where that runaway comment came from. That was well out of order. I can't apologise enough. Hell, can I make it up to you? Look, pull over to the Chocolate Fish café and let me shout you a coffee and a big sugary chocolate cake, your favourite. In fact, anything you want to order. I owe you big time. Sorry."

"I should think so, Freya Isobel Nilson. However, I will forgive you because I know how sleep deprived you must be. I do remember that part of our 'little soldier' weekends away in the hills," he says with a touch of sarcasm. "By the time you were on watch and exercising most of the day, there was little or no time to sleep. I think that was part of the exercise, to push you to the limit, break you down then build you up again the way they wanted you to be. However, a free coffee from my favourite Bionic Woman, now that's an offer I can't refuse." A BMW four-wheel drive with a Yummy Mummy from the Bay pulls out, leaving the Beetle a perfect parking space right outside.

"There you go, no more walking for you today, Fin," he says, calling her by her childhood nickname. Then he jumps out and like a true gentleman swings open the rusty old door onto the pavement. "Madam, this way," he announces, as he guides her through the front door of the busy little café.

Much to Zac's amusement, Freya dives into the choice of cakes. She obviously hasn't had any treats for the last three weeks and goes hammer and tongs at a slice of passionfruit cheesecake followed by Louise cake and a large flat white. They talk and catch up, and as Zac notices Freya's energy levels starting to slip again, even after the huge sugar fix, he realises it is best to get her home to his mum's for a shower and a good night's sleep.

Freya's parents have recently sold their lovely Lowry Bay home and gone overseas to do their OE. Rather late in life, but all the same, they quite suddenly upped sticks and headed for Scandinavia. Freya's architect father Nils had recently been to a co-house hui and had found out that Denmark was the best place to learn more.

He had grand ideas of starting his own co-house community but wanted to see for himself how the Danes had successfully done this. His wife Sarah, Freya's mum, was always up for a challenge, especially if it involved travel. With Freya being their only child and now highly independent, why not? The real estate market had been booming and they got an offer on the house they simply couldn't refuse.

With all of their worldly goods, including Freya's, now in storage in the Waitarere Beach bach, Freya had no base any longer and no excuse to visit the Bay. Most of her friends, except Zac, had moved on.

However, Freya's godmother Zita, who happened to be Zac's mum and good friends with Sarah and Nils, had a soft spot for her god-daughter and always kept in touch. She was like a second mother and insisted on Freya calling in at least once a month when she was in town, to let her know what she was up to.

Those visits had paid off with Zita extending the invitation to her to come and stay and share her tales of the adventurous Outward Bound escapades.

Zac pulls into the side road just off the Marine Drive into the cute little cul-de-sac where his parents have lived forever, noting Freya's half-closed eyes. He drives the Beetle down the tree-lined driveway past the swimming pool and comes to a standstill. "Okay Sleeping Beauty, we're home."

Zita, hearing the Beetle roar up the driveway, comes running out. The distinctive engine sound was always a bit of a giveaway when sneaking home late at night. The Beetle being the spare family car as Zita would never part with her.

"Fin, look at you,' she says, giving the girl a huge hug and kiss on each cheek. "You look like you need a good week's sleep and you're so thin, did they not feed you on that course? Come in, come in. Zac, be a darling and take her bag for her. Come in and tell us everything." She glances at her again and changes her mind. "No, you pop into your room and have a nap. We'll have plenty of time to hear some tales later."

Without arguing for a change, Freya lets herself into her room. "Oh my god, a real bed, real walls, a roof… oh this is heaven. Night Zita," she murmurs, and within seconds she is asleep.

*****

"Chute, come over here, man," the heavy-set navy blue suited man calls out, a billowing cloud of cigar smoke escaping from his mouth.

The black suited Judge Chute with a tightly folded copy of the *Capital News* tucked tightly under his arm changes direction, answering, "Good god, it's you Prendergast, underneath that cloud of noxious fumes."

Prendergast takes a sip from his crystal cognac glass before replying, "Good fellow, now tell this whippersnapper the real reason for the 'Earthquake Strengthening Act' that we supported. Sorry, where are my manners; Chute, this is Church, Donald Church. Church – Chute."

Church stands as he takes the proffered hand. "Pleased to meet you, Your Honour."

"We are not in a courtroom, Church; Sir will do." Turning to Prendergast, Chute remarks, "Still disobeying the doctor's orders, are we?"

"That quack wouldn't know his arse from his backside," Prendergast splutters. "Besides, I didn't call you over for a medical consultation; please enlighten my new client."

Pouring himself a generous measure of cognac, Chute takes a seat, eyeing up the younger tall man. He takes note of the well-tailored expensive grey suit before explaining, "Well, if you are going to utilise Prendergast's services, you should know that although he charges like a wounded bull, if you are in my courtroom, he will get the correct result."

"I'll bear that in mind, Sir," replies Church.

Chute turns to Prendergast. "We need to talk about the Wakefield result after this."

"Yes, yes, Chute, that special piece of artwork is being prepared for transportation to your residence as we speak. I would anticipate delivery tomorrow, old chap."

"Good, good." Leaning back in the leather armchair, Chute takes a sip of the cognac. "Hmm, you ordered the Paul Giraud, I see." Taking another sip, he continues looking at Church. "Now a developer like yourself, yes I know who you are, Church, your reputation precedes you." Turning again to Prendergast he adds, "We will talk after this."

"Please go on, Sir," Church offers.

"Now the practical applications of the 'Earthquake

Strengthening Act' is that in the fine print – the subsection escapes me, but Prendergast knows it well – it states that heritage buildings are not immune," Chute takes another sip, "and that if the cost of earthquake strengthening exceeds fifty-one per cent of the value of the building…"

Prendergast interrupts, "… then you can take your wrecking ball to it and build one of your new high-rise apartments!"

Church sits back in his chair. "I thought there was a loophole somewhere, damn that is fantastic information, thank you gentlemen." He shakes his head in wonderment. "Who knew it would be this easy; I have a property ripe for this type of development."

"Now we never met, Church, or awkward questions could be raised. Now I think it's best you run along," Chute says, dismissing Church.

Prendergast stands. "Chute here is correct, Church, we had best meet in future elsewhere, away from the Club."

Church stands and walks off, passing another table of suited men drinking tea and reading newspapers, feeling humiliated. *Those toffee-nosed wankers don't know who they are dealing with,* he thinks to himself, vowing to get them one day. But for now, he plans to use them to his advantage.

Waiting until Church is well out of earshot, Chute turns to Prendergast. "Damn it man, he is one dangerous criminal, what are you doing taking him on as a client?"

"He's just a property developer, Chute. He has money to spend, why not spend it on my excellent legal services? Besides, Brenda is wanting another six months on the yacht in the Caribbean."

"I don't know why you married that gold-digger,

Prendergast," Chute remarks. "Thirty years younger than you, she is not from one of the first ships – no breeding or class."

"Watch it, Chute," Prendergast warns. "I'm just trying to set my later years up for a life of ease."

Chute chuckles, raising his glass. "Living a dangerous life more like it. Well good luck to you, my friend."

*****

"Smyth, don't make it obvious but look at who Judge Chute is talking with at the moment," Tombe quietly whispers to his colleague.

"That damn crook Prendergast," spits Smyth. "But I'm not sure who the tall, thin, grey suited gentleman is."

"Me neither. Certainly not at this angle, but if we end up in the same courtroom as those three, we know Prendergast will have Judge Chute's ear," Tombe comments.

"And we will have one hell of a battle for our client," Smyth finishes.

As Smyth pours them both another cup of tea, he comments, "Probably some property deal, as his firm has a long history of dubious land transactions."

"Hmm, one interesting mix is 'Russell, Whitaker and Prendergast', definitely the old school tie brigade," Tombe adds before asking, "Tell me Smyth, you being the history buff of our firm, what is their background?"

"Well, old man Prendergast, that one's great-grandfather, was the infamous Judge Prendergast of the 1870s who presided over Wi Parata v the Bishop of Wellington. He called the Treaty of Waitangi 'worthless' and a 'simple nullity' as it was signed by a group of savages who were not capable of understanding what they had signed," Smyth answers. "Racism and the belief of English superiority was very common back then and was often used to take Māori land illegally."

"Well not much has changed really, has it? Especially after the land grab for the Kāpiti Expressway," Tombe replies. "What about Russell and Whitaker?"

"Wealthy Auckland-based families, again back in the 1800s heavily involved in land acquisition from Māori and sales to settlers, as we both know, very dubious transactions back then," Smyth continues. "From memory, their actions in the Bay of Plenty may have had something to do with the Battle of Gate Pā. They made their fortunes and their families have remained in the upper strata of society ever since."

"And their offspring continue the family tradition, I suspect," Tombe muses. "Perhaps I'm being unfair, but 'forewarned is forearmed' as they say."

Chapter 2

Wake up Sleeping Beauty

Freya eventually wakes up, and unsure of what time it is, climbs out of bed and draws the curtains. As she looks out at the gorgeous garden, she realises this is what she wants – a real place, a real garden, a real bed. She's sick of the constant couch surfing, crashing here and there.

She recalls the last three weeks; what a mind bend. She looks into the mirror and hardly recognises herself. Her mind flashes through all the physical and mental challenges she has just gone through and wonders how life can be the same.

She stares intently into the mirror. "Who am I?" she says aloud to her reflection, and starts singing the old song her parents used to sing: "What's it all about, Alfie?" Zita hears her singing and knocks on the door.

Freya opens the door and they both smile at each other. "Well, little Miss Sleepyhead, nearly twenty four hours later! Why do I think life has suddenly changed for you? I have a feeling we have a lot of talking to do, young lady. Are you ready? How about having a shower? Wash off all that weariness of the last three weeks of exploring the South Island and when you're freshened up come into the kitchen. I'll have an extra strong coffee and some of your favourite goodies for you." Zita leaves Freya to get ready.

"Where's Zac?" Freya asks when she meanders into the kitchen.

"He's gone. He had to get back up to Auckland where his work has him most of the time now," Zita explains. "I do miss him, but it's good to have you back in town after all your travels."

"Oh, I feel so bad," Freya exclaims. "I wasn't exactly very nice to him yesterday. I wish I could have seen him again."

"Now never you mind, young Freya. You know what you two are like. I am sure he is used to you egging him on. You know Zac is as strong as nails, he won't have taken anything you said personally."

All the same, Freya feels bad with the way she treated him. Zac has always been there for her, but she just seems to take him for granted. She just hasn't known life without him and with her new insights from her course, maybe she needs to show that appreciation a bit more.

Freya thinks about how sometimes people should be careful what they focus on and ask for, as the universe has a way of delivering not necessarily what you want, but always what you need to learn to grow from.

"So, my girl, what have you been up to in Te Waipounamu since I last saw you a whole *three* weeks ago? You look different. Spill, my *alskling,* what's been happening?" Zita's fondness of her goddaughter is plain to see; Freya is the daughter she never had. She adores her two boys, Zac and Rufus, but she has always wondered what it would have been like if she and Marty had had a girl. Zita had gone to Chilton St James, the local girls' boarding school with Freya's mum, Sarah, and they had become the best of chums.

They had married and stayed in the neighbourhood and both had their kids at the same time. They sent them to private schools and had doted on them when they were home for the holidays, taking them down to the beach for swims, teaching them to row out on the harbour. They had gone to all their celebrations, twenty-firsts, engagements and weddings – well, Zac and Rufus's weddings. Freya, however, was a dark horse; she had never settled down, too much of a free spirit.

"Now Fin, where do you want to begin?" Zita asks, passing her a large plunger coffee. She puts muesli and toast on the table for breakfast, as well as an inviting piece of homemade carrot cake.

"Auntie Zita, there's too much to say, but in a nutshell, I am so glad I did it. At times it was my worst nightmare getting up early every morning and wearing the same old clothes, getting lost in the bush, trying to learn Te Reo so quickly – that language is very different – plus sleeping on the ground or on those hard marae floors, but man was it worth it. I wouldn't change it for the world."

"You and early mornings – that would be a shock for you, you can't get to the train in Levin for 6.45am let alone get up at five most mornings! Why you stay at that old bach in Waitarere Beach, I don't know. Zac was telling me you were up running at five o'clock or some ungodly hour, and that's when you weren't on watch. How did you do it?"

"Well, like anything new it was really hard at first, but you kinda get into the groove. Also, one of the instructors was pretty easy on the eye so that gave me an incentive to get up. Mind you, not half embarrassing, having a cutie pie staring at you when you look like some washed-up hippie appearing out of an old kombi van each morning, with a sore back and walking weird, wearing the same smelly clothes to bed as you did during the day. You don't half stink while you're in the bush."

"What was the highlight, what did you really learn about yourself?" asks Zita.

"Well, I've realised I'm made of stronger things than I thought. I do have a lot of stamina and I just realised how goddamned determined I am, I don't give up easily. In fact, I had all this energy and get-up and go I didn't know I had. And as I was the oldest on the course, it felt kinda good when I kept up with the rest of the group."

"Tell me something I didn't know! Just when did you *not* have a fierce, determined streak in you, Fin? You have always been that way." Zita laughs, but then turns serious. "You are very fortunate you have this amazing inner strength and resilience – now don't you forget that, especially when things get tough – give yourself a break, you are stronger than you believe."

"Yes, you're right. I guess what I'm saying is I under-rated myself. I guess I was too busy listening to all those creepy old schoolmasters and matrons and some pathetic bosses, thinking as they were older they must be wiser and therefore their words were gospel. You know the type of reports or appraisals you get, the standard ones: 'Freya would do better if she applied herself more. I wonder if she does have that latent potential that most students have. I still don't see any …'"

"Come on Fin, you are far too much of a free spirit to have taken all that nonsense seriously, surely?" Zita probes.

"Well, Zita, a few things happened while I was away which I won't go into now, but it really made me reassess my life, my values, my upbringing and worldview. I mean look at Mum and Dad suddenly upping sticks and taking off on their OE, back to Scandi of all places.

"They swore they would never go back there after everything that happened. It made me look at the Te Ao Māori world differently too. Well to be honest I am a beginner with this Māori learning, but man my mind is buzzing – I just realise that the sky is the limit. I have so many ideas running through my head, I don't know where to start."

Zita questions her goddaughter further. "Okay, what's different this time, Freya?"

"This time I am going to follow through. I want to change my life; I am sick of plodding along doing the right thing to please everyone. This time I am going to dance to my own tune. I want to explore my whakapapa more, on the Māori side, on Mum's side. This trip on Outward Bound meant following in the footsteps of our ancestors, our tupuna; it was incredible. The stuff they went through, they were strong people, a bit like Dad's Viking side of the family. But I want to find out who my ancestors were, what motivated them, what drove them? As well as all my plans for Portobello."

"Wow, you *are* all revved up. So, where do you start?" Zita asks.

"Well, first of all I need to see the lawyer and find out

if they've sorted out granddad's estate yet. Then, I've got some ideas that I may need to see the bank about, which will hopefully open up a whole lot of other ideas I've had. I had a lot of time to think while we were on those bush hikes!"

"That sounds really exciting, Fin! Bloody lawyers, banks, probate, it's time consuming and money wasting, it's a pity your grandfather's estate hasn't been all sorted yet. That would have helped you nicely, getting your feet on the ground. You two were such peas in a pod, I know he would've been so proud of you Freya, of what you've achieved so far and where you're heading."

*****

"Oh, this is lovely Martin," Clara exclaims while taking in one of the most expensive restaurants on the Wellington waterfront.

"I'm so sorry Clara, but I've just seen a colleague who shouldn't see us together," Martin cuts in, quickly adding, "come on, I'll make it up to you."

"Who is it?" Clara asks.

"Prendergast, a complete incompetent, in the navy-blue suit, not sure who he's with, but let's find somewhere else," Martin replies.

Clara takes in both men at the table as they head off in the opposite direction.

*****

"A dozen oysters, with the apple and cucumber mingnet thanks." The tall, grey suited man bungles the French pronunciation.

"That's *'mignonette'*, my dear fellow," corrects the navy-blue suited man in impeccable French. He turns to the waiter and says, "I'll have the same please, *garçon*," adding, "and can we get a bottle of Bollinger La Grande Année on ice please?"

"Certainly Sir," replies the young waiter as he scribbles in his order pad, "it will only be a few minutes." He turns and walks towards the bar, muttering to the maître d', "He called me *garçon* again, what a tosser."

"Ah, a much more suitable place for a discussion, Church," Prendergast comments. "You will be able to see your next project on the Petone skyline before you know it."

"Well that's what I pay you for, Prendergast," Church replies. "But you are right, we will be able to see it from here this time next year, I just need the title to come through as soon as possible. Now what's the hold up?"

"It seems, my dear chap, that the old bugger Wolfe has left the building to his granddaughter, with a rather large mortgage over the property," Prendergast says. "So, a cheeky offer direct to the granddaughter might be in order."

"What about the bank?" Church asks. "Could we get them to foreclose on the outstanding mortgage, and I could then pick it up for a song in the tender process?"

"Well, you could if you knew the bank executives," Prendergast replies, as two black suited men approach the table. "Ah, here they are now, let me introduce you to Mr Rudd and Mr Howard…

Chapter 3

First the Lawyer, Then the Cute Banker

Freya tidies herself up, throwing on her most conservative outfit she owns, reserved just for funerals and interviews – her black suit, white shirt and black high heels all proudly purchased from one of her favourite charity shops, Nurse Maude in Christchurch. She decides to take the bus into Wellington and meets with her grandfather's lawyer, Mr Tombe.

Freya was Wolfe's favourite; her parents believed it was because they were likeminded, both free spirits and very artistic and creative, always coming up with hare-brained ideas. Even when Freya was a child they would sit around the kitchen table designing all sorts of wild and wonderful creations. Naturally it came as a huge shock when one night recently her grandfather passed away, sitting slouched at the table with his ruler and pencil, designing yet another grand house, his passion.

Freya had thrown herself into Outward Bound on the rebound, as she wanted to get away and make sense of his death and the aftermath. Wolfe dying was a major life turning point for her and she decided something physical and mental was exactly what the doctor had ordered.

Freya thinks back to the awkward family meeting just over a month ago, where the lawyer revealed her grandfather's will.

The family were all seated in the Smith, Smyth and Tombe executive offices on Lambton Quay in Wellington, all ready to hear what Wolfe had left them. Wolfe and his wife Lois had next to nothing.

However, Wolfe had built and owned several of the hundreds of grand designs in his fifty years of architecture, with only one Art Deco block of apartments and offices in the main street of Petone remaining. Both very stylish in their day and still in vogue with the classical architecture coming back into fashion.

Mr Tombe hurriedly scuttled into the mahogany-clad office to greet the family. "Good afternoon everyone, I apologise for my tardiness but I needed to collect all the relevant information for our meeting and didn't want to leave any stone unturned.

"Firstly, I must give my condolences for your sad loss. Wolfe's passing was greatly unexpected, wasn't it?" He paused for a minute and then continued. "He was definitely a fine man and it was always a pleasure dealing with such a gentleman; he was definitely one of a kind, a true gentleman through and through. I don't think they make men of that calibre anymore."

The family made pleasantries and then Mr Tombe finally addressed the reason for the meeting. What did the old man have, and who got what, if anything?

To break the ice, Nils, Freya's father said, "Mr Tombe, thank you for your kind words, but could we get on with the contents of my father's will?"

"Yes of course, Sir", he replied, tearing open the documents with an old-fashioned silver letter opener. There was complete silence as he read the contents out and then reached the important part: "There is only one beneficiary. Freya Isobel Nilson."

There were gasps of shock in the room. "Can I ask the rest of you to leave the room, unless you would like anyone to support you, Freya?" continued the lawyer, looking at Freya's father.

"D-d-dad," Freya stuttered.

Freya and her father learned that the only main asset Wolfe still had to his name was Portobello, the block of Art Deco apartments in Jackson Street, Petone. She was in shock, and thought back to a conversation with Wolfe a few years ago after Lois died, when he joked about leaving his worldly goods to her. *'Freya, you are the only one who really understands me, you know we are like two peas in a pod, we are one of a kind. I want you to have Portobello. I trust your judgement, your intuition; you know how important the building is to me. I know you will not sell it to make a quick buck like the rest of the family.'*

That was almost a month ago, and Freya now is back in the same room and reflects on how much has happened since then, with her parents now overseas, and Outward Bound behind her.

Shaking her hand enthusiastically, Mr Tombe greets her. "Well Miss Nilson, it is so good to see you back from your adventures in one piece. Please come through as we have a few things to discuss."

Taking a seat in front of the large mahogany desk again, Freya asks, "Have you discovered anything else, Mr Tombe?"

"Well, it would appear that Wolfe had taken a mortgage out on Portobello and that the bank is wanting to foreclose on the property, sooner rather than later," Mr Tombe responds.

Freya, shocked, asks, "What do you mean a mortgage? There can't be. It's the only building my grandfather had left and he's had it for ages, so there's no way there would be a mortgage, would there?"

"Well, the facts are this Freya. Your grandfather left a mortgage behind on the Jackson Street property. It is quite significant, especially for someone like yourself who has no other income. That is unless you have suddenly won Lotto, or found yourself a significant other who can help you out, or perhaps you have landed yourself a full-time permanent job? From the bank's point of view, if you can't settle the debt, they want to foreclose and sell the property," Mr Tombe explains. "I have contacted the bank's head office and they are intractable – they were very rude. However, I have set up a meeting for you with Simon Brown, Wolfe's old bank manager. He's about your age and is sympathetic to your situation; there may be a way for you to continue to hold onto the property if you co-operate with the bank. Please keep me informed of your meeting's outcome, so I can file the deed settlement with the Land Transfers Office, as I will act on your instructions, *not* the bank's."

Mr Tombe hadn't messed with his words, giving her a full and frank update in one fell swoop. Freya leaves the office in a state of shock, like a stunned mullet. There is a lot to take in and process.

*****

The large man in the pinstripe suit paces back and forth, muttering to himself, "Damn agents, never on bloody time."

Looking at the corner site containing an old Art Deco building, he mentally calculates the site's square footage. Frustrated, he crosses the road and paces out the building's street frontage, stopping to write the figure in a tatty old notebook. Then he rounds the corner and paces the side street frontage, stopping again to note the other figure. Doing the math, he mutters to himself again, "Hmm, not bad, only a little out, I didn't see just how far back this rear yard area goes."

A tacky sign-written Real Estate car pulls up beside the pinstripe suited man and the electric window rolls down. "Mr Damien Bradshaw?"

"Yes," he answers.

"Please hop in, that particular building is not yet for sale," the Real Estate agent replies.

Opening the passenger's door, Damien gets in. "I suspect it will be on the market soon enough," he remarks, as he pushes the button to close the window. "Now what would happen…"

A brown suited man carrying a battered brown briefcase walks past the car before it takes off down Jackson Street, comments to his colleague, "Penny, that's Wolfe Nilson's place, wouldn't we at the bank know if it was on the market? Mr Tombe, the lawyer did leave me a message, remind me to check it when I get to the office."

Ignoring her boss's comments, Penny replies, "What I've been trying to ask Mr Brown, is can I have maternity leave, as I've just found out I'm pregnant."

"Congratulations Penny…" Simon replies now distracted and he completely forgets to check his messages.

*****

With hope in her heart, Freya finds herself back in Petone, in the bank manager's office, seated across from Simon Brown.

Simon is a conservative yet charming man, completely grey, with a complexion to match from clearly spending too much time within the vaulted walls of the bank. He is the Branch Manager of the local Post Office Bank, having started off as a bank teller in the days of the New Zealand Post Office and working his way up through the ranks and all the bank's mergers.

Simon has been a loyal and faithful employee for the last twenty-five years, a rare commodity in today's corporate world, priding himself on being a valuable member of the local Petone community.

Freya's grandfather Wolfe was with the Post Office Bank and dealt with them for all his architectural business matters, as well as his personal affairs.

Simon greets her hesitantly, startled by her stunning looks. Her remarkable poise and presence has quite an effect on him as he tries to regain his composure and introduce himself. "Thank you so much for coming in to see me, Freya. Please call me Simon. How are you?" he enquires.

"I feel really good, thanks, as I've just returned from

three weeks in the South Island doing Outward Bound. It was a major challenge, I feel great, but I am a bit physically and mentally drained, not to mention sleep deprived. I'm looking forward to starting my new life and jumping into my new project, getting Portobello shipshape."

"Well, ah yes, that's what I wanted to see you about. There are a few hurdles to jump before you can take possession of the property," Simon says reluctantly, and a little too nervously.

"It's like this, Freya. Your grandfather left a large mortgage behind on the Jackson property. I'm being instructed by head office to sell the property." Feeling somewhat heartless at Freya's crestfallen face, Simon decides to change tack. "However, if we can find some way that you can service the mortgage, perhaps I could sign ownership over to you?" He searches her eyes, hoping for some good news that would make this relatively large obstacle go away.

"Mr Brown, I mean Simon, how long have I got to come up with a solution? I have some ideas." Freya, being used to challenges and using her newfound self-confidence, decides there and then that she will eat humble pie and ask her previous boss if the Senior Advisor role is still up for grabs.

The job didn't exactly light her fire, but the money did. She decides she can sell her soul for a bit longer and sit in on those long, tedious meetings if it means keeping her grandfather's property. "If I come up with a high paying job, how much would I need to service the mortgage?"

Taking a real shine to this feisty young woman, Simon eagerly replies, "Well, let me see… if I gave you an interest-only mortgage and your job covers those payments, and you come up with a business plan for the property that can be bringing in money within a couple of weeks to start repayments off the principle, then we might just have a deal, young lady."

"Wow, that's a big ask, but I'll do just about anything to pay off that mortgage. Anything to get the building and honour my grandfather's wishes to bring the old lady back to life again," Freya responds, pulling out her phone. "Do you mind if I make a call?"

Freya remembers the last conversation she had with Dimitri, the head of the project she was working on up at Education House. She'd said to him, "I would rather walk on burning coals than return here, Dimitri. No offence, the people are great, but I will be collecting my pension by the time we make traction with the government on this initiative." She hopes she won't regret this now.

She finds his number in her contacts that she fortunately hasn't had time to delete and puts a call through to him, half hoping he won't answer and the other half hoping he does. The phone rings and finally goes to answer phone, she reluctantly leaves a message. "Hey Dimitri, how are you? You must be in one of those extremely important mid-week meetings that never end… Anyhow, guess who this is? I bet you thought you would never hear from me again. It's Freya, I'm just back from my wonderful three weeks on Outward Bound, and I'm all raring to go, I've missed you, the team…" She pauses and can't believe she has just said the last sentence. Where on earth did that come from?

She composes herself and tries to sound a bit more genuine. "Look, I have some ideas about the project going forward, please give me a buzz. I look forward to your call, Dimitri. Have a nice day." She hangs up and feels like throwing up, not sure if it's from nerves or from the thought of going back to a place she thought she would never ever have to return to. *Well, like James Bond used to say, never say never.* Just then her phone rings – the caller display reads 'Drama Queen Dimitri'.

"Hey Dimitri, thanks so much for getting back to me. I know you're not big on small talk so I'll get to the heart of the matter. Did you listen to my message? No… well how would you like me back on your team again? Creating magic… Is that Senior Advisor role still going? Okay, but I want a pay rise, how about… Fantastic, when do you want me to start?" Thinking this is going really well, Freya switches to speaker phone so Simon can hear the conversation.

"Freya, I thought I would never hear back from you. What's with the change of heart? You know coming in from Foxton every day and all your dramas with your transport issues just won't cut it this time around. I do need someone who is local and someone I can rely on. We've got to a crucial stage and I need someone to be able to work around the clock, be on call, and the deadline means it would only be for the next three to six months."

Freya can't believe her luck, that is exactly what she wants. She knows Simon is listening in and all he is concerned about is how much can she make to cover the loan. "Well, Dimitri, it sounds great. You know me, I burn the candle at both ends – long hours are not an issue for me. Location isn't either," she says, wondering how she is going to suddenly relocate herself back to Wellington, especially now the rents have gone sky high and her parents have sold the family home.

She thinks on her feet. She can move into Zita's spare

room. That bunker of hers is just sitting there empty since Zac left home and is now just a sewing room. She can use it while she waits for Portobello to become available and stay there for a while. She's sure her godmother won't mind. Taking a punt, she says, "Yep, location, hours sorted, so just one thing left to sort. The money! For doing these sorts of anti-social hours, and over time, what are we looking at? Or would you like me to wave some figures around and see what we come up with?"

She doesn't need to do much waving or negotiating, and by the end of the phone call they have settled on a win-win contract, for all parties with a starting date of tomorrow.

The conversation puts a smile on Simon's dial; Freya and Simon shake hands and she leaves the bank.

*****

Outside the Post Office Bank, Freya walks off in a bit of a daze down Jackson Street, nearly dropping her phone as she texts her besties Sven and Clara: 'I'm back and wow so much has happened already, we just have to get together tomorrow for a celebratory coffee, at morning tea break – that's right, I'm back working. Sven, text us the details of that groovy new café and it's my shout! Xx'.

Looking up from her phone, Freya sees the pale pink exterior of her grandfather's building. *Well Wolfe, we just might pull this one off yet,* she thinks to herself.

As she walks purposefully towards Portobello, Freya sees a familiar face seated across the road at a footpath café table.

"Leo!" Freya calls excitedly as she rushes forward to

give the elegantly dressed gentleman a massive hug. "It's so good to see you!"

"My dear, you have quite taken me by surprise. Freya darling, it is very good to see you. Have you quite finished with all that physical nonsense, bounding about or whatever it was?" Leo enquires as he straightens his jacket pocket kerchief and resumes his seat.

"I sure have, Leo," replies Freya as she takes a seat. "I learnt a lot about myself, but now it's time for the next adventure."

"Well, let's have a coffee and take a look at your palm while we wait," Leo says as he leans back and calls through to the café, "Another soy latte and a flat white here for my charming companion please, Shelley."

Leaning across the table, Leo takes Freya's left hand and looking intently, starts deciphering the lines. "Hmm, yes, and now the right hand please. Yes, yes, of course, hmm."

"Leo, you old rogue, unhand that delightfully striking maiden," a conservatively dressed older attractive woman calls as she approaches the table.

Leo's face lights up. "Why, it's Evelyn, my fellow traveller of the mystic paths!" Leo stands up formally. "Please take a seat and join us, darling."

"Don't you 'darling' me, you old scoundrel," Evelyn growls good-naturedly as she takes the offered chair. "What fanciful tales are you spinning this poor wee thing?"

Freya laughs out loud as the jesting continues between them. "You two are such a hoot!"

After introductions are made, coffees arrive and the conversation continues. Freya looks across the road at Portobello and its pale pink exterior with blue trimmings around the wooden joinery and can't help thinking it resembles a large French ice cream gateau, white with blue and pink icing.

Portobello, as it was originally named, had been one of Wolfe's first commissions for himself back in the day, and she was gorgeous, a true honey. She was three-storeyed with elegant bay windows and balconies on two sides of the building; one with views to die for of the ocean and Wellington Harbour, and the other side looking out over an adorable overgrown orchard and tree-lined public park.

All his buildings were designed for all-day sun and nearly all the rooms were bathed in sunshine. As a result, the building was permanently like a hot house – so hot they needed to have the French doors out onto the two balconies open for fresh air most days.

Freya, sipping her coffee and listening to the interplay between Leo and Evelyn, a couple of old friends that Wolfe had introduced her to, then pulls out her diary and starts making a 'to-do list'. It's Wednesday, only halfway through the week and she's only been back two days. She wonders where the rest of the week is going to lead her.

*****

"Mission accomplished Mr Church," Damien advises over the phone, "I'm texting a photo of the report to you now."

"Excellent work Damien, so the price was right?" Donald asks.

"The cheeky bugger asked for more, but soon shut up when I showed him a photo of his daughter at school," Damien replies.

"Good, we should have this property deal wrapped up in a couple of days, now how are you going with that insulation scam…"

Chapter 4

Back at Ed House

It hadn't taken much persuasion with Aunt Zita to let Freya move in for a short while. Zita was delighted, now that Zac and Rufus had flown the nest, she was only too happy to have her favourite niece back with her. There was never a dull moment with having Freya around and something had significantly changed about her. Zita was keen to see which new direction her goddaughter's life was bolting off into.

Zita had dashed around making the bunker look homely and filled it up with snacks and goodies, that way Freya could feel self-contained without having to traipse into the house every second her stomach suffered from hunger pains.

With Freya living in Zac's old room, Zita privately thought that maybe this would be the time they got together; she had always secretly wanted the two great childhood friends to unite. She'd been so disappointed when Zac had gone off and married his first ever girlfriend after leaving King's College in Auckland, and what a disaster that had been! And Freya had got distracted with the vet from the rural town of Marton while still at school. Zita just needed an excuse to get Zac back down from Auckland, and decided to start preparing Rufus's old room just in case her son needed it.

*****

Thursday morning at 7am on the dot, Freya has clocked in and is sitting at her old desk in Education House. She has found her old lanyard, and is surprised to discover the password on her laptop still works.

At 7.30am Dimitri walks in, coffee cup in hand, and does a double take as he sees what he thinks is an apparition of Freya typing away furiously at her old desk.

He clears his throat as he approaches Freya's old pod. "Good morning, Miss. What brings you in at this outrageously early hour? The only good thing about the time is we are over halfway through the week and this time tomorrow night I will be sunning myself at the beach with a Piña colada in one hand and my toy boy in the other. What's your excuse for breaking a habit of a lifetime and being here at this ungodly hour? Did your flatmates kick you out of that Foxton Beach dive you call your fixed abode?"

"Dimitri the charmer, as usual. I have a couple of answers for you. Not Foxton but Waitarere Beach, and it is *not* my fixed abode, although I still have half my things in storage up that way. In fact, I have moved back to more familiar roots of Lowry Bay. Since leaving Auckland, I wanted to hunt around for something a bit more down to earth and the family bach fitted the bill nicely; I did love those charity shops up that way. No, I have decided in the interim to return to Lowry Bay, where I'm staying with my godmother. And as you know, it is only a half an hour door-to-door ferry ride away to work. So yes, I can be on tap for you all the hours you need. Nothing is a problem. As for your toy boy, that's far too much information. I don't need to know about your out-of-hours activities, just your office hours activities will suffice."

Looking a little taken aback, Dimitri sighs and smiles. "Really, do go on. You are obviously on a roll, please don't let me stop the female flow."

"I appreciate it. Now I have a question for you. I have started typing up some ideas for you – I wanted to do something worthwhile as I was officially on the clock over half an hour ago. After all, I know you want bang for your buck. So, let me know if you would like me to share the ideas now, or if you have something else you would like me to start on? How about an update on what has happened the last three weeks since the cat has been away?"

In no time at all it's as if she has never been away. She and Dimitri are talking to each other again like a husband and wife duo who are far too familiar with each other, at times finishing off each other's sentences.

Freya could do the job blindfolded, which is great as this gives her plenty of time to plan the next stage of Portobello. She makes a few phone calls in the private Ed House meeting rooms to check in with Simon and Mr Tombe to make sure everything is business as usual. No matter what is going on behind the scenes she needs to hurry things along and get her name on the title as soon as possible and take possession. She has an uneasy feeling in her stomach, but she just can't put her finger on it. Somehow, she feels that the finance is not going to be the last obstacle she's going to stumble across.

*****

Freya is happily talking with Sven and Clara over coffee, updating them on the latest news of Outward Bound and her inheritance, completely ignoring the incessant phone beeps as they tirelessly make their presence known. After a while, curious to see who is being so persistent, she checks the messages to see it was Simon. She has herself a source of income now, what else could he possibly want? Not feeling up to hearing any bad news, she decides against returning his calls for now.

"Well gals, it's great to be back. I've only been in town for three days – I came in early and good ol' Zac picked me up from the ferry, and guess where I'm staying now?"

It doesn't take long for Sven to work it out; replying in jest, "You're staying back at Gill Road and you're loved up with Zac, you have finally seen the light and you're having his babies in his bunker."

"No, I am *not* having his babies, or anyone else's babies," screeches Freya, a little too loudly. "You know that is the last thing I want, so wash your mouth out with soap. No, I am back working at Education House with Drama Queen Dimitri and his merry band of followers."

"You're joking, you're a public servant again? Never, not after what you said last time. My god, I hope you've got a decent enough excuse to justify that huge move," replies a clearly shocked Clara.

"Well I do, but I won't get into it now. Look, DQ is giving me a chance and it will help pay the mortgage on Portobello until I can get that project moving. I'm earning good dosh now, so it makes it worthwhile. Anyhow, the Education project hasn't moved since I left, so DQ Dimitri is desperately needing some fresh ideas on how he can get the project and himself in front of the Minister. He says before he retires, he wants at least one of his ideas to come into fruition.

"He really is a kind soul and if I can do that for him, plus get my dreams for Portobello off the ground, it will be a win-win for all concerned. Look Sven, I won't be catching the Kiwi Con until I need to move my stuff out of the Waitarere bach, and for the next wee while I'll be living back in the Bay, so it will be the ferry for me most days. Well, until I get it down to a three- or four-day week like you, you shifty cow."

"Well let us know if you need any help," Sven says, "but it sounds like we need a girls' weekend soon, these coffee catch-ups are far too short!"

"Count me in for that too," Clara says. "I'm tied up this weekend with extra judge work, but hey, let's stay in touch."

*****

After coffee, as Freya is walking back to Education House, she finally listens to Simon's urgent message. 'Freya, you are not going to believe this, but I need you to pop into the office urgently, I've had a bit of bad news. I really don't think Portobello is meant to go ahead. I have never come across this many obstacles before. I would rather not discuss this on the phone or leave a message. Please call me urgently.'

Pushing the urgency of Simon's message to the back of her mind, Freya spends the next few hours at Dimitri's beck and call. She marvels at how motivated one can get, knowing that something is just short-term and it's leading to something bigger. Freya is suddenly reminded of how much she enjoyed the brainstorming, the joking and working with Dimitri. Out of all her bosses, he would have to be the best, but all the palaver that went with the day-to-day grind did make it challenging. However, she decides this will definitely be her last stint with the public service, and this time it is for a worthy cause.

She's quite happy to put in the long ten-hour working days as she is getting paid by the hour, and the commute home is only half an hour. Previously it took her two hours by train and car, by the time she walked to and from the station.

Suddenly she realises it's one o'clock, and she has to find time to meet Simon at the bank. She wonders why he's left another three messages, and thinks it's so unlike a banker to get hooked up into the fuss of everything.

Checking Dimitri's diary, she sees he's in back-to-back meetings for the rest of the day, so she picks up her laptop and case and marks her calendar as 'out of office meeting' and catches a train out to Petone.

It's only a fifteen-minute train ride, and no one will miss her for an hour. Besides, she can always say it was her late lunch break, if questioned.

"Hey Simon, what's up?" she asks as she walks into his office. "What's so urgent that you have to ring me so many times in one day?"

"Freya, please sit down. I don't know how to tell you this, but there has been a new development. The council has provided the bank with their engineer's report stating that the building is an earthquake risk. Due to this report, head office believes that the value of the property has dropped to only just cover the outstanding mortgage. As such, they have no option but to sell Portobello to a property developer to recover the outstanding debt. They have instructed me to turn down the mortgage agreement we signed."

A crestfallen Freya pleads, "Oh Simon, what are you telling me? That you're going to renege on our deal? Come on, on what planet is this fair?"

Simon squirms in his seat and looks very uneasy. "I am sorry Freya. This decision has been made way above my pay grade."

Frantically thinking on her feet, she persists. "What if I got a second opinion from a reputable engineer? My friend Zac McLean-Smith is up in Auckland, but I'm sure he could fly down this weekend and write a proper report that said the building was structurally fine. Wouldn't that mean the property value would be higher?"

Then sensing Simon wavering, she adds, "Are you telling me you are not going to fight this one for me? Is this not one of those principles that you live by, being a true local bank manager working for his community? I'm sure I can have my engineer look over Portobello this weekend. Come on Simon, just give me a chance."

"Okay Freya, let's see," says Simon, feeling stung about the community comment. He gives himself a moment to think, not wanting this girl he seems so taken with to walk out of his life forever. "Look Freya, I'm going to go out on a limb for you over this as I don't like how head office is dictating this, let's do this the right way." Then an inspired plan formulates quickly in his mind. "Okay, how's this: I suggest you arrange for access to the building via your lawyer Mr Tombe, and I'll need a detailed engineer's report on my desk Monday morning, along with your business plan. That building is currently untenanted and is not producing a cent, so your business plan will need to be good. Hang on a moment," he says, shuffling through his desk file drawer. "Look, here's a couple of generic business plans on a flash drive, but they show examples of what the bank needs to see."

"Oh, thank you for your compassion, Simon, I'm not going to let you, Wolfe or myself down on this!" Freya replies with conviction. "I'd best get on with it and get back to work!"

As she walks down Jackson Street, Freya rings Zac on her mobile as her first port of call, as always in times like this. He is the level-headed one, knowing how to stand in his own rangatiratanga and be heard.

Besides, he knows how to fight council planning bureaucracy and his surname usually works a treat as well, coming from an old well-to-do Wellington family, the MacLean-Smiths no less. Somehow that hyphenated name really cuts it in all sorts of circles around Wellington.

"Zac, hi darl, it's me again. Sorry, I know I've talked to you more this week than I did nearly all last year. It's urgent; I need your body and I need your brain. Have I got you at a good time or are you doing one of those Health and Safety tricks and hanging off scaffolding on some high-rise building in Queen Street?"

Zac responds in a serious tone – clearly there are bosses or clients around and he can't goof as easily as he usually does when around Freya and her friends. "I'm actually at the council offices in your old hood, on Waiheke Island. We're just going through the final plans of a souped-up house extension over here for that old TV announcer. You know, Mr Hose-skin."

"Wow, not my old stomping ground?" reminisces Freya. "That seems light years ago now; oh god, I wish I was still there. Life was so simple back then. I've only just got back and things have suddenly got far too serious. Shit Zac, what do I do? I feel the whole world is against me and I think I'm going to have a serious meltdown if I can't get you down here to help. I am so sorry the way I talked to you… Please, please can you help me?"

"Fin, what on earth have you got yourself into? Of course I'll come down, but how can I help? You need to tell me what's going on down there."

"Oh, what I didn't tell you is that Wolfe left me Portobello, his building on Jackson Street. My dream is to restore Portobello to her former glory, and it's all going down the drain. First the banks wouldn't give me a mortgage until I had some sort of income. So, I did it, I'm back working with Dimitri at Education House and for twice as much. They agreed to the mortgage, then they got some council engineer report to say the place was not structurally sound and would never stand in an earthquake, and as we lie on a hundred fault lines, they're saying it's a wreck and therefore condemned, then they want to sell her to a property developer. But I've convinced Simon, the local bank manager to hang off until I can get a second engineering decision, which he wants on Monday. Please can you get on a plane and help me out?"

"Wow, that's a lot to take in, but I get the gist of it. I'll see if I can get away early. I'll make a few calls, but tell Mum to make up the spare bed," Zac replies. "Right, gotta go, the client and the council officers up here are staring at me funny."

Chapter 5

A Sense of Belonging

Freya ferries into work on a blustery Wellington morning from Eastbourne into town. She didn't sleep a wink as her mind was doing overtime over Simon's last conversation. He just wasn't his usual self; it was like it was someone else talking on his behalf, then switching to work out a solution, along with his very Jekyll and Hyde-ish behaviour. She wondered if he might fancy her.

She stops for a coffee on her way to work at a colourful caravan cart. The owner chats to her as he prepares her caffeine fix. "I've really enjoyed serving my regulars for the last two years, especially the chatty crowd that pile off the Eastbourne ferry each day. They are a little different, that lot – they don't wear the same dull drab black and brown colours that most of the commuters wear, especially the ones you see piling off the trains. I used to do my gig down at the railway station and enjoyed the Kāpiti crew that came in and further afield, but I have taken a liking to this crew down here. The ones that battle the rough Wellington seas to get to work each day. How long have you lived over at the Bay?" he asks Freya.

"Well, off and on since I was a wee tot, but I moved away up to – now don't hold it against me – to Auckland for a while, have you heard of a place called Waiheke?"

"Yes, I have. In fact, my family are living up in Auckland, but we have visited Waiheke, very beautiful. But I am hoping to relocate them down here. Well I was, once my caravan business got going, but now the council have brought in all these new rules and regulations – compliance this, tick box that. It's just another way of revenue generating and keeping the poor man down. I also think they're not that into foreigners and even though I am a second-generation Turk here, they would rather we all buggered off and went home." He clearly feels a bit overcome with what he has just said. "Wow, where did that come from? I am so sorry, I had no idea I was going to say that. I didn't even know that's how I felt, it must've been parked away in there," he says, pointing to his head, "brewing itself up a storm like that Wellington Harbour today and suddenly, you walk past and cop it. Sorry. Anyhow, I didn't catch your name?"

Freya, with her poker face, calmly responds, "No worries. I'm Freya, and you are?"

"Micco, but you can call me Micky if you like, sometimes it's easier for some Kiwis."

"Turkey, aye? What a wonderful place. Well, I haven't been back since the nineties but I loved the people, the beaches, the lifestyle and culture, and of course the Turkish carpets are spectacular. I brought one back when I was there last."

"What, you didn't bring back a handsome Turkish man wrapped up nicely in your magic carpet?" Micco jests.

"No, I missed that boat, Micky! Sorry, I'm going to use Micco, it's much better. But I did match-make my travelling bestie at the time and she ended up marrying him. Anyhow mate, I've gotta get going – it's only my second day on the job. But listen, I love your coffee, your branding, the dinky caravan, the whole works. I may have an idea for you. Will you be around tonight, when the ferry leaves again?"

Micco's dark eyes darken even more with excitement. "Of course I will be. Somehow I think we will be talking more, and you will be getting to drink more of my strong coffee. I will save you some of my favourite Turkish cake. Catch you later, Freya."

Freya strides off down the Quay and makes her way to work, an idea starting to form in her head. She has a spot out the back of Portobello in mind, with some street frontage for a coffee caravan and a little courtyard area next to the orchard. Micco could be her first potential tenant, she muses, planning to share the idea with Simon on Monday as part of her business plan.

By the time she swings through the grand entrance of Education House she has almost forgotten Micco and is deep in thought about another key player in her life, Simon. She jumps onto her pod and logs on so her little green light will show up online for all her nosey co-workers to notice.

Not everyone is excited to hear Freya is back. Her sudden departure last month had left them up shit creek without a paddle and they had had to pick up the slack and work for a change. Then, just as they had decided on her replacement, she suddenly without warning appears back again, in her old pod with Dimitri falling all over her, rushing off for coffees and their very important meetings that no one else can attend. Then out of the blue, all these crazy ideas appear on all the whiteboards around the office, with Dimitri taking the credit. Of course everyone knows where the ideas have come from, put out by the fact that their own ideas are not even hitting the dizzy heights of the very same whiteboards.

Freya, with no time to spare as she has a business she wants to get started and bureaucrats and banks and councils to deal with, realises that if she puts her thinking cap on, she can do most of her day's work in the first hour. She gets out her A4 pad and starts mind mapping, drawing a bubble in the centre of the page of each project Dimitri has put his hand up for. Then she prioritises what she believes is the most important and most realistic project. It can't be too out there, otherwise the crusty old egg-stainers won't take it on and it will be yet another waste of taxpayers' money, another year, another project, more inaction and more ideas left as an archive on some drive somewhere in cyberspace never to see the light of day again.

An hour flies past at the speed of light and there is still no sign of Dimitri at 8am. She checks his outlook calendar that he has kindly given her access to and sees that it is shaded purple, meaning out of office. He has left no reason for his absence, although Freya wonders if the dinner and spa with the toy boy went exceptionally well and he is treating himself to a huge lie in, or lie on, whatever the case may be.

Dimitri had a habit of starting each meeting off with the graphic details of what he and Kostas had got up to and all the ninety-eight different positions and locations they had tried out their new 'scenes of passion' in. To be honest, the first few gossip encounters had been interesting, but they had all got a little too crass for Freya's mind to digest, especially on an empty stomach.

Trying to get the thought out of her head, her mind shifts to Simon and what he might be up to. She decides to ring him now before Friday flies by and she picks Zac up from the airport.

She dials through to Simon. "Hey Simon, how are you today?"

Simon still sounds a little off. "Oh, hi Freya, good. Well that's not entirely true – I do need to explain myself. I don't think I made myself and the situation very clear yesterday. Look, I am sorry for all this cloak and dagger stuff, but can I see you in person again? I really don't want to waste your time or your mate Zac's time and have him fly down here all unnecessarily."

"Yep, sure Simon, but I can't keep leaving the office; is it possible for you to meet me in town?" Freya asks.

"I'm sorry Freya, but hey, how about we compromise? I have a set of the keys to Portobello and I know you are dying to have a look inside, how about I meet you there? Look, I can't get away from all these tiresome meetings until after lunch, but how about two-thirty? What time is your mate flying in from Auckland?" he asks.

"Look Simon," replies Freya, "I know you really respected Wolfe, and you have been very helpful with me, so I know you have our interests at heart. You're not the sort of person who would go back on his word, but I sense there is more than meets the eye here and you can't talk on the phone. You know this council engineer's report saying the building is not structurally sound is absolutely ridiculous.

Wolfe built his livelihood on his reputation and word of mouth… Portobello was his favourite – there was no way he was going to short-change on that project." Freya finally stops to take a breath.

This is what Simon loves about Freya – her true passion, her sheer determination, her unstoppable ideas, her love and commitment towards her grandfather and his dream Portobello. He wishes she could see him in a different light, fully aware that in her eyes he is a stuffy, boring conservative banker. He wants to be honest with her about his feelings for her, but realises that first he has to be honest with her about the business side of their relationship. He just hopes she takes it well.

*****

"At least put the helmet on, Mr Church," the pinstripe suited man pleads. "You know what would happen if Worksafe turned up."

"Oh, give it here then, Damien," Mr Church replies. "Bloody OSH inspectors! A man should be able to do what he wants on his own property."

"I've heard they are on the warpath at the moment, what with the recent earthquake," Damien explains. "They shut down the downtown cinema car park rebuild last week due to someone not wearing a Hi-Viz."

"Ridiculous, as if a Hi-Viz is going to make any difference," Mr Church says. "It's just another unnecessary expense for the property developer." Looking around the construction activity, he asks, "The bones are looking good, are we on track for stage two?"

"Well we had better be, I've got half of the apartments

sold already," Damien replies. "Such a stroke of genius of yours, Boss, to bully those recent widows out of their homes and into your retirement apartments. How do you get all the names?"

"Ha, I've got a couple of temps in different offices, one going through the death notices in papers and trolling the funeral homes' websites, then the other matching the names to council and land court records to see what property they owned. Then I send that list to you and Thomas, to approach the widows and offer to buy their homes and rental properties," he explains.

"You have certainly made it easy for us," Damien comments, "especially with the official looking Tenancy Services letters demanding immediate upgrades of insulation to their rental properties. It's just too much trouble for the old dears, most of who have never seen a bank statement as their dearly departed husband looked after all the finances."

"After a week of flyers for these retirement apartments being placed in their letter boxes, it's an easy sell for Thomas and you, Damien," Mr Church chuckles. "And when they won't sell, then your little potion comes in handy, and I scoop the properties up from the estate as the children just want the money pronto so they can take an overseas holiday."

"As I said, Boss, sheer genius," Damien comments appreciatively.

*****

Back at 'Ed' House, the day flies by. Dimitri comes and goes, with just enough time for Freya to type up a summary of her ideas that becomes 'His' proposal. She jazzes it up into the 'required' font and report template that is expected of all good public servants and sends it off to meet its unrealistic deadline, knowing there will be no one in town on a Friday afternoon, let alone the ministers to ensure it meets its deadline. However, they had played the public servant game for the week, well Freya had for her first few days back and that was all that mattered. Dimitri had a permanent smile on his dial, so all was good in that quarter.

Dimitri stops to see Freya before leaving for another round of networking with fellow Senior Advisors and Managers, on his daily coffee circuit. "You know Freya, you should come some day; it is so much fun finding out what all the other government departments are up to."

Freya responds, "Is that an order or just a fly-away suggestion? I'm sure it will be worthwhile and one day when I have grown up and you haven't got me running around like a blue arse fly, I will follow suit, but seriously, for now we have too many fish to fry up here on our floor. Besides, I don't want to steal your show. They love you and your pink tie and your dramatic stories. And anyway, I'm happy to blend up here amongst the wishy-washy white pods, doing a hard day's work so you can stick to your 'Hard Day's night'."

Dimitri laughs, and hamming it up, sings as he leaves the building: "It's been a hard day's night and I've been working like a…"

*****

Freya feels a bubble of excitement that she can't put

her finger on. Is it the weekend coming, being back at the Bay, the shit that's happening with Portobello, or…? She just can't work it out.

She texts Zac to ensure his flight is on time, and he confirms that he's landed safely and he'll catch a taxi and meet her at Portobello, hoping to make it there by three.

Freya catches the 2.10 to Petone, so she can get to Portobello just in time for her two-thirty with Simon, who is always punctual.

Walking up Jackson Street, Freya catches her first glimpse of the delicious looking three-tiered ice cream cake building from a different angle, from the train station end of Jackson.

Pausing for a moment, Freya is blown away by the building's beauty, and for the first time takes in the reality of her situation. There her dream stands, tall and proud with all the panache and class of a bygone era, finely dressed, good structure but needing a lot of TLC to get her back up to her former glory. To Freya, Portobello looks just as elegant as the gorgeous Art Deco buildings that downtown Napier prides herself on.

Proudly admiring her new baby, she basks in the glory that Portobello is nearly almost hers. She silently thanks Wolfe for making it happen, and knows that good things will follow, with other good people. Portobello has been like a lighthouse, shining brightly and attracting all the right people and steering those on the right path, and she knows it will again. She believes that the hurdle she is facing is just a temporary glitch, and she is determined to overcome it.

She starts reciting her daily mantras to herself as she continues to walk down the busy street. The business district is filled with the excited buzz of a Friday afternoon.

The public servants she had seen during the week, previously dead men walking, have now transformed into groovy Bohemian locals walking with purpose down the street. She sees Leo, her favourite palm reader, sitting outside his local café, sipping on no doubt his tenth soy latte for the day. Despite having his back turned, busily engrossed in one of his palm readings, he still feels her presence. He turns and looks up and waves with his trademark cheery grin, his flowing Jesus Christ locks blowing in the Wellington westerly and his faithful young barista Shelley bending over him offering him another Danish pastry, on the house.

As Freya approaches the building at exactly two-thirty, she spots Simon at the grand entrance, anxiously glancing at his watch. He looks up and breaks into a warm smile as soon as he sees her. They greet each other with a formal handshake, and enter the building. "You first, Freya," he says, allowing her to go ahead of him over the threshold.

"Oh Simon, I had forgotten how gorgeous this was. It really is delectable – like a French gateau, or better still a Danish pastry, or one of those fancy Swedish cakes. Anyhow, please tell me what the latest is, and how we can make this venture work? It's two-thirty and there are only two and a half hours exactly before close of business for another week." She looks on with her pleading eyes and yet again Simon gets lost deep within them.

He tries to compose himself, aware that if he loses it now, she won't appreciate it. He tells himself to keep to the matter at hand; there's too much to lose. "Okay Freya, I know you are an intelligent young lady and don't suffer fools easily, so I will put you out of your misery. It's good to talk here, away from prying eyes and wagging ears. What took me by surprise, and I certainly didn't see it coming, was the formal directive from head office, which is not normal."

Freya jumps in. "Oh no, not one of those 'That's strange, that's never happened before' episodes. My friend Sven loves hearing about those all the time. However, I sensed something in your tone when we were talking earlier. Okay, lay it on me, what's the real story?"

"I can certainly see where you're coming from, I do feel your pain," Simon smiles, before going on. "When I got that first directive from head office that the settlement of this property was not to go through due to the serviceability of the mortgage, and then when I ticked that box as you got yourself a job and had sufficient income to service the mortgage, then they hit me with the second directive. That the building is condemned due to not meeting the engineering/earthquake standards, and that they had a property developer in mind. That's when the penny dropped, but now that I have extended the time and you have your mate coming down for a second opinion, they have got a little pissed off."

Freya laughs at Simon's sarcasm and exaggeration, which is out of character. He suddenly has this mischievous spark in his eyes that she's never seen before, or perhaps it has always been there, but she'd never noticed it. She admits that in his own eccentric kind of way, he really is quite an attractive man. He had taken his little John Denver circular glasses off and for the first time she catches a glimpse of how he looks under that conservative demeanour. She imagines him in a pale blue shirt, a jazzy bright tie to bring his eyes out more, and if he wore contact lens or glasses that had been created by some designer in this century instead of last, and maybe a snazzier haircut, he may just cut the grade for good looking.

"Look, off the record Freya," says Simon, interrupting her thoughts, "I believe someone doesn't want this deal to go ahead. You have to promise me this will not go further than these four walls?"

"Yes, of course, I promise what happens on tour stays on tour." She winks and encourages him to go on and misbehave and break his confidences.

"Okay, there has been a bit of interest in this place. I walk past here every day from the station to get to work and I have noticed a few people hanging around. As the property has been empty for some time, I was afraid it may be vandalised or broken into. You know, with the shortage of accommodation in and around Wellington, it wouldn't be surprising even in this day and age to get squatters. It's very handy to Wellington and you know Petone does attract us likeminded Bohemian types, and it would make a great shelter for someone. Anyhow, I have seen this speculator, some real estate agent and his entrepreneurial mate standing around looking at it, and rather too closely for my liking. Donald..."

Freya blurts out, "Donald Trump?"

"No, close, but with the same hairdo and complete lack of ethics," he laughs.

"You're joking – no one could replicate that hairdo. That is definitely a one-off. It's such a turn-on though, isn't it, Simon? Would your wife let you have a hairdo like that?"

Simon, a little taken aback, answers, "Seriously, you don't fancy that hairstyle, do you? And no, I don't have a wife. Now someone as observant as you would have noticed I don't wear a wedding band on that finger, surely?"

Freya admits, "I haven't noticed, but seriously, that is a bit old-fashioned; the wedding band on or off means nothing nowadays. Are you saying you're not married? A great catch like you?"

Simon reluctantly comes clean. "I was married, but she died. It was a long time ago." He sees Freya's embarrassment, and wanting to clear the awkwardness quickly adds, "I am well over that part of my life now, but I still would like to find someone else one day."

Now it's Freya's turn to feel awkward. She wonders if Simon is trying to make a pass at her – is this his way of letting her know he's available? The idea sounds rather appealing, but then she chides herself – it would only add complications that she doesn't need.

Before she can embarrass herself, she quickly changes the subject back to the matter at hand. So, who is putting these roadblocks in and who are these real estate shysters? What are their names? What's their claim to fame?"

"Just some investors who obviously have a bit of clout with the chairman of the bank. If it is Donald Church, we could have some trouble, but I have an idea on how we can bridge this gap." Before he has time to finish, the doors swing open and Zac walks in. He's almost unrecognisable, dressed in a smart suit, looking as if he's come straight from some important Downtown Auckland meeting.

Freya does a double take, and it does not go unnoticed with Simon, who suddenly feels rather insignificant. Simon realises he doesn't stand a chance with Freya as long as Zac is around – it's clear that she only has eyes for him, even if she doesn't know it herself yet.

Freya's eyes indeed light up and she runs over to give her mate a big hug and kiss on his cheeks. Zac grins like a Cheshire cat. He feels a surge of familiarity yet excitement; it's always fun to be around Freya even if it's like a roller coaster ride at a theme park at times, but the rides are certainly worth it.

"Hey Fin, I hear you've kicked me out of my bed at home – I am now officially homeless," then turning to Simon, he introduces himself.

Simon pipes in, "Hi Zac, it's nice to finally meet you. Well, if we don't get onto this case here, Freya will be homeless and if I don't watch my back, I could be jobless. As my friend Alex likes to say, 'Time is of the essence.' We have exactly two hours to get this show back on the road and get this building back into the rightful owner's hands. I have just told Freya – or Fin as you call her, that there are some local entrepreneurs that believe they have first dibs on this place; they have the cash, the clout and the bank chairman's ear. I've bought us until Monday to swing this ship around and get her back on the right path."

"Okay Simon, you have my undivided attention. Let's sit down and get this sorted together. You know our Freya always loves a win-win solution," Zac replies in a business-like manner, "and as my brother always says, 'United we stand, divided we fall'."

Chapter 6

Let's Swing This Ship Around…

Simon reluctantly returns to work, leaving Zac and Freya behind to sort out the structural issues. He needs to come through for her, and decides he'll do his best to find a loophole so he can get the mortgage through to thwart those head office plonkers.

*****

"Well, Fin, you know you have Simon eating out of your hand, don't you?" remarks Zac, as soon as Simon is out of earshot. "He is so besotted with you. It must be breaking his heart that he can't help you out. Mind you, this way he does get to spend more time with you…"

"Don't be ridiculous Zac," Freya replies. "Do you really think he might fancy me?" Then more forcefully, "No, I think it's more to do with head office stepping on his toes."

"I would like to get to the bottom of that and find out

what's really happening. However, no time for jumping on bandwagons that are, for now, out of our control. The only thing we have control of right now is getting this engineer's report reversed. Show me the report and all the files you have on the building, photos, plans, the whole works. I assume you popped by the council and got all the records on the place?"

"Of course I have. Do you think I would give up that opportunity to get all the paperwork on this piece of land? I knew if I didn't hurry up, someone would take the important files away and they would conveniently never see the light of day again."

Zac laughs out loud. "Don't tell me, let me guess. Okay, it was like that time you tried to get all the files on that lifestyle block you were interested in, in Levin, the council suffered a fire back in the day and all the plans, consents, alterations etc. had all gone up in smoke?"

"Yes, how did you know?" she asks.

"Because that excuse is standard operating procedure for overworked and underpaid council workers the length and breadth of the country, and you offered sweetly to do her work for her?"

"Well yes," Freya replies bewilderedly before going on, "more or less; she did say that they didn't have an Archives department, as that facility was no longer in existence due to budgetary costs. So I went back yesterday while she was on her lunch break and asked another council worker at the desk if he would be kind enough to give me the new address of their Archives department. I said I was from their small brother department, Wellington Regional Development Advisory Services and just doing an inspection on one of the greater Wellington properties.

They gave me an address in Lower Hutt which just so happens to be around the corner from here, so I popped in and got what I needed. Wolfe's plans from back in the day, all elevations, alterations, consents, the builders' names, the materials used, the plumbing/piping, drainage, the foundations, the piles, even down to the type of fireplace they put in, the type of taps, and the balconies. There is even consent for a small structure on the flat roof above, and the best thing," Freya says excitedly, shuffling through her papers, "check out these old black and white photos of the construction process."

Freya's excitement is contagious and Zac gazes in amazement. "That looks like you can see extra steel reinforcement… here, look at this one showing the timber joinery, and this one of the concrete foundations, the rollers! I tell you, Fin; this was cutting edge tech for back then and still is today!"

"And the building even won an architectural award! Look, here's a photo of Wolfe getting the plaque from the local mayor in some ceremony. Wow, it was right here in this very room!" says Freya, looking around the dining room.

"If I'm not mistaken, that's Mr Galbraith Senior himself, presenting the award," says Zac. Looking at Freya he adds, "You know, Fin, his son is the deputy mayor at the moment."

"Zac, if you can't make this non-compliance sticker go away, I am going to check out Mr Galbraith Junior. I am sure he would not be impressed to hear that an award his father gave out for best architectural building in the area has now been condemned by his fellow council plebs," Freya threatens.

"It's okay Fin, it won't come to that," Zac assures her. "Trust me. But yes, if you need to dig up the dirt from the past, we'll cross that bridge when we come to it. Okay, I have some serious work to do here if I'm going to produce some figures and statistics for Simon in the next hour so we can try and get this project of yours back up and running again. I'm dead tired, I had to get up at five this morning so I could do my full day's work before I caught the plane down here, can you go and grab us some coffees – a large espresso please?"

"Yes Sir, coming right up, Sir!" Freya teases. "And some chocolate to keep you going, perhaps?" Laughing, Freya continues, "I know just the place, it's my new competition. I'll be back in five."

Zac yells out, "Yeah, make it twenty, I know how you can't resist a good long chat when one comes your way. Take as long as you need, catch you soon." He opens his leather shoulder satchel and takes out his tape measure and camera before heading for the quirky spiral stairwell down to the basement to check out the foundations.

Freya takes off to see if Leo her palmist mate is still at 'Cheekos' across the road. As luck would have it, he's still there, even at this late time of the day. She knows Leo is not into crowds and with the Friday workers coming out for the weekend he's usually long gone and back in the safe surrounds of his house by now. However, she sees him sitting out on the promenade and gives him a big friendly wave. He smiles back.

"Hey Leo, it's great to see you," she says, bending over to hug him. "Don't stand up, it's okay, I know you are a gentleman, enjoy your coffee. How's business? I see you're still attracting the masses. That word of mouth has got out of control – you are always busily staring into some damsel in distress's palm."

Leo looks up and puts out a hand to invite Freya to sit with him. He has been talking and analysing women's hands since ten o'clock and it is now three-thirty. "Please take a seat my dear, I feel like a small recreation break. Now tell me what's happening across the road with your grandfather's building?" he asks, as he starts rolling another cigarette.

Freya laughs. "I forget that you and my grandfather went way back..."

"Why, of course I knew that. However, the copper plaque on the building clearly states who the architect and the builder were. You would have to be blind or absentminded not to notice that. It had been neglected for quite some time, but someone who I suspect was you shined it up and it really catches the eye now, especially when the sun is out on that side of the building. It's like a beacon, a lighthouse showing you the way. But yes, do go on."

"Well, my granddad left it to me, but there have been a few hiccups, and getting settlement and the title changed over to me is proving very difficult. Someone clearly thinks they deserve it more than me – some developer – and the council have planted a big 'condemned' sticker on it. The council engineer believes it could be an earthquake risk should we have one and I need to get an engineer's report to prove them wrong. That is clearly a load of crap. So, I have got my engineer mate Zac down from Auckland checking it out now.

"I just wondered, could you please take a look at my palm to see what the future holds with regards to this building? It is my new life. I want to bring the building back to its former glory, give her back the life and dignity she once had. Wolfe never had the money or the time to do it, but now he's gone this is the least I can do. It's like a legacy for him, and I want to honour his work. Besides, it was a pact we had together."

"My darling girl, anything for you. You may not be aware, but I once had the good fortune to live in a Wolfe Nilson house and it was extremely durable. Why, my first wife and I rode out a few earth trembles back in the day. I recall that one of Wolfe's trademarks was 'earthquake proof'. Now let's look at your right hand first."

Freya displays her hand and Leo answers her questions in a matter of minutes. He reveals that yes, she will be the landlady, and the building will be grand yet again. Then he reveals something about her love life; something she wasn't banking on. She turns a darker shade of red and suddenly feels very hot. "Don't talk silly, Leo," she says uncomfortably, "it will never happen with him, no way…"

Just then Zac appears. "I knew you would be a while. Have you even got around to ordering the coffees yet?"

Freya turns red yet again as Leo's steely eyes assess her reaction. "Hello young Zachary MacLean-Smith, it has been some time. How are you?" he asks.

"Great, Leo. Look, I would love to stop and chat, but my boss here has forgotten what she came over for. Excuse me I must get a caffeine fix into me."

Just then Shelley emerges from the café with two cups of coffee, "Here you go guys, I saw Freya get waylaid, hope a couple of flat whites will do."

"Thanks, you're a star!" Zac replies, then continuing turns back towards Leo, "I've been up at Freya's favourite island in the Hauraki Gulf, Waiheke. I tell you, the characters have changed a lot up there since Freya's hippie days. If you don't mind me saying, the Bohemian type artists have diminished a lot and there's more of those Auckland yummy mummies and their husbands and lovers in their four-wheel drives roaming the island now. Anyhow, excuse me Leo." He turns his attention to Freya. "Freya, I have some good news that I've got to share with you. It's going on four o'clock and I think we need to pay your Simon a wee visit. What do you think?"

They say their goodbyes and hurry over to the bank before it closes for the weekend. They find Simon beavering away in his office, now in shadows as the sun has gone behind the building that blocks the afternoon sun.

"Simon, our clever clogs Freya here has the building files from the council – the archives no less, as well as photos showing the sound foundations. I've also taken some photos, run my tests, taken some measurements and I would give the old girl a six out of five. I don't know who this turkey is that signed it off, but this 'Earthquake Risk' certificate is not worth the paper it's written on."

"Zac, that's great news," Freya says excitedly.

"In fact, Simon, I'm sure this is a set-up. Someone else wanted the building for a steal. I would like to make a formal complaint about this, but I'll let it go for now if we can get this loan and settlement through immediately, tonight by close of business," Zac continues. "Perhaps you would like to pass my words onto your chairman or whoever is still in the office at this time of day on a Friday who can authorise this without any further dramas. We don't want it to get costly and embarrassing, legally or media wise, do we?" Zac smiles at Simon. To be fair, Simon is just following head office orders and Zac knows he's been trying to help Freya out.

"Look Simon, to save any embarrassment we can leave the office now or just sit out in reception if you would feel better, but we've spoken to the lawyers and they're all ready to release the keys tonight. They're just waiting for the last details from you," Zac finishes.

Simon replies, "Of course, Zac. You know I have Freya's best interests at heart. If this wasn't going to go through, I had found a loophole to buy some more time. But let's see if we can do one better than that; leave it with me and I'll meet you at Portobello with the news."

*****

By 5pm that evening, Freya Isobel Nilson was the proud new owner of Portobello. After a quick trip to the local charity shop, Freya had a couple of old Formica tables and quirky chairs already set up, along with mismatched champagne flutes. Sven, along with Clara, Zac, Simon and Leo and his dog Timmy, had gathered together. Sven had brought in some red and white spotted bunting and hung it up. Clara had brought some flowers.

"Thank goodness you bought the good stuff, Zac!" Clara comments as he pours the Daniel Le Brun.

Leo had got his dog sitter to drop off Timmy and together they stand to propose a toast: "Three cheers for Freya, one fine determined young woman. Here's to Freya and her plans and to Portobello and everyone who sails in her!

Chapter 7

Bubbles at Portobello

It's just like old times, all the besties together gassing away about the latest goings-on in and around town. Due to the usual unnecessary build-up towards the end of the year, no one has had time to have a proper long conversation over a bubbles or two.

Sven, a.k.a. Samantha Svensson has been busy in her new role at the Big Super (BS) Ministry in town, just around the corner from Freya's Education House. All government departments are huddled together in one square mile. Clara, a.k.a. Flat White has been working at the High Courts for the Judiciary Advisory Board (JAB). Typically, Clara is the most excited about her job and can't stop talking about all the judges and how the older ones are very good looking and, in her opinion, so gentleman-like and can't do anything wrong! Sven is talking about the latent potential the place has up at the BS Ministry and how good it is to be working with their old boss Bernard again.

Leo, however, is the most amusing. He and his gorgeous Border Collie Timmy are as animated as each other and Timmy is synched in with every action – verbal and non-verbal – his master Leo makes. His lovingly brown eyes just stare on in sheer admiration as Leo has them in fits of laughter talking discreetly about some of his palm readings and the dramatic reactions of certain female customers. He doesn't charge for his time and expertise; he is just fully fuelled with multiple soy lattes and slices of cake in return for his craft. Besides, helping people and being of service is his calling – it is a gift and therefore no money is to be exchanged; Leo feels strongly about this. This is his way of enhancing the planet and its lost souls.

Sven is intrigued by Clara's positive comments about the judges and poses a couple of questions to get a clearer picture of what is really happening up at High Court House. "So Clara, tell me, what's the Colonel's secret? Or should I say the Judge's secret? What's keeping you content and happy up in those quarters? Or do we not want to know?" She nudges Freya with a twinkle in her eye.

"Sven, seriously, I love it. I really love going to work. You know how you and everyone else moan about going to work and get all septic on a Sunday as Monday-itis starts setting in twenty-four hours before you've even landed back at work? Well I don't suffer. My colleagues, bosses, my team are just brilliant. We are all on the same page rooting for the same things," Clara replies.

"Are you sure that's not the only thing you and *your* team are rooting? You wouldn't be rooting an old crusty judge would you, by any chance?" Freya has her doubts about Flat White's pure and innocent words and wonders if it's just one of those exterior superficial facades Clara is good at putting on.

"Freya, why do you always think the worst of me? You always think there's something else going on that I'm not admitting to. Just because you and Sven go deep doesn't mean we all have to," Clara pouts.

"Oh, rivers running deep, aye, Flat White?" Sven chimes in. "Hell no, I would never put you in that category, and of course I would never delve into Clara James' innermost feelings, stirrings or fantasies. Hell no! You just keep them parked away in there nice and tidy like a government filing system. You never know, another couple more bottles of good ol' Daniel and we could be just about ready to excavate the first layer into the chasm of Clara James' real inner self. Then stand back everyone," she adds, rather too sarcastically.

Clara's lack of authenticity after all these years infuriates Sven, and sometimes she just can't hold back. If only she wasn't so materialistic and tried to get in touch with her real authentic side a bit more.

Clara gives Sven an evil glance. "No, Sven, don't let the bottle go to your head. Just because you've had a couple of glasses doesn't make you the head shrink of the BS Ministry."

Freya attempts to rescue the situation by changing the subject. "Anyhow, what has your hiker boy Jack been up to on the weekends lately? Are you planning to conquer Mount Everest? I hear Kathmandu is the place to go. So, when are you two off? Good old Kathmandu, what to do?"

Flat White doesn't seem to hear and carries on glaring at Sven.

Zac, a little tipsy, chips in. "Now, now, ladies, let's focus on the celebration instead of going on about ourselves. This is a little party to celebrate Fin getting across the finishing line with her bureaucratic battles – the kind of thing that you girls thrive on at your jobs – and she won. I would now like to propose a toast, and Leo, feel free to follow suit."

Zac stands up on one of those dodgy tables that Fin scored from a charity shop only an hour or so ago and raises his glass. "Here's to the cleverest little cookie I know in town – I'm in awe of the determination and persuasion she portrays, and it paid off. Here's to Portobello, us, and all those who sail, sleep, eat, drink, bonk, whatever, inside her. Three cheers for Portobello and Freya."

"Hip, hip, hooray, hip, hip, hooray, hip, hip hooray…" they all chorus, and Timmy barks his contribution too.

The clinking of glasses and raucous laughter can be heard from down the road while Timmy continues to bark excitedly. All five really do look a sight: Leo in his smart pants and purple silk waist jacket and bowler hat, long Jesus Christ hair now tied up in a man bun, beard and moustache. Timmy with his Scottish Stewart Tartan dog jacket wrapped around his waist, Zac in his very posh Auckland suit, Freya in her long flowing flowery charity shop skirt number and white camisole, Sven in her little Rarotongan flowery sundress, and Flat White in her executive navy blue suit and high heel shoes, the most smartly dressed. The Fabulous Famous Five they called themselves that night, along with their dog Timmy.

"Okay Leo, speech, speech, speech," chants Zac, encouraging him to stand up. "Come on old boy, up you get. Well actually, you and the bubbles look far too comfortable and we don't want you jumping up on the table and creating our first Health and Safety hazard for the building. Besides, we haven't created the robust, best practice Health and Safety Register yet. A from the chair speech will be just fine."

"Freya, darling, I am absolutely delighted and ever so privileged to be here today celebrating with you this momentous occasion. Seriously darling, I feel Wolfe's spirit here. Now for those of you in the room who don't believe in this," Leo says, looking straight at Clara, "please don't be alarmed by what I have to say. From the minute we came in here I could feel him. Wolfe is definitely here tonight.'"

"Where, Leo, where?" interrupts Freya excitedly. "Please point him out. I thought I felt the hairs on my arms stand up before, but didn't want to say anything. I didn't know what it was."

Leo points to the corner. "Why, I believe Wolfe is just over there, my dear. If I'm not mistaken, that is his unmistakable big Cheshire grin," Leo continues, smiling and acknowledging his old mate Wolfe. "But then you knew that my dear, as I saw you looking over there from time to time. I think it is time for you to start having faith in yourself and your special gift, and I believe this is the time for you to go deeper within yourself and trust your intuition. Now I won't embarrass you any more in front of your friends, but I would like to do another reading for you, a top-up, shall we say. A lot has moved and changed with you and your destiny in the last month, and we keep getting interrupted when we sit down for a reading. You are vibrating at a higher level and as a result attracting more positive events and people into your life."

"Let's give these two a moment," Zac suddenly announces, "and with your permission, Freya, I'll take the girls on a little rooftop tour."

As the others leave the room and head for the stairs, Freya sits next to Leo. He takes her hands and examines them intently. "I don't normally let on to people that I can 'see' sometimes, but I use palmistry as a way to connect and listen to what messages come through. I don't want to freak people out and say I can feel and see things."

"Well, I'd really appreciate what guidance is available from the spirit world, as it has been a roller coaster since Wolfe passed," Freya concedes.

"Yes my dear, but seriously, those trials and tribulations were there to test you, to make you heal and grow. There will be more, but that's life – nothing you can't handle. Right, now let me see," Leo starts. "It is great that you have won the big prize, but I want you to know that this huge exciting adventure and dream will also come with its own setbacks and challenges. It will be like one step forward and two steps backwards, but that is life, my dear, and I don't want you to feel discouraged by this. You know why? Because you are highly protected, Wolfe is on this journey with you. He may be on the other side, but he is here with you and your other tupuna; they are all here. You have to remember that Portobello here for dear old Aotearoa, our lovely country, is a very old building. It is also on a very special piece of land. There are a lot of people who have passed who had a lot to do with this building. Look, I have an idea. Let's do a blessing and cleanse the place, put the right intentions back into her, restore her spiritually back to her original blueprint/DNA. What do you think?"

As Freya gets to her feet she feels very emotional, as she knows her grandfather is with her. She is a very spiritual person and has some psychic tendencies, but she keeps them well under wraps. Ever since she had her own near-death experience in the car with her grandfather when they were on the way to the big Wellington department store Kirkcaldies, she has felt a presence, like a protection, a guiding light around her. Sometimes when she gets too stuck in the mediocrity of everyday life, she puts up her barriers and forgets that she actually holds the answers, she knows what's right and what's best. She knows she must just meditate, breathe, take time out and go within, but she finds it hard to do this when racing around with the busyness of the twenty-first century.

She leans over to Leo and gives him an almighty hug. "Thanks Leo, for grounding me as usual, giving me that reality check I need from time to time. You are so right – I forget I have it all covered, so to speak. Yes, I must remember I am my own GPS, I punch in the co-ordinates and I know where I am going, who I am. I just forget, and I tell you, that three-week hīkoi completely turned my whole life upside down. It's like I'm going through a defrag, or a cleanse, and now I'm building up my mainframe again by getting rid of what I don't need and attracting more of the greens that make my heart sing. Okay, I'll stop this soppy stuff now. But it's not the alcohol talking," she adds, glancing towards the door as she hears the others coming down the stairs. "It's me, Freya talking."

Freya stands as her friends enter the room, and grasping her glass says, "Kia ora my little whānau, thanks so much for coming. I do want to have a few words and thank each and every one of you."

She takes a sip of water, composes herself as emotions are running high, and continues. "Today is a very, very special day for me. As you know my granddad and I have dreamed about the reincarnation of Portobello, and as of today she can rise again."

She pauses and looks at Zac. "Thanks Zac for making this possible, for flying down here only a few days after you had left and getting the engineering report through. And thank you for putting up with my acid tongue, my thoughtless words. I really will try to curb my tongue more."

Zac nervously shuffles his feet, and for a second or two looks a little overwhelmed.

"Here's to Simon our absent friend," continues Freya, "who unfortunately couldn't stay – he has been a godsend making sure the finances went through, even aiding Mr Tombe to get the formalities and the deed signed off."

Then she looks at her bestie, Sven, and says, "To Sven, for being my inspiration – you taught me girl how to keep following my heart no matter what, and that I have done."

Then she turns to the colourful duo. "Here's to Leo and Timmy for being my guiding light and always checking in on me."

Freya continues her speech, turning to Clara, determined not to forget anyone. "And Flat White, thank you for being in my life for so long – you do crack me up and thank you so much for reapplying your lipstick before I made this speech. You always show the rest of us up by looking immaculate with your flawless make-up and style."

Facing everyone once again, she announces, "Now, Zac and I are going to be around this weekend, starting our designing and renovating stage. I'm getting some supplies in tonight: food, wine and even my own personal coffee cart, so if any of you want to recreate any of those TV home renovation programmes, then this is the place to come. And I promise, you will not be disappointed with the cuisine, coffee or the conversation."

Everyone applauds with enthusiasm, more toasts are made, and the party continues.

"Thank goodness Wellington has a real public transport system here; the ferries, trains and the buses are a godsend." Sven hastily adds, "I mean not as good as the *tunnelbana* in Stockholm, but still, it beats Auckland hands down."

"I know what you mean," agrees Freya, "but I do miss my Waiheke ferry, especially Friday night drinks." She looks at her watch. "I'd be getting into my second glass of bubbles on the 'Cat' on the way home to Waiheke at this time, with the old crew. I loved that thirty-five-minute commute. So pretty; the Bean Rock Lighthouse, looking over at the golden sands of Mission Bay and Kohimarama, my favourite beach, past the old Naval base of Motuihe and feeling the sun on my face on those summer evenings on the top deck."

"Come on Fin, don't get all soft on us and start pining for the big smoke, you closet JAFA – you are back where you belong now, back in Wellington. You just got lost for a while in Auckland, but you've seen the light now," pipes up Flat White, adding the traditional catchcry, "There's nothing like Wellington on a sunny day!"

Leo gets up and Timmy yelps in agreement. "I really have to get going, I am way past my bedtime, it's almost seven o'clock and I need to get Timmy home for his tea. You know us older folk have a routine to stick to. And I've been out longer than usual today doing all those readings. It must be that time of the year; everyone needs to know where their life is heading and what they should be doing as Christmas approaches. Should they jack their job in?

Should they stick with that relationship or start with that one? Should they put their digs on the market, because there is something bigger and better up the road? Oh, c'est la vie. That is one of the few things we can be sure of – change, death and taxes. Okay my darlings, on that happy note, it's time to hit the 'frog and toad'. Come along Timmy." Leo farewells them all with hugs and kisses and makes his way to the bus stop one door away, bound for his plush homestead in the leafy lush suburbs of Lower Hutt.

"It always takes one to break the party, so I'll take this as my cue to leave as well," says Clara. "I have a lot of paperwork I still need to get through this evening as I haven't finished off my working week yet. I must fly. Thanks a lot for the quality bubbles, Freya," she adds, kissing her on both cheeks before she leaves.

"Why are you are off to do paperwork on a Friday night?" asks Sven. "Flat White, are you sure that's the only thing you'll be 'doing' tonight? You're not doing one of those judges as part of your paperwork routine, are you? Or maybe a ménage à trois with hiker boy and the judge together? Anyhow, I thought those judges were all from out of town and would have flown back to their wives up in their tree-lined suburbs in central Auckland by now?"

"Funny ha-ha, Sven. No, you don't understand. I have a lot more paperwork to do now since I've been promoted – I can't be just like you guys – clock in and then clock out the second I get there for my own personal agendas," Clara retorts.

Freya notes how much of a prude Clara has become recently. She's so up herself and so distant and doesn't even know it. It was okay when they were younger, being closed books at that stuffy boarding school as everyone was like that, but now surely it's time for her to stop defining herself by her external assets, the car, the house, the job, the clothes, the holidays, the brands, the...

Nevertheless, Freya tries to be empathetic towards her. "Sure, Flat White, you head off, darl, it's been a busy week and if you still have stuff to do, then go. Will we see you over the weekend? It would be good if you could drop by. I would appreciate your skills in the interior decorating department – the way you've got your place looking is inspiring. Would love it if you could spread some of the same magic around here. Anyhow, I understand if you're busy. Ciao for now." Freya hugs her friend and ushers her out the door.

As soon as the door closes Sven proceeds to offload. "I'm sorry Freya, I just don't have the patience for that girl right now. She is so distant and always so 'busy, busy, busy' doing god knows what. Her job's not even that significant. One of my old acquaintances works down there and says she's basically a glorified secretary to those uptight, up-themselves JAFA judges.

"You know what?" she continues, "I think when all this madness is over, us three should go on a holiday together. You know, go back to Raro or even further afield. I know you're real busy now Freya, but even just a trip up north – we could bypass Auckland and maybe go up to the Bay of Islands. Just a girlies weekend to regroup, check in with each other, have a phones-free, internet-free weekend."

"Yeah, don't count me out," says Freya enthusiastically. "Let's see how we get on here; I still have to come up with a concrete business plan. The stopwatches are on and I want to get this place looking good and have clientele and positively prosperous businesses humming in here by

Christmas. I know, no pressure. You know me – I'm like a dog with a bone when I'm in the groove, doing what I want to do. Sven, you do the research if you want. I know you have lots of time on your hands at work, so if it's just a weekend away or something, then let me know what you come up with."

"Okay Fin," interrupts Zac, "you have me until Sunday: two days, two nights. What do you want from me?"

Sven roars with laughter. "Now that's an offer you can't refuse! I would take that one up before he changes his mind, but I didn't see a bed upstairs, Freya."

"Enough of that, Sven," Freya jumps in, her face turning a bright shade of red. "It's business, pure business. Besides, we're just good old friends. Okay, let's see," she says to Zac, who is looking a little crestfallen, "Simon had an old business plan on a flash drive; can we try it on your laptop? Let's see what we can do with it – add to, delete, modify and throw some figures into the equation and see what we can come up with. Then when we've had enough of that boring stuff, let's get physical and start clearing up this tip and design some of the floors and rooms. I could do with some ideas, guys."

Sven gets up to go. "Hey kiddo, what was that about a coffee cart? You haven't dragged that old Oxford caravan of yours back down here have you, and turned it into a coffee cart? What was her name? She was orange… oh, Fanta, wasn't it? Have you got Fanta stashed outside serving coffees around the back in the garden?" She takes a peek out the window to see if anything has landed in the garden since she arrived.

"No, but I met a Turkish guy, Micco, the other day. I get a coffee from him when I'm on the Wellington wharf commuting on the Eastbourne ferry. You know how much I love Turkish food and Turkish coffees."

"Yes Freya, and I remember how much you love Turkish men. Remember that Abraham fella you got loved up with in Selchuk that time on the Turkish coast? And then the one whose name you couldn't pronounce down at Izmir – you called him 'the gentleman'. Of course, I remember your fascination for anything and anyone Turkish. So, what's the story?"

Freya hurriedly tries to brush Sven's words off before Zac has time to comment. "Well I had a more serious chat with him the other evening; he's the one with the caravan to die for and he has to move his coffee business on due to the good old City Council bureaucracy. He shares the same values and ethics work-wise as I do, long story short, he, his caravan and charisma arrive tomorrow."

Just then, she hears the roar of a van and looks out the window. Micco and his bright turquoise caravan are backing in. "Well there you go, he's moving in tonight! Obviously the council were true to their word, his time on the wharf was up today and so he's checking into his new location tonight. Good on him. Zac, do you want to go out and welcome him, show him where the facilities are? I think this party is over. Time to sober up, get some coffees into us and make a plan."

Freya walks Sven to the door. "Doll, thanks for coming. I'm going to get some grocery supplies in, finish off some *real* paperwork tonight here with Zac, and get a reasonably early night's sleep back at Zita's so we can get into the charity shops tomorrow. I'm hoping to buy a few more things for Portobello, print off some flyers, have a bit of a working bee, but a well-fed working bee. I hope you can make it." Her voice almost drowned out by a passing freight truck.

Sven takes off, promising she'll be back tomorrow. Zac is downstairs with Micco. Leo has texted to say he is safely home. Clara and her Mercedes no doubt got home safely to the dizzying heights of Kelburn.

*****

The truck driver reaches for his phone, quickly dialling a familiar number. When the receiver answers, the driver talks rapidly, "Damien, there's a stack of activity at the boss's property on Jackson Street, lights on people inside and out and a coffee caravan of all things."

"Coffee caravan? Thomas are you on the sauce again?" Damien asks.

"I'm straight and I've got that insulation on board, can't afford to get pulled over under the influence with this load," Thomas replies.

"Damn, I thought the Boss had the title sewn up today, seems that's not the case, I'm not looking forward to breaking this news," Damien says downheartedly.

"That's why I phoned you and not him, good luck with that mate!" Thomas bids.

*****

Freya is now all alone for the first time. She plonks herself down on the large orange beanbag she found in the cupboard and gets out her pad, pen and highlighters and starts flicking through the business plan on Zac's computer. She opens the different versions up, but finds it contains too much corporate jargon. She decides to leave it for Zac, as he's a whizz in that department.

She takes time out to reflect and look at the corner where Leo sensed Wolfes' presence. Closing her eyes, she stills her thoughts and reaches out with her mind, and imagines she hears her grandfather whisper *Good girl.* Excited and tired and not sure if she is imagining things Freya goes back to the computer thinking to herself, *I wonder if I should check this out with Leo?* She creates a new folder and in capitals types in PORTOBELLO, then underneath creates some sub-folders: Business Plans, Agreements, Flyers, Potential Partners, Finances and Budget.

She grabs the huge roll of butcher paper she found in the kitchen cupboard and spreads it out on the wooden floors. She throws her inspiration and adrenalin into her creativity and starts for the first time in a long while jotting down ideas, projects and sub projects. Freya is confident she'll be able to whip these ideas into action, resulting in an outcome – unlike most of the ideas at work that get archived away into an electronic musty vault, the Cloud.

She takes her lipstick-stained champagne glass and lifts it to propose a toast, addressing the corner of the room; "Well, Wolfe, we made it. Here we are, weeks before Christmas and I am the proud new owner. Here's the piece of paper from the charming Mr Tombe to prove it. Now the real adventure begins. Please stick around, and just sometimes show me a sign that you're still here, or that I'm on the right track."

As Fin throws herself into updating the design and layout of each of the three floors, including the roof, she gets a faint whiff of jasmine, Wolfe's favourite climber. She is so ensconced she doesn't notice Zac sitting in the corner, quietly working away with his own pen and paper. She looks up and shrieks in surprise. "Zac! When did you come back? You gave me a fright! I thought it was Wolfe making his appearance known. How long have you been there for? How's Micco?"

"Now Fin, I am a bloke, remember, I can't multi-task and answer all those questions at once. I've been here five minutes. You looked so cute sitting there on the floor, like a kid with crayons and colouring book; I just didn't want to interrupt you. Yep, Micco is all good. You marked out clearly where you wanted the caravan to go and on what angle, so it was even hard for us blokes to stuff that up! Have a look out the window. He'll be up and running in a few minutes, promising to deliver your favourite coffee and kebab. I think we all need a bit of sobering up and some food. I haven't eaten anything decent since I left Auckland airport besides those yummy pre-drink nibbles earlier."

He looks at his watch. "Wow, that was a few hours ago. Man, times flies when you're having fun and I'm with you," he smiles.

Freya jumps up nervously. The evening is still hot from Wellington's summer day so she opens the French doors to the balcony facing the garden. "Oh, I'd forgotten how pretty the orchard and garden are. They're seriously in need of some TLC, but I love the overgrown wild look, all the wildflowers and the self-seeded vegetables and plants, the tall fruit trees laden with fruit. Let's have dinner down there, shall we? I've made a start on how I want each floor to be, nothing too detailed. I've left the finer details like the measurements, finances etc. up to you. What have you done?"

Zac shows her a couple of arty flyers, with the new

logo and branding ideas for Portobello. "I'm with you, Fin – let's make this simple. Life can be simple; we humans just specialise in over-complicating everything. Let's not recreate the wheel. Instead of you running around being the mother of everything – the Maître d', the Head Receptionist, the Head Barista, the Course Co-ordinator, I like the idea of contracting out to all these specialists – they can be your tenants. So, let's have a series of tenancy agreements, a bit like you've done with Micco downstairs. They lease the space off you. You design what you want and what image you want them to portray, what service you expect, and they bring in their expertise, their clients etc. Then you sign them up to pay rent plus you get a share of their profits. That way it's all under your brand, so if they don't fit in with our values or go off on their own merry way which doesn't align with us, then they change or you march them down the road. What do you think, Fin?"

"Oh Zac, I love it. You know I can't be bothered managing people and being their mother, their matron, their manager or whatever. They are all adults. Now what do you think of this type of layout and suite of businesses?" She shows Zac the floor layout and what each floor will deliver.

"Okay, the basement will be earmarked for wine associations – it's perfect for storing wines, and they can do their wine tasting down there, as well as the conferences and the barista crafting and coffee tasting sessions," she explains excitedly. "Then in the nook behind the mock bookshelves and secret door (like that Jekyll and Hyde bar in Edinburgh), we can have the 'crème de la crème' of all libraries, along with the readers' and writers' retreats. I just met this cool chick from the Beach Book Festival last weekend up in Kāpiti and she runs a Romance Writers' Club every month. I think if we get more of these cool types of clubs and associations, we can have like a revolving door of different clubs, courses and characters coming and going, and that room can be used day and night, and weekends. So the space would be in constant use with different energies, vibes and people – a real sense of community!"

"Yes!" says Zac. "Not to mention the spondoolies that will be floating through the door. And the upstairs accommodation will be like one of those overseas airport hotels or 'Ladies of the Night' knocking shops, with businessmen and women being serviced in their lunch hours or lonely evenings away from home."

"Zac, I can't believe you said that! Is that legal?" asks Freya, taken aback.

"Well if you do your 'bookaroom.com' you talked about, it's up to you what guests you have here, and it's up to them as paying guests what they do in the room. Could be rooms rented out by the night, like the traditional motel, or it could be by the lunch hour, whatever. Now your council hasn't put a regulation in for that yet, have they, young Fin?" Zac winks.

Fin squeals with delight. "Oh my god, you're so naughty! Come on, let's go downstairs and have dinner with Micco before he gets bored waiting for us."

They walk down the spiral staircase from the second-floor veranda to the newly erected gazebo, chairs and caravan now parked in the garden.

"This staircase is in much better nick than the one down to the cellar. Might have to look at that one over the weekend," comments Zac.

"Is there any way we can have little en suites for each

of the rooms, and can you look at that over the weekend as well?" Freya asks Zac as they approach Micco.

"Hey Micco, good to see you again, welcome to the neighbourhood. I'm so glad you've arrived! Now what treats can I buy off you this evening? Show me your menu."

Micco gives Freya a big hug instead of the formal handshake. "Thanks Freya, I think we are going to work well together. I have signed the paperwork and given it to your man here. I have a menu, but can I surprise you? I think I know what you and your man would like, please take a seat at one of the tables and I will bring over your dinner shortly."

Not wanting to spoil the mood by correcting Micco on calling Zac her 'man', Freya lets it pass. Zac pulls a chair out for her and she sits down amongst the red and white checked tablecloths. The waterproof bunting is up and it's like Micco and his caravan have always been there. They all fit in perfectly amongst the wilderness of the pretty garden courtyard.

Freya lets out a huge sigh just as Micco puts the coffees down for them. She raises her cute hand-painted cup, and stares into Zac's gorgeously adorable brown eyes. "Thanks, my knight in shining armour. It's really special for me that you're here for my first night, that you helped me get through that council and bank drama, and you're here now for two whole days to help me get all the business and design and compliance side done. Imagine where I'll be when you come down next? Whenever that is, of course. No pressure. I know you love Auckland and you've got your new life sorted up there. But you know Wellywood and I, not to mention your family and home, are only a short plane ride away. Okay, *salute, prost...*"

"Anything else I can do for milady?" Zac replies in an aristocratic voice, "Perhaps slay a few dragons while I'm in the hood?"

They both burst out laughing as Micco brings over the food, exactly what the doctor ordered, and they tuck in. "Man, this tastes good. I wish your cooking was as good as this…" jokes Zac, and they continue to banter and discuss their future plans in the warm, Wellington evening air.

Chapter 8

Basement Discovery

Zac and Freya, exhausted and feeling the effects of the week, return upstairs and lock up before heading home in a taxi. Zita greets them excitedly at the door. "Great to see you home so soon Zac, I hadn't planned on seeing you until Christmas. I'm sorry but I've given away your favourite bachelor pad to Fin. I hope you don't mind. I just thought it made more sense having her staying in town for a while as opposed to all that unnecessary commuting. I've got Rufus's room made up for you. Nice and cosy up there, so you shouldn't be too shell-shocked by the drop in temperature after the humid weather conditions up in tropical Auckland. Now, what's with following Fin around the countryside, eh? I can't believe your timing, you two. You leave Waiheke Fin, and Zac moves in. Then Zac, you move out of Lowry Bay, Fin's parents follow suit and then Fin moves in. Next you'll be moving into Petone when Fin moves out, or maybe next time you'll both stay in the same place at the same time. I can't keep up with you young people."

Zac rolls his eyes, leaning over to whisper in Freya's ear, 'She's such a chatterbox."

"Well to be fair," Freya says, smiling at Zac's comment, "my parents are hardly setting a good example, taking off at their age and stage in life by selling up their worldly goods and doing their OE again, not to mention leaving me homeless."

They talk for a little longer until everyone darts off in their different directions to get a good night's sleep so they can start early and refreshed.

*****

The early morning quiet of Lowry Bay is shattered by the roar of Zita's old Volkswagen Beetle as Zac and Freya zoom off around the bay, across the bridge, down the parade and onto Jackson Street. They arrive at Portobello in no time, parking in a small alcove around the back, next to the old garden shed.

Micco is already up and running, attracting a roaring trade with early-morning coffees for the retailers who have already opened up their shops for Saturday business and the market stallholders who need a pick-me-up before they set up their stalls.

"Morning you two, yes the early bird does catch the worm. I was the first coffee shop open this morning. I've already had to call in my son to help me out. It's another corker day and I think we are going to be selling our Turkish treats like good old hot cakes off the shelf. I've already put an order in for more just to keep up with the morning trade.

Just call out if you need top-ups." He hands them their two favourite coffees and cakes which they take upstairs.

"He's such a nice guy. I just love his passion and enthusiasm to do his best and give the customers what they need, or in some case what they don't even know they need until it's halfway down the hatch," Zac comments, taking a bite from the Turkish pastry.

Freya agrees as she finishes her slice of cake. Then gets down to business.

"Okay Zac, you're in charge. I'm a bit overwhelmed with what there is to do, I'd be really happy if you could steer this ship this morning, just until I get my feet on the ground. Here, I've started a checklist if it helps – can you prioritise and add to it as we go along?" Freya asks.

Zac skims his eyes over the list, nodding. "Very impressive, Fin. Who would have thought you'd have been into checklists and clipboards? Those times in government departments have paid off after all."

"Funny ha-ha. Right, let's see what we can knock off in two days. I'll be going back to work on Monday for a break. Anyhow, I get paid on Thursday – my first pay day in a month, that should keep Simon happy."

"Great, so you have the finances sorted – can I have a look at the mortgage agreement you've signed? I just want to see how much you have to pay back each week and if your current salary is going to cover that. We should check the conditions too, and make note of the penalties you may incur if you pay back more than you should, or not enough, etc. Do you have a copy of your employment contract? And has Simon sighted it?"

He peruses the financial technicalities while Fin goes through her database of potential partners and clients.

She cross references the ones on her laptop with the ones on her phone, wondering if her list is large enough. She suddenly has an idea and remembers the piles of paper, flyers, pamphlets and letters that have been pushed through the letter slot in the front door; mostly from a variety of people promoting their businesses. She goes through each one and puts them carefully into piles. She makes a pile for those who are promoting their business associations, clubs, courses and workshops. Then one for local retailers: the shops, restaurants, bars, and a separate pile for interest. She reads them all with fascination. She had no idea such clubs even existed, and she can imagine some of them renting out her space for as little as two hours a day, to a full weekend on a regular basis. She decides to go through these individuals and businesses with Zac later, but in the meantime, she wants to look at how she can utilise her space effectively.

Then she plans to go back to her butcher paper from last night and titivate the plan of each floor; she'd like to finish them off before Zac comes back to her with more questions about the money side of things.

"Look Fin, it all looks okay to me, but I'm just not sure of some of the legality and words around some of the clauses. It would be a good idea to run this by your accountant or lawyer, just to make sure there are no hidden costs or fine print."

"Accountant? Oh my god, I've never really bothered with those sorts of things," remarks Freya, looking slightly disconcerted. "And as for the lawyer, Mr Tombe, do you think he's almost past it? Okay, I'll add this to my list. Now let's leave that boring stuff and get onto how we're going to fill up these spaces. Let's start with downstairs and have a look at these piles of mail I've sorted out. They're all local businesses. Some may be quite interesting…"

"I think you will find that although Mr Tombe may be older, that experience means he knows how to do things the right way," Zac reassures Freya.

Now in full on organisation mode, Freya spills her ideas out to Zac, "Okay, so is outside almost sorted, with Micco and the alfresco dining and coffee? Any room for a garden bar, do you think? Micco says he does have a food and liquor licence if that helps?"

"Now that's a great idea, let's check if Micco is up for that, perhaps a roof top bar or get him to run the kitchen?" Zac contributes.

"Oh yes, his cooking is fantastic! Now I think having an in-house gardener is a bit extravagant, but do you think we need an in-house security guy-cum-receptionist, house manager or whatever you want to call it? Someone who lives onsite who can make this happen?" Freya asks.

"Yes, in time my dear, but maybe a bit of a luxury for now. There is only one stream of income coming in, and that's your contract work. You know you could always move in, once we've got some furniture sorted? Then you could keep an eye on the place," Zac suggests.

"Hmm, I like that idea. Maybe I could put my Aikido green belt into practice if I need to get heavy with any prowlers in the middle of the night."

"Now that's something I'd like to see, want to practise with me *grasshopper,*" Zac smiles, suggesting with an Asian accent.

Posing in a mock Aikido 'ready' stance, Freya shoots back, "Try it bud! Anyway I don't know how I would be, running the hotel and some of the rooms by the hour though. It would be funny, wouldn't it, if I recognised any of the clientele? Wellington is a very small town, especially after Auckland, so… oh, it doesn't bear thinking about! Okay, moving right along! "What about contacting those businesses and clubs?" Zac asks.

"Yes, I can do that by email and phone during the week when it's quiet at work and I haven't got Dimitri breathing down my neck," Freya replies.

"Also, we may have to fix the staircase down there and make it safe so that it fits Health and Safety regulations – we don't want anyone breaking their necks," Zac states.

"Or worse still, their heels going through the staircase. You know I love these lighthouse-style spiral staircases, but they are a bit dodgy and it is so dimly lit down there. Great to create the scene for a romance writers' club or a wine tasting event, or a cosy murder mystery, but I think we need to install those dimming lights and add reading lamps to make it cosy, but also so people can see," Freya adds

"You don't want to be killing your clients off by not being able to see where they're going. Anyhow, we can create an atmosphere like those cool underground cavern bars you have overseas. Somewhere inviting and cosy but with the option to create the mood to full-on lighting if you need to run a meeting, so the poor old folk can read the minutes and agenda in front of them," Zac agrees.

Freya after poking around in the basement, "Gosh, it's so dusty, remind me to bring a bucket and mop next time I'm down here."

Zac adds this to the list, along with a reminder to check out the staircase and the lighting. Tick, then up a floor to the ground floor at street level.

"I think a big boldly painted door, like red would look grand," suggests Freya.

Zac jots down *'front door'*. "Okay, your call, but that's something you can do without me, maybe after work you can express your artistic talents, let's give that a 3 for the priority list. How about 1's for what's important now and 2's for jobs to be done in the next few weeks that you can do on your own without an accommodating gentleman and engineer free of charge like me. And naturally a 1 means this weekend, before I go."

"No, you are definitely not free, Zac," Freya insists. "I am not taking you for granted. Look, we haven't discussed this yet but perhaps like a business arrangement – you can't just not charge me for your time. I want you to keep a logbook of the hours you're putting in and your hourly rate, plus GST. This is all above board," she demands, thrusting a notebook into his hands.

"Freya, I could never charge you. You know that. I'm only too happy to do this for you, I mean what are friends for? And I know how important it is to you. Besides, it's a novelty seeing you so grown up."

Freya, for the first time, breaks down and cries. "No Zac, I am not going to take advantage of your kindness, generosity and talents. No, I have taken advantage of you for far too long. It's just not happening."

Zac grabs Freya's chin and lifts her face gently up to his. "Hey Freya, what's up? Why are you *really* crying? Come on Fin, you can tell me. I'm not going to shoot you down in flames for opening up and being real."

Freya, a thrill running through her body from his touch, composes herself and allows Zac to wipe her tears with his red polka dot handkerchief, the one he always carries in his pocket. She bought it for him once as it matched her old favourite red and white polka dot sundress.

She reluctantly opens up, wanting to be more honest with Zac, and with herself. She is so over suppressing her feelings and thoughts only to have unplanned outbursts because she can't control her emotions anymore. Besides, after watching Flat White's display yesterday, she doesn't want to become like her.

"Zac, you are being so kind, and you are always there for me. You're so clever and creative, and the way you're so generous in giving your time and skills reminds me of my granddad – he often helped people out without charging them. It's no wonder he ended up in financial difficulties. People took advantage of him and I don't want that pattern to repeat itself, if you get my drift. In fact, Zac, I don't know what I would do without you." Then her face suddenly lights up. "Hey, I've just had an idea. How would you feel about going into business together? Let's be business partners! I never thought I would say that to anyone, as you know I have a trust issue. But I absolutely one hundred per cent trust you. Let's do fifty-fifty. What do you think?"

Freya looks at him, and afraid of rejection interrupts before he has a chance to answer. "Listen, don't answer right now – as you always say, just percolate on that and see what you think before you fly back to Auckland tomorrow. Okay, where were we?"

Zac goes quiet, thinking about the generous offer, while also trying to sort out his growing feelings for her, "Fin, I can give you an answer right now. I would love to go into business with you. But I do have to finish off what I've started up in Auckland, I can't leave the boys in the lurch.

I do need to go back, but maybe we could review this in the New Year or before we break for Christmas. You are more than capable of running this show by yourself and you know I'm only a phone call away. Okay, let me think about it some more, I'm not saying yes or no right now," Zac smiles, "now wipe those eyes Fin and let's see what we can achieve this weekend."

"Thanks Zac," Freya replies, then composing herself continues, "All right, let's carry on…"

"Let's go for the ground floor, that's easy-peasy. That's just going to be your average restaurant/bar-cum-café. Right?" he asks.

"There will be nothing 'average' about anything we do here," says Freya enthusiastically, her eyes shining with determination. "It will be the eatery though, so we need to put in a little bar there. I know the kitchen is pretty small, it's hardly commercial size, but I would rather have a small and intimate cosy restaurant versus a huge sausage factory-type place, where you concentrate on just bums on seats. Okay, I will add that to the plans. I like your idea of offering Micco the restaurant/bar-cum-café."

"Maybe we can have one of those dumbwaiters, where we can zoom food and drinks up and down in the lift for the guests upstairs? What do you think Fin?" Zac asks.

"Great idea Zac," Freya beams, "and we have those office rooms on the other side."

"Well, I'm guessing the front one could be a retail outlet, but we may need to put another door onto the road, rather than this one central entrance; so one retail, one back-room office then?" Zac suggests.

"Sounds great. Okay, upstairs to the next level, let's go and check out the accommodation floor," Freya says, walking up the stairs.

"This is the floor I think I find the most intriguing so far," says Zac as he trails behind her. "I really want to know what you're planning up there. What is your definition of accommodation, young Fin? Or have you been reading too many Mills and Boon books?" he teases.

"I'll have less of that from my business partner," Freya shoots back, "Now what are your suggestions?"

"Right, there are five rooms up here – two of them have balconies, one with a harbour view and the other with a garden view. And then there's a tiny 'Romeo and Juliet' balcony, like the ones in Europe, where you can open the doors but there's no room to stand outside. You can still get the general feeling of indoor/outdoor flow though, and that's the side where you can look out at the setting sun. Maybe if you're looking for names for your rooms, you could have 'Harbour lights', the 'Garden Room' or 'Jardinière', and then the 'Night Sky Room' or the 'Astronomer's Den'. I don't know; you're better than me at conjuring up names."

"No, I like it Zac. These would be the crème de la crème rooms and cost more as they have the balconies, and then the other two are for the 'budget' travellers. Perhaps we could reserve these as cheap rooms for the pimps and pros – if they're not interested in the view (other than the horizontal kind) then we could put mirrors on the ceilings," she smiles mischievously.

Zac looks a little shocked. "So you like my idea?"

"Absolutely," Freya smiles as she continues, "By the time we charge out each of those two rooms at two hundred dollars an hour we'll end up making more on those as the turnover will be faster. However, if we get the Richard Gere and Julia Roberts' *Pretty Woman*-type prostitute, then they'll want the balcony rooms. Do you remember that scene in *Pretty Woman,* where Richard – sorry, I should say Edward ⌐ almost wet his pants when she climbed onto the edge of the balcony, took her hands off and said, "Look Edward, no hands!" That was so romantic, it was the best movie I've ever seen. Well, maybe back in the day. The hotel suite had the luxurious bath, and then they… Oh Zac, this is so exciting, I can really see this happening!"

"Alright Fin, let's stayed focused," chuckles Zac. "Okay, there are five decent-sized rooms here and one and a half bathrooms – do we want bathrooms in each room? You did mention en suites earlier. I think it'd be a good idea, as today people are a lot more private, they really want their own bathroom and some like their own kitchenette, so they don't have to go out and share the facilities with others. Leave me to it for a few minutes while I measure up the rooms to see what a decent size is for a queen bed, sink, shower, loo, and one without."

"I'd love en suites for all the rooms if possible Zac, I'll check the curtains, see you soon." Freya replies as she wanders off to measure the windows in each room for curtains. Some rooms already have curtains which are so dated they could be back in fashion again as 'retro chic'.

She decides that with a bit of dry cleaning or gentle washing the curtains could be brought back to life. Even the bathroom is okay with its pink porcelain Art Deco bath and sink and matching toilet. It wouldn't take much to polish them up and make them look brand new again. The other bathroom is Art Deco-style as well, but in yellow.

*****

"What do you mean another engineers report!" Donald Church explodes over the phone, "I thought you said the council one was enough… Well we will see about that… Okay, just wait a minute, let me try something this weekend and we can talk more about getting ownership signed over to me on Monday… Thanks."

Donald quickly dials another number, waiting impatiently for the call to connect.

"Boss?" Damien answers.

"Damien, I need you to source some special kit for a job tonight, is Thomas with you?" Donald asks.

"Yes, we're stacking the insulation into the warehouse, so he can get the truck back to the wharf tonight, why?" Damien queries.

"We will need his lockpicking skills tonight on this job, I'll be coming along to make sure it goes without a hitch," Donald explains.

"Okay boss, what's the special kit you need…" Damien queries.

*****

Zac joins her again with his pencil behind his ear and his tape measure swinging off his belt buckle. "Okay Fin, what have you found this time, some more delights? Are we sledgehammering any walls and doing a Kirsty off *Location, Location, Location,* or are you leaving everything as it is?"

"Well actually, these bathrooms are very original and haven't been touched; even the wallpaper is original. Maybe strip the wallpaper off one of the walls and keep this one a feature wall with the original paper. I think we should leave the original tiles around the bath and vanity, what do you reckon? Look, the toilet still has the old chain from the ceiling to flush it; do you think it just needs polishing?"

Zac laughs with amusement at Freya's enthusiasm. It is definitely contagious and even Zac starts talking it up energetically and adds a spring to his step as they walk around the floor. "Look at those chandeliers – a little damaged but aren't they absolutely gorgeous. They won't take much to fix, we can salvage parts from another one from a charity shop," Zac enthuses. "What other changes do you want on this floor, Fin? How many customers are you thinking of and do you want it like a hotel, so they come down for breakfast, snacks or meals? Or do you want the rooms self-contained like modern day living, everything at your fingertips and you just sit in your room with your WiFi code and just stare into the screen all night constantly scrolling through your social media?"

"Well when you put it like that, I want to go back to the olden days, when there was a sense of community and family. You sat at a table and shared your day's stories with each other instead of staring into a screen of some sort. Let's bring back the old-fashioned family-style hotel.

"Okay, you're in charge Fin, let's do that. The old-fashioned family and travelling businessman's hotel, and they go downstairs for breakfast, or order room service if they can't be bothered with the niceties. Okay, that's all floors done." Zac finishes scribbling down some notes as a reminder of what he needs to do, fully aware that Fin will be off on another tangent shortly.

"Not so fast my boy, follow me!" Freya replies, leading him upstairs to the rooftop. "The crème de la crème is yet to come! This turret is the cherry on the top of the gateau cake – I can see all sorts of things going on up here."

"What, like the rooftop bar I suggested?" Zac asks.

"No. Well yes, but this is where I can see Leo doing his readings, the astronomy club meeting and stargazing when Mercury is retrograding, when the moon is full, when the eclipse is happening, when Matariki our Māori New Year takes place."

"When the moon is in the seventh house and Jupiter aligns with Mars…" Zac sings.

"How groovy the lyrics from 'The Age of Aquarius?" she asks. "I'm sure my parents used to bop around singing that tune."

"Yes you are right. Clearly my singing is a hit. Right, back on task you've convinced me. The roof top is where anything goes, basically."

"Yes, and we can have those huge sun loungers up here like they had on the *Titanic,* and on a fine sunny Wellington day the guests can come and sunbathe… and the like." Freya is in full brainstorming mode. "People can enjoy the sunset, the Wellington Harbour. We can run all sorts of classes up here, a bit like downstairs, but the ones up here will be more of a spiritual kind. You know, physically closer to heaven, for example the Theosophers one evening and then the Philosophers another. We can have yoga, meditation and mindfulness classes too. Sven was saying that even government departments are catching on about the importance of mindfulness now. Maybe Evelyn could pop up and do some classes on her numerology. I think the turret is very apt for anything with a spiritual bent."

Briefly stopping for a breath, Freya barely gives Zac a chance to get a word in. "Could we put a gazebo up here? Like pin it down with a big sturdy steel frame, but put up the canvas awnings and those plastic covers for the windows, and add a brazier on cold Wellington evenings? We have all the safety rails and the Art Deco surrounds, so it should tick all the boxes for the Health and Safety Gestapos at the council. Now have we got enough fire exits? Are those spiral stairs on this side of the building enough to meet that standard?" Seeing Zac frantically writing in his notebook, Freya finally pauses. "Okay, I'm done Zac. What have I missed?"

"I think you've covered everything. Okay, there are a few alterations I need to make, but nothing serious, just a few additions and you can do the interior decorating and get the furniture sorted. But have you decided how you want to run the accommodation side? Do you want to run it yourself or have that outsourced? I do think we need an in-house receptionist/house manager/security dude, whatever you call it. We mentioned it before, and they need to live onsite –that could be you initially, if you want to?"

"Okay, all good, I think I'll do that. Now it's time to go shopping. I want to see what second-hand goodies I can find – paintings, furnishings, crockery, maybe the odd rug, bedroom chair, tables and chairs, glasses. Can you think of anything else we might need?" Freya asks.

"You will need new beds, sheets, towels and the rest for the guests, but we will need a few other things sorted first," Zac adds.

As Zac and Freya start down the stairs they hear a loud banging on the front door.

"Hey, can anyone join in or is it just a party for two?" Sven calls out as she lets herself in.

"Yay! You made it!" Freya cries with delight. "Perfect timing Sven, we're just about to head out to the charity shops!"

"Well that sure beats the cleaning I was expecting! What are we waiting for, kids?" Sven asks.

The girls pound the streets of Petone picking up bargains and then take the VW further afield to get some bargains on beds and bedding with same day delivery, while Zac phones his tradie friends making some good deals on the plumbing.

Before they know it it's seven in the evening and they've achieved a lot. Arriving back at Portobello, they start unloading the VW's contents into the garden shed, Zac giving them a hand, "Sorry Fin, no sign of Flat White – maybe tomorrow."

"She must've got busy with her own life, and that's okay," Freya comments.

"We need a serious word with that girl," replies Sven. "I'll start planning our weekend escape when I get home. Catch up for coffee on Monday?"

"Sure will babe, thanks for helping today," Freya replies, waving Sven off.

Zac organises one of his gym mates Stan with a van to drop off the goodies for them on Monday as they lock up. Meanwhile, they decide to have a swim in Lowry Bay for old times' sake. The tide is in and the moon is sparkling on the waters; the little raft that they swam out to as children is still within easy reach of the shore. They nip home, jump into their togs and swim out to the raft, where they belly flop off the side, into the ocean. They swim for a long time and do cartwheels off the raft like the old days. A group of people down at the old boat shed are having a party and the voices echo across the bay. Zita comes down with a picnic hamper and they all sit around drinking and eating. Then they eventually head back home, dead tired.

*****

A small man in a rumpled black suit sits in a grey car parked opposite Portobello. He reaches for his phone.

"Damien, it's Thomas here… they've left, and the coffee guy out the back is packing up… Okay, I'll see you and the boss back here at 1am… yeah, yeah, I've still got it." He disconnects the call and drives off down Jackson Street.

*****

Sunday flies by as they finish some more shopping and they post their flyers out to those they feel would add value to Portobello, the sort of organisations and people they believe would be like-minded.

With Zac returning to Auckland on the late flight out, there's time for one last visit to Portobello.

They pull up in Zita's VW Beetle, and as they approach the main doors Zac comments to Freya, "You know, I want to check the council engineering report, Fin. I've got a feeling that it was a contractor and not council staff that did the report."

"Sure, I left it in one of the rooms upstairs, Zac…" Freya replies, then finding the door slightly ajar, "Hey, I'm sure I locked up last night."

"Hello, is anyone here? Hello?" Zac calls as he gingerly walks inside. Suddenly the hairs on the back of his neck rise and he feels a chill run down his spine. "Fin, just hang back a bit while I scout around." Trusting his instincts, Zac scans the ground floor and then heads towards the cellar door. He slowly makes his way down the stairwell while Freya stays on the ground floor, just in case someone is lurking upstairs – maybe squatters.

Zac suddenly screams out, "Freya, don't move! Stay where you are!"

"Why, what's happened?" Freya calls back, frightened.

"Now is not the time to ask questions, just stay put. There's been an incident and I don't want you tainting the scene. I don't want you to see this, Fin, so please, for once in your life just listen to me and know I've got your best interests at heart. I need you to check if you have reception on your phone and call the police. I'll be up in a second."

Freya, struggling to stay calm, nervously dials 111 and waits patiently for the operator to pick up before asking for the police. A pale-faced Zac appears at the top of the stairs and takes the phone from her. "Hello, I would like to report a death please." The operator asks the usual set of questions to clarify the caller and the address.

Zac answers the questions calmly. "There is a man's body, in his early forties, I'd say. I have checked his pulse, he is dead. I don't know who he is…"

Freya stands still in shock, waiting for Zac to finish on the phone, before asking, "What do we do now Zac?"

"We wait for the police, don't touch anything, in fact, let's go and see Micco," then noticing Freya is tearful, Zac reaches forward and puts his arm around her shoulders, and leads her outside, "Come on Fin, there's nothing we can do for the poor guy."

"Oh Zac, that poor man…" Freya stops, and turns back towards the stairwell, feeling the hairs on the back of her neck rise and a chill runs down her spine. Then she hears her grandfather's voice in her head *It's okay Fin, I'll help him.*

"What's up Freya?" Zac asks.

"I thought... never mind, lets go," Freya replies, whispering in her mind *Thanks Wolfe.*

*****

Micco walks over to the table in the courtyard with a tray of glasses and an ornate bottle containing a milky liquid, taking a seat with Freya and Zac, Micco announces, "I think we need a little rakı, purely for medicinal purposes."

"What is rakı?" Freya asks.

"It's a delicious traditional Turkish drink made from aniseed and twice distilled grapes," Micco explains as he pours a small measure into the three shot glasses.

"Will I be able to drive Freya home after this Micco?" Zac queries.

"We could ask the officer to breath test you before you go," Micco quips, "but you should be okay after one or two, now down the hatch, *Şerefe!*"

*****

The police officer in charge walks over to the table as they finish their drinks, "Thank you for your initial statements Mr McLean-Smith and Miss Nilson, as the detective assigned to the case arrives tomorrow, he may want to talk with you further."

"I have to be back in Auckland tonight for work tomorrow Constable Patel, I can change my flight to help out the best I can, is it possible to deal with any more questions over the phone or in Auckland?" Zac asks as notices Freya welling up again, he puts a protective arm around Freya's shoulders.

"I'll b-be alright s-soon Zac," Freya sobs.

"I'm sure that will be okay just double check your contact details in your statement, but we need you back here at some stage sir. Unfortunately, as the building is a crime scene, we can't allow any access, officers Moreau and O'Malley are cordoning the building off now and we will have a police presence here until Forensics are finished," Constable Patel advises.

"Oh no, our plans are still upstairs," Freya exclaims.

"Don't worry Fin, I'm sure I can get a copy from the council," Zac soothes.

"Can I still run my coffee business Constable? I'm sure all your team will appreciate the best coffee in Petone!" Micco asks.

"Well, I don't see why not," Constable Patel replies, then turning to Zac, he adds, "you may want to take Miss Nilson home as she is still in some distress."

The rest of the evening becomes a blur as the police cordon off the building as they are leaving.

Chapter 9

Injunction and Bombshell

Freya flings herself into her new Monday work routine in an attempt to block out all the events from the weekend. With thoughts of the murder, property settlement, Zac, Simon, mortgage and council earthquake reports to worry about, she is thankful to have a job to distract her from everything. Work seems trivial, and for now she needs to operate just in first gear. Working in overdrive for the last week and being constantly on alert has taken its toll, so establishing a regular work routine is a welcome reprieve.

It seems like an age since she's been through the government doors of stifled creativity. Dimitri has had an argument with his boyfriend and life is hell in the office. It's only 9.00am and the atmosphere could be cut with a knife. Everyone has their heads down, avoiding eye contact with Dimitri; it's not worth losing their pay cheque risking 'handbags at dawn'. Everyone is too scared of not meeting their own mortgage payments or rent, so they just smile sweetly and pretend that everything is right with the world, while Dimitri throws his mouse pad and keyboard into the air after one phone call too many doesn't go well.

After his outburst, Dimitri seems to forget where he is and lights up his cigarette before catching the lift down to the basement car park. There's a collective sigh of relief as soon as the lift doors close. Then everyone bursts into laughter at the sight of the fire warden wearing his red 'Fire Warden' cap and yellow Hi-Viz jacket, carrying his fire extinguisher as he looks around frantically for the source of the smoke.

Amidst all the drama, Freya notices she's received a missed call from Simon, and wonders what he wants. She rings through, unaware that things are about to get a lot more complicated.

Simon relays to her what's happened. "Look Freya, I know you have enough on your plate, but I want to keep you abreast of everything that comes to hand. I know you can handle it that is why I'm not keeping anything from you. Mr Church, the property developer has put a High Court injunction on the property over the ownership of Portobello."

"What! You can't be serious!" Freya exclaims.

"At this stage, as long as you make the payments it remains yours, and I believe that you still have access to the property. But you may want to contact Mr Tombe to confirm that – I've emailed him the details," Simon continues

"Oh my god, I have to go to court for Portobello?" Freya cries.

"Look Freya, I'll get you what information I can, this is

just not right," Simon adds.

"Thanks Simon, I appreciate the heads up," Freya gratefully says.

"I'm sorry, I have head office's lawyer on the other line, I have to go. Try and have a good day. Phone Mr Tombe now and get him on the case. Take care, and stay in touch," he says, before ringing off.

Freya thinks about the infamous Mr Church being the developer; she's heard of his dodgy property deals around Wellington. She wishes Zac was still here – he'd been out of town less than twenty-four hours and now she had to deal with this nightmare on her own.

Her phone rings again, but this time it lights up as an unknown number.

"Is this Freya Nilson? It's Rex Croft, I'm the investigating officer at your property."

"Ah yes, it is, how can I help?" Freya replies.

"I'm just phoning to say that the whole building is now a crime scene and all access is closed off. I'll also need you to walk me through your movements inside the building over the weekend," Rex advises.

"Sure. Look, I'm at work at the moment, can I call out there later today? Also, you will have noticed a Turkish coffee caravan in the rear courtyard – can you please let him stay open? He's just moved there and has nowhere else to operate, I'm sure you and your team will appreciate quality coffee while you're investigating," Freya pleads.

Hearing the honesty in her voice, Rex hesitates. "Well, it's highly irregular… but, I guess as the criminal access appears through the front door, the rear courtyard area is technically not part of the crime scene. Okay for now, but we can talk about it further when you get here, Ms Nilson."

"Thanks so much, I'll be there as soon as I can," says Freya before ringing off.

Freya is grateful for small mercies – with Micco being able to stay onsite and in business as usual, it means that she may still be able to get into her shed and store what she needs for the refurb upstairs. She hopes she can use the back entrance to get into the building soon.

That would give her enough to get on with until Zac comes back and the police finish up their investigations. Freya can't believe someone had to drop dead inside her slice of paradise – couldn't he have done it somewhere else?

She texts Sven: 'Up for a coffee later? I'm stranded in the office today and so much has happened in my world; I could write a book about it.'

She doesn't hear back from Sven, so contacts Mr Tombe to investigate and protect her interest in Portobello, before she gets on with the day, making the best of an awful situation. She goes to text Zac but decides against it for now, as he hasn't got back to her about the business partnership yet. She decides that all this shit is happening for a reason – it's her karma to sort out.

Dimitri is out so she prowls the internet and Trade Me for fixtures and fittings under the Art Deco section, striking it lucky with a great find. There is a demolition site of an old Art Deco building, and according to the advert, if she gets there within the next twenty-four hours, she can take all the fittings for free before the demolition starts.

She's dumbfounded that some people can just destroy history like that, and not even realise that the contents are valuable and stylish, just waiting for a new home. Clearly they don't have any taste, she muses.

She rings Zac's mate 'Stan with the van' to help her pick up yet another load so she can store it in the shed. By another stroke of luck, Stan is on a mission in the Hutt near where the demo site is, and he can swing by and grab them. "Thanks mate, it's a box lot from the Trade Me auction, I owe you. Just drop them off at Portobello later this arvo. Micco will be there and he can open the shed for you. Cheers again."

Feeling a bit guilty about not updating Zac, Freya calls him and tells him all the latest news.

*****

It's almost close of business and it's still only Monday. As Freya reflects on how exhausted she is, Sven finally comes back to her with a text: 'Hey girl, sorry, been in meetings. I'm free now if you still wanna talk.'

Freya picks up the phone and calls her old mate. "You know what, Sven? I am exhausted; I don't know if I can continue like this, too many roller coasters, is it all worth it? Now there has been a murder in Portobello and the police have closed her off, it's all hush hush, so you didn't hear it from me."

"Oh my god! You're not joking are you!" Sven exclaims.

"I think I need that get away pronto."

"Leave it with me, darl. I've felt a trip brewing for some time. I think it will be great just the three of us girls. I have some ideas – I'll get back to you."

Sven puts her idea into action and books the weekend away for the three besties. She calls Freya back by the end of the day, confirming dates and times, but doesn't divulge where they're going or what they're doing. All they need to do is turn up at the airport, and Sven will take care of the rest.

Freya marvels at what a tonic Sven is. She feels much better now she has something to look forward to. It makes her realise how much she needs to get away. Just four more working days and then she's away, on a jet plane…

Clara is in two minds; she can't drag herself away from her highly important job, but Sven lays a guilt trip on her. "Now Flat White, remember the pact we made in Sweden? We would never get into that groove again of working until we dropped and burnt out. Now you don't want history repeating itself, do you? All work and no play make Clara James a dull girl.

Besides, Freya really needs us right now. I mean there's someone who has the balls to follow her dreams and is pushing through all the red tape and getting setbacks left right and centre. I think getting away from the situation will put everything into perspective, and I think the destination I have planned will really resonate with her – a blast from the past but with a twist."

"Okay, okay, you've convinced me, you can stop the guilt-ridden words and manipulation. You're starting to sound like my mother, so please stop while you're ahead," Clara grumbles.

Sven feels a tad guilty. "Hell, sorry Flat White, am I being an energy vampire? I'm not sucking you dry, am I?"

"No, you could never pass for an energy vampire, you and Freya are too much on the 'empath' spectrum; you care too much to be categorised as an energy vampire. It's just sometimes I get a bit triggered when people get pushy, and I see my mother's narcissistic traits in them. She's very clever in telling me what I should and shouldn't do and then making me feel bad when I don't follow her golden words of wisdom. Besides she's now choosing the latest fashionable retirement village. Anyhow, let's not waste airtime on that subject."

"Yep, fair enough, and sorry about triggering anything nasty for you," replies Sven. "I should know better – I remember her drama-laden performance at your twenty-first party, when she made it all about herself… Man, that seems light years ago now, doesn't it? Okay, enough, we can go there if we need to over a few wines one night."

They ring off and Sven starts sending emails and making phone calls to get the accommodation sorted. She giggles to herself, confident that Freya will never guess what she has planned. She decides to have a bit of fun, and sends her friend a text: 'Hey, guess what? You know how you love guessing games? Well, you have four days to guess where we're off to. PS: No pressure! xx Sven.'

*****

The first picture Freya gets in her head is a golden sandy beach with palm trees. She decides to work on this picture over the next few days and records her dreams in her dream journal.

*****

"Oh my god!" Rex exclaims, immediately stopping the examination of the black backpack lying next to the bloody body. "Start clearing the building, Patel, I've got a call to make." He slowly backs away from the backpack and dials through to his partner.

"Charlie, I've got a situation… no, I'm not being dramatic mate, I've just opened the backpack beside the body, and it looks like dynamite… no, I'm not bloody joking!" Rex shouts. "Now I know I'm meant to get the bomb squad in, but I've already moved the backpack and looked inside… Yeah, as I was trying to say, doesn't look like a detonator is attached at all… Yeah, I agree, looks like amateurs… I know it's a risk, but it would save a hell of a lot of time… Okay, okay, I'll phone the chief and report it… Thanks mate, hope to see you soon as I could do with a hand down here," he adds, before hanging up.

"Sergeant Croft? Are you okay down there?" Constable Patel calls from the top of the stairs.

"Yeah, fine Patel, is the place cleared yet?" Rex asks.

"Yes Sir," Constable Patel replies, then showing some initiative, "Do you want me to get the coffee caravan moved as well?"

"Don't call me Sir, Patel, I work for a living," he says, before adding, "bugger it, Patel, do me a favour and order us a large coffee, I'll be up soon."

Gingerly reopening the backpack with his disposable gloved hands, Rex looks inside, confirming that nothing is attached to the dynamite. He carefully removes two sticks of the explosive, some priming cord, wire and a small timer attached to a simple detonator, grateful that he'd done a stint with the disposal squad and knows what he's looking at.

Keeping the items separated, he re-tapes off the area and heads upstairs for a coffee, making another call. "Boss, it's Croft here… just found some explosives… don't worry Sir, remember I was part of the Bomb Disposal Unit a few years back, it's safe… I know it's not protocol, but it will sure save time and money on the investigation… Yes Sir, I'll phone them now, I just wanted to keep you in the loop."

"Good man, Patel!" he says as he walks into the back courtyard and takes the coffee from the constable. Then he makes the call to the Bomb Disposal Unit.

*****

Freya rings through to Zac during the week. "How's it all going up in my old hood?"

"You will never guess where I've been assigned to up here."

"Okay… Kohimarama, St Heliers, Mission Bay?"

"No. Close, but no cigar," Zac teases.

"My old stomping ground?" Freya queries.

"Sure is, Doll Face," Zac replies.

"What did you just call me?" Freya asks. "Doll Face?"

"Ah, yes… sorry about that," says Zac, feeling like a bit of an idiot. He was sitting on a beach having his lunch and had felt so relaxed and mesmerised by the boats and the water he just said the first thing that came into his head. Realising he has put his foot in it, he quickly tries to cover his slip up.

"Yeah, you know what I mean, Fin. You always loved your porcelain dolls and doll collection, so I was just calling you Doll Face. You know how you loved collecting all those different dolls from each country you went to."

"Oh, right, okay then," Freya says, with a hint of disappointment in her voice. "Anyhow, the girls and I are off on a mystery weekend. Sven has organised it and we don't know where we're going, but I reckon it has something to do with beaches – golden sand, palm trees, sailing boats.”

"Ah, it sounds like where I am." He looks around and all he can see is a long strip of golden sand, turquoise water and palm trees…

Chapter 10

Waiheke Bound

Friday afternoon finally rolls around, and Sven has managed to keep the weekend getaway destination a surprise for Freya. Even Clara has no idea where they're off to. They're well and truly ready for the 'Trinity Trio' to have a catch-up. The name stuck after they met at Speech and Drama classes back in their school days, where they acted out their frustrations and dreams to achieve their Trinity College Speech and Drama exams each year.

Clara has been acting strangely lately, and Freya has been struggling to deal with the latest brick walls surrounding Portobello. She updates the girls in the back of the taxi. "There is still no word from Mr Tombe at the High Court, and that arsehole Church has his high-powered lawyer trying to put another injunction in. On top of that, that detective Rex has only allowed limited access to Portobello, so there's not much I can do." Clara is too busy thinking of her shopping exploits and doesn't hear the reference to the police and what has gone down at Portobello.

"Hopefully your gorgeous Zac can sort something out," Sven says, lightly elbowing Freya in the ribs.

Clara suddenly joins the girls in their conversation after daydreaming. "He's one hunk of a man, Freya," Clara agrees.

"Settle down girls! Besides, we're just good friends," Freya protests.

As the three girls jump out of the taxi, Wellington Airport is already filling up with locals trying to escape the forecasted stormy weather that lies ahead of them. Catching a plane in and out of Wellington can be dodgy at the best of the times, the weather usually windy due to its infamous cool southerlies and strong northerlies. In high winds, the runway feels too small to land a plane, especially when the winds are rocking the aircraft from side to side. If the pilot doesn't put the brakes on in time and even up the wings, it's a high probability they could end up surfing the waves of the local Lyall Bay Surf Beach that sits right next door to the runway.

Sven, wanting to keep the destination secret for as long as possible, checks everyone in on the automated self-service kiosk and then hurriedly leads them through to the departure lounge. The screen clearly says Auckland, with a departure time of 2.00pm.

Dimitri had not been too happy about Freya taking off early on a Friday in just her second week of being with the department, however, the Minister had been delighted with his proposed ideas (which were in fact Freya's), so Dimitri decided to let it slide.

Initially Clara had protested about the weekend away

as she had a mountain of paperwork to catch up on after stopping for drinks with the girls at Portobello the previous Friday.

But her reluctance has now been replaced with enthusiasm as they plonk themselves down in the departure lounge, ready for the boarding announcement. "So Freya, it looks like we're all on for a girls' retail therapy weekend to Auckland. I love the shops up there, especially Parnell, such gorgeous boutique stores, not to mention the bars. Even Remuera Road has some cute little shops down that mall. You know I lived up there for a while. I didn't last long though, I missed Wellington too much. And the real estate prices have got too crazy now. Even I couldn't afford to buy up there. Well I could, but it would be some tiny house on the outskirts of Auckland, like south of Pukekohe. I don't think they have a huge selection of shops, restaurants and bars out that way. So, I will stick with Wellington."

"The prices have settled now, though," remarks Sven. "Yep, even I've done time up there, very briefly. I do like what you've shown me Freya, especially Kohimamara Beach. I loved going to the little changing shed down there and meeting all the locals. Remember when we went that year to their pre-Xmas barbeque and all the cute retirees came out in full swing with their 'bring a plate' and BYO drinks…" Sven is interrupted by the intercom. "Okay girls, here's the boarding call!"

*****

As the girls board their flight northwards, Zac is racing through the check in kiosk to get to his plane on time, thanking the Air New Zealand hostess, he finishes his call,

"Isaia, can you check if Paulo is free this weekend too… Thanks bro, I'll owe you big time… Oh blue label is your favourite… Catch up tomorrow bro."

*****

The plane lands on time and they jump into a taxi heading for downtown Auckland.

"Oh, can I guess the surprise? Are we staying at the Hilton, Sven? You know that's my favourite place to stay!" Clara gushes excitedly.

They head across town via Onehunga, missing the heavy bumper-to-bumper traffic, and after an hour they arrive at the ferry terminal.

"Oh Sven," Freya exclaims with a tear in her eye as the taxi parks up next to the wharf dedicated to Waiheke Island passengers. "Waiheke Island, one of my favourites! Thanks so much!"

It's only been a few months since Freya left her beloved Waiheke, and already she notices both new and familiar faces on board the Quick Cat. Some of the regulars are standing up at the bar ordering their usual drinks as she strolls up and slips into the queue, quite naturally. It feels as if no time has gone by at all.

She can't help thinking how different it is to queuing up at the train station for the dear old Kiwi Con. Over the last few months since house sitting between Foxton and staying at the family bach at Waitarere Beach she had got quite accustomed to catching the Palmerston North to Wellington commuter train each morning. Depending on which house she was minding she would catch the train at either Shannon or Levin. With the train ride being over one and a half hours, it was at least a two-hour commute door-to-door. She enjoyed the peace and quiet that house sitting on lifestyle blocks gave her, and the companionship of the dogs, cats and free-range chickens, not to mention the horses and curious cows. But she also enjoyed the hustle and bustle of having a café, a bar and shop or two within a stone's throw. There was also the option of staying at Waitarere Beach in the family's bach, but she preferred animal-sitting where she could enjoy wide open spaces in the country.

Recognising some of the old crew at a corner table in the ferry's busy bar, Freya leaves her Wellington mates behind with a nod, and heads over to the table with her bubbles and crisps firmly in her hand. "Hi gals, room for me?"

Her Waiheke mates look up and do a double take. "Freya, what on earth are you doing here? Have you moved back to the island? Have you seen the light?" the red-haired girl asks.

"No, but I am very tempted." Freya turns and waves at Sven and Clara. "We've just come up for a surprise girls' weekend, needed to get away from the capital and what better place to escape to but good old Waiheke. So, spill, what's happened since I left the island?"

They all catch her up on the gossip of who has swapped partners, who has moved onto the island and who has defected.

Clara and Sven, not wanting to intrude, quietly retreat to the sheltered deck out the back and sip on their bubbles, taking in the view of the Auckland city, the Sky Tower and Ferry building as it all slowly disappears from sight.

Sven breaks the silence, "You know, looking at this

amazing view, how could one leave the place? What an awesome way to commute each day. It beats sitting with all those stuffy public servants on the Kiwi Con every day, where you don't make eye contact with each other, let alone start up a conversation. Everyone seems super friendly on board."

"To be fair," replies Clara, "it *is* a Friday night, it's summer and a few of the regulars are enjoying the odd tipple. You know, the end of the working week, sun and booze – it can make the rattiest person really happy."

"Yes I guess you're right," agrees Sven. "It's just sometimes all the train commuting into Wellington kinda leaves you feeling a bit depressed, especially in the winter. It's like catching the old tube in London, everyone huddled up together." She suddenly points to the lighthouse close by. "Awesome! That's the Bean Rock Lighthouse Freya talks about. Wouldn't it be fun to stay there one night?"

Clara is keen to know where they'll be staying as she doesn't like being away from the comfort of her own bed and all the luxuries that entails. "So, to quieten some of my anxiety, Sven, what amazing accommodation have you sorted for us tonight? A hotel, a tree house, Airbnb, someone's shady basement beneath their main bedroom and we have to listen to them watching TV all night?"

"Flat White, oh ye of little faith, you will just have to wait and see. I don't want to spoil the surprise when we get there. Can you handle the local bus, or do you insist on a taxi? If we take the bus, we'll have more money for drinking later." suggests Sven, always the one to penny pinch and make money go further for the finer things in life, like bubbles.

"I'm not that bad, Sven," Clara replies. "I'm not that

much of a snob, am I? Just because I didn't backpack around and stay in dodgy dives and kibbutzes like you two did together overseas? You know, I did a stint on an ashram in India once."

"I didn't picture you being the communal type. Well, you have to admit you were always getting out of should I say the 'intrepid' side of the travelling. If anything was too adventurous, like trains or hostels, you would make an excuse and we would end up meeting you the next day. You were always looking rested and refreshed compared with us. What's an ashram, anyway? I don't remember you telling us about that, Flat White," Sven asks dubiously.

*****

"I've got a lot riding on this deal Prendergast," Donald warns.

Looking around to make sure he isn't heard, Prendergast hisses, "We both have a lot riding on this deal Church, I can't make that last injunction stick, but it will buy us time over the weekend."

"If that injunction won't work, what am I paying you for?" Donald demands.

"That injunction Church, is to push the case out of reach of the lower judges, that way our friend Chute gets the case to adjudicate over," Prendergast explains.

"This had better work…" Donald threatens.

"Strategy my boy, strategy, besides I have an ace up my sleeve, a certain Police Commissioner, now have some patience and we will have this wrapped up next week" Prendergast placates.

*****

The ferry starts to slow down as it approaches the Matiatia Wharf and everyone piles off in an orderly jovial manner. The weekenders fumble with their suitcases, remove them from the luggage carriers and wheel them up the wharf to the bus. Freya joins the girls again and they get three tickets for Palm Beach and board the bus. They take off and start ascending towards the little village of Oneroa.

As they arrive in the village, they look out the window and spot one supermarket, a Four Square, a Red Cross charity shop on the right, and some cutesy bars, restaurants and dress shops. They take in the view on the left of the gorgeous Little Oneroa Beach of golden sand and the inviting turquoise water.

They thank the bus driver as they leave the bus at Pope's Corner and start walking along Hauraki Road. Sven stops a couple of houses away, checking the details on her phone until she finds the number she's after. "Okay girls, this is home sweet home for the next couple of nights." She ushers them through a quaint little gate attached to a white picket fence.

Clara, clearly shocked, exclaims, "Sven, you've done well! Look at that awesome view! Wow, ocean views, a sandy beach at the bottom, and I think I can even see an ocean liner out there. This is adorable. How much are we paying for this little number? It's huge. Have we just got the downstairs?"

"No darl, we have the whole house, this is all ours. It's a three-bedroom cottage. No en suites though, Flat White, I hope you can cope with that!" Sven replies with a wink.

"It's a typical old seventies cottage, back in the days when en suites didn't exist, but I think we can handle a shared bathroom after all these years we've known each other."

Freya recognises the house straight away. "Wow, this is Anna and Michael's house, isn't it? Well, I should say their holiday house. Don't they live here off and on during the year, in between their little trips overseas?"

"Yes, it is, Freya. I remember you mentioning them and their house to me ages ago, so I made enquiries to see if they'd be here for the weekend. As luck would have it, as it's not quite Christmas and school hasn't broken up, it's empty. It has an amazing wraparound deck, with all-day sun, and those fabulous sea views. I think we'll be getting into some serious sun lounging out there. But it gets better. They've been kind enough to let us use their car – it's a typical old Waiheke car, but it's a car and we can run around in it and go to the market and get in our supplies. They even said we could take it back to the ferry and leave it down there as they're coming back over on Monday."

Overwhelmed, Freya hugs her friend. "You know, Sven, you are so damn thoughtful; you're definitely up there in the empathy stakes. You know how I'm highly sensitive, and I don't like staying in noisy places, all hemmed in and typical suburbia, and this is perfect. Just look how it's surrounded by trees and native bush – it's so private, and I remember how quiet it is. It's like going through a secret portal. Once you go through the gate you feel like you're in a different place altogether, tucked away from the big wide world out there."

There's a buzz of excitement in the air as Sven opens the door and they step inside.

Freya loves being back on the island; she didn't realise

how much she'd missed it – it really does feel like home.

"Okay, let's have a look upstairs," says Sven. "Now due to all the shite that's been going down lately with Freya, I would like to suggest she gets the front room with the view of the sea. What do you say, Flat White?"

Clara looks in and enviously agrees. "Yes, but I think we can have PJ parties in there and we all get to share the view."

"Deal," they all agree, before heading to their respective rooms to unpack.

Sven can't help worrying about Freya and is determined to make the weekend as perfect as she can. She had always thought Freya was the fey one but realises she has got her all wrong and her friend has found her true calling. She hopes the weekend will be an opportunity for opening up and some good old-fashioned downright honesty, and perhaps she'll be able to soothe Freya's nerves, and get to the bottom of Flat White's angst.

Sven pops downstairs and opens the ranch sliders onto the deck as the house is quite stuffy after being locked up all week. She picks some roses from the garden, and then puts the jug on to make some plunger coffee. She gets out the muffins she purchased on the ferry and lays the table for a late afternoon snack. Everyone is feeling a little jaded from the working week, followed by the flight and the two glasses of bubbles on empty stomachs on the boat.

As promised, Anna has left two pizzas in the freezer so they can avoid the queues in the supermarket aisles with the other holidaymakers on the island. Sven puts the two bottles of bubbles she had in her carry-on bag into the fridge to chill, and then heads back outside to raid the vegetable garden. She picks a few lettuce leaves, capsicum, cucumber and tomatoes and throws a green salad together. The evening is fast approaching, and it is still hot and humid – typical Waiheke temperatures, very different to further down the North Island.

"Okay girls, evening attire is lava-lavas – too hot for PJs, when you're ready come on down for coffee and muffins on the deck," Sven calls up the stairwell.

Freya and Clara both have the munchies as they haven't eaten since lunch.

"It's a strange time to be having afternoon tea at six o'clock in the evening, I know, but I think we need a sugar and caffeine fix. We must make the most of these two nights while we're here. We're catching the red-eye flight from Auckland to Wellington on Monday morning, and as it's too far to commute I've booked us a B&B back on the mainland for Sunday night. So, here's to two action-packed nights on the island. And remember, we do have a car, if you want to head down to a bar, that's cool, but I think we can get up to more trouble talking and drinking here without having to share a bar with the masses. What do you think, Freya?"

"Yep, all good with me," replies Freya. "Okay, let's get this show on the road. Coffee, black, please."

"Flat White, how are you having it at this time of day? Straight and black, or straight and white like your judge friend?" Freya asks, determined to waste no time in finding out about Clara's wayward love life. She had been with Jack the hiker for aeons, they had done everything together – well, almost everything bar getting married, having children and buying a house together.

"Okay girls, let's set some boundaries, ground rules like we used to in the old days," interrupts Sven. "So, agree or disagree with me. Let's go for respecting each other, one person speaking at a time, whatever goes on here stays on tour, and let's be honest and open and cut the BS and PC crap. Agreed?"

Clara and Freya nod in agreement.

"Okay Flat White," continues Sven, "you have the talking stick. And remember, we are not in a downtown Wellington or Stockholm meeting now, so no need to go for sentence fillers or corporate jargon – just get down to the fast and dirty in as few words as possible, unless it's funny, disgusting and we need all the build-up and adjectives to paint the scene. Okay, sorry Flat White, that was the last interruption. Take it away, girlfriend."

Clara hesitates, and then decides it's time to come clean with her besties. "Look, the coffee and cake were great fillers, but if I'm going to spill, I need something a little stronger. You know I don't eat much, don't bother with the pizza, let's just crack open that vino that's got my name on it, okay?"

Chapter 11

Clara Spills

lat White, wanting to avoid any more interruptions, heads inside from the deck and skates across the kitchen lino floor in her bed socks. She grabs the Lindauer Special Reserve from the fridge, glances at it, and takes it back to the table. "Sorry guys," she sighs, "this is like some of the men we've dated – it's not top shelf, but it will do for a one-night stand."

The other two roar with laughter; they've all had their fair share of mediocre men, who once they had woken up beside the next day, knew that their expiry date was up. Freya holds the champagne flutes out as Clara, with Sven's help, pops the overly dry cork and starts pouring. She passes the glasses around and together they raise them and chant their traditional, *"Salute, prost,* cheers."

"Okay Flat White, that's given you enough time to conjure up the story of your lifetime, but please remember the rules this weekend – only honesty is the theme, so no porkies. Right, what's up with Jack?" demands Sven.

"Well, to be honest…" Flat White begins, a little sheepishly.

"Yes, that's what we said, and remember, no fillers to pad the sentences out – you know it's like saying 'Well me personally', or 'Just between you and me', or 'Well off the record…' Now they are all unnecessary time-wasters…" chides Sven.

"Okay, okay. Jack. My 'Irresistible Jack', I'm just not feeling it anymore. I don't know what's happened, but as the song goes, 'I've just lost that loving feeling'. I never thought it would happen. Back in the day, I just found him so goddamned gorgeous, I just couldn't keep my hands off him. He had a body to die for, charisma in bucket loads, and his bank account and assets made the whole package pretty goddamned gorgeously irresistible."

"Hell, Flat White, can I interject?" says Freya. "To be fair, he still is all of those things – well he was last time I saw him biking through town in those skimpy shorts showing off those hairy tanned legs. How can you go off that?"

Clara yet again hesitates and looks down at the floor while hurriedly trying to take another drink. She suddenly looks incredibly vulnerable and Freya feels bad for putting her on the spot.

Sven breaks the awkward silence. "Hey Flat White, you know we're not being nosey for the sake of gossip and juicing up our conversation. We genuinely care. You just seem very different. Preoccupied, like you're physically with us when we're together, but not mentally or emotionally; you seem distant and we're just concerned. Look, do you want me to go first? Not that I have anything very exciting to say."

Clara looks up again. "No, it's all good. Okay, now remember we're not going to be judgemental or too prudish, are we? I know you think I'm purer than the pure driven snow, but I think you may be a little shocked. Okay, now no interruptions – anyone busting should go now. So, let's fill up our glasses; this may be a bombshell."

"Flat White, you have our undivided attention. We are in suspenders on the edge of our seats."

"Well, I've been doing a lot of hours for JAB lately, and most of it is legit as there are so many cases, and you know the usual crap – budgetary costs so of course salaries are the first to be cut. And after the last round of restructuring, refreshing or rebranding, whatever you want to label it, the ones who didn't lose their jobs, like me, well, we were the ones who had it the worst. You know how it works; you get this false sense of security where you think you're incredibly lucky, especially at this age and stage in life, with ageism and sexism, that you still have a job. In reality, you have to do several people's jobs for the price of one. Then eight hours of official work turns into an unofficial ten hours and more just so you can keep up with the minimum required. Well, I've been spending a lot of time at the office, helping the judges out with their notes. Then because most of them are up themselves and living in the past, you end up playing their secretary. Then suddenly you're doing their filing, bringing them their lunch, typing their notes and travelling halfway over town with them and before you know it you've started early and finished late and it becomes a pattern."

Freya jumps in with a legal quip. "Flat White, I need to interject, my client is getting way off topic; can you please bring her back in again, and stick to the question?"

Everyone, including Flat White cracks up laughing. "Yes, Your Honour, I do beg your pardon," Clara winks at her friends. "Well, like I said, most of them are crusty old arrogant tossers, but there's one who is just so adorable. I mean he's nothing to look at – well that's not fair, he is in a cute gentle giant way – but if you saw him walking down the street you wouldn't get all hot and sticky below."

The girls shriek with laughter.

"Now there's the old Flat White I remember!" Freya snorts. Clara is hilarious when she's half pissed and her alter ego Flat White emerges. Just like any other Friday night she doesn't hold back on her words when a few drinks are under her belt.

"He has that middle-aged portable table that hangs over his belt, but if you can get past the flab, he is oozing charisma. Highly, highly intelligent, knows everything there is to know about NZ Law, all the cases that have been and gone, and coming. I've seen him in action, and it is such a turn-on. He's like a dog with a bone – you can see that he's sniffing out for any loophole. You simply cannot pull the wool over his eyes."

"Okay Clara, does he have a name?" asks Freya. "Will we have seen his name in the papers, on TV? If I had gone to Law School, would I have seen his name? Are you saying he's like Martin Shaw, Inspector… Gently?"

Sven interrupts. "Oh yes, for those of us who used to get glued to their chairs watching Bodie and Doyle in *The Professionals* with their sexy Ford Capri car like mine, my favourite was Doyle, with the curly hair and olive skin. Doyle was the man. That's why I named my car after him. Anyhow… whoops, my turn to go off script. Would he have looked like Inspector George Gently back in the day, with that twinkle in his eye because he still knows how to give it to you in the sack?"

Flat White blushes as she clearly thinks of her bed scenes with him. "Yes, kinda. And funnily enough his name is Martin. Just like Martin Shaw the name of the guy who played Doyle in *The Professionals* and who also played Inspector George Gently"

Sven can't help but interrupt again. "Oh my god, not the one and only Martin Jacobsen? The top lawyer back in the day who flew up through the ranks real fast and then became judge before bouncing his way up to the dizzying heights of the High Court bench? Not him, Flat White, you're not screwing a celebrity judge?"

"Yes madam, guilty as charged."

"Holy shit, Flat White!" Freya screams, unable to hide her shock.

"WTF!" Sven splutters, nearly spilling her drink. "I am trying to be careful what I say next as we must keep to the rules I just laid down in this court of law. Can we have a recess? I need to reconsider my case."

Freya steps in. "Well congratulations, Clara James, you little dark horse. Who would have thought? So, you are screwing the judge on the judge's bench, that's the extra 'paperwork' you've been racing off to do?"

"Trust you to twist it and make some innocent, genuine romance sound so sordid," Clara remarks, looking a little abashed.

"Well, Flat White, is he married? Come on is he or isn't he?" asks Sven.

"Well yes, kind of…" replies Clara.

"FFS Flat White," Sven exclaims. She grabs her purse

and fishes inside, pulling out a packet of Pall Mall and her old orange BIC lighter. "He is 'kind of'…?" she asks sarcastically as she lights a cigarette. "So he has half a wedding band, no wedding band, or the full Monty wedding band then?" she queries, flicking ash over the deck rail.

"Yes, he is married, but he's not happy and before you shoot me down in flames and tell me I am naive and stupid, he is leaving her. It's over. Yes, they still share the same house, for the sake of the dog Sebastian; they can't agree on custody. Plus a few other things. But it's serious, gals, I think I'm in love, I think he's the one." She sits back into her chair, looking a lot more relaxed now that she's got this off her slightly flat chest.

"Hmm, that will be why you've lost the loving feeling with Jack. Because Martin has overstepped him in all the stakes, except maybe in the age stake," Sven bites.

"Well, funny you should say that. He should have retired by now – he's sixty-eight, but due to the shortage of real decent judges, they keep asking him to come back," Clara explains.

"I read about him not so long ago, doesn't he live in Auckland?" Freya asks.

"Ah yes, affirmative," Clara replies.

"And as we just happen to be in the Auckland region, where in Auckland is he? And are you thinking of popping over and seeing him? Maybe it's his wife's weekend off and she's away?" Sven grills.

"Oh, of course! A judge – a High Court Judge. He lives in Remuera, doesn't he? On Vicky Ave?" Freya jumps in, trying to release some of the building tension.

"Yes Freya, how do you know that?" Clara asks.

Putting on an upper-class English accent, Freya replies,

"Because, my dear Wellingtonian, when you have lived in Auckland for as long as I have and contracted around enough, you get to know the best real estate addresses and where certain folk live." Then dropping the act, she continues, "No, seriously, I used to live in a flat just off Victoria Avenue, called Chatfield Place, and I used to see his big Remuera tractor a.k.a. Range Rover, drive past every day while I was waiting at the bus stop. Now I think I need a cigarette after that confession," she adds, turning to Sven with her hand extended, the girls being social smokers. "It takes a lot for me to be blown away and for you, Flat White, to be the one that does it. That is a remarkable achievement. So, are we popping over to Remma's tomorrow for a spot of shopping?" she asks, lighting a cigarette.

"No, we are not. I've promised I'll stay in the background for now. I don't want to jeopardise our future together by being one of those ditzy females and coming out in public. In fact, I was sworn to secrecy that I wouldn't tell anyone, not even you guys. So your lips are sealed, okay? I think I need one of those too, Sven."

It's been a highly stressful week and Freya can't believe that here she is back on Waiheke Island again, the island where Zac just happens to now be working. She finds it quite ironic that this weekend he's back in Lowry Bay at his parents' house, for her sake no less, where she would have been if it weren't for the girls' weekend away.

She sucks hard on her cigarette, drawing back every ounce of nicotine, and blows it out. "Wow, that feels good. First one since before Outward Bound!" In her mind, she goes through all the events of the last few weeks – the unexpected mortgage Wolfe had on Portobello, the investors playing their corrupt games, the council condemning the building, being served the papers, having the locks changed, and then the dead body at the bottom of the stairs.

Freya draws long and hard on her cigarette again, and before she knows it, it's finished and it hasn't even touched the sides. She lights up another one and thinks about Zac. He seems so far away. He must've been in the traffic heading for Auckland airport while they were driving into catch the ferry. She thinks about what he's doing down in Wellington to help her with her Portobello and wishes she was there now to help him. But she knows she has reached breaking point. She needs to be as far away as possible from all of the drama on Jackson Street right now or she may do something she will later regret. *That bloody developer Church and his bully boys!* she thinks to herself.

Flat White steps inside and paces around the living area as she takes out her phone. Sven shakes her head as she looks through the window.

"Who do you think she's texting?" she asks Freya. "Jack or Martin, or both? What do you think about that?"

"That's certainly one out of the bag. God, married men at our age. I thought we got that all out of our system back in the day," Freya replies.

"Aren't we too long in the tooth to be getting down with an old married man, and then putting our life on hold for them to leave their 'dearly beloved wife'.

"The one who 'never understands them' as they so often say?" Freya interjects.

"Oh god, I can hear those lines all over again," recalls Sven as her eyes tear up. "I remember holding onto them as if they were gospel. Especially when I would start getting impatient and say, 'But you said you were leaving her last weekend, I can't wait that long, when are you going to tell her?' Oh god, poor Flat White."

Sven suddenly notices the distant look in Freya's eyes. "Oh, sorry girl, what's on your mind, Freya? Besides the big court case?" And then inspiration suddenly takes her by surprise. "Oh my god, I just got it. Do you think old Martin Jacobsen here could help you? Or maybe not – we're not even meant to know he exists. Okay, let's flag that idea for now. What's up?"

"It's just Zac. Our unbelievable timing. It was just something his mum said the other day to me about how I live in Waiheke, he lives in Lowry Bay, I come to Waiheke for a weekend, he flies to Wellington. He's been so kind. Then there's Simon the banker who's bent over backwards for me. He's such a sweetie and I think he may have feelings for me. He's single, available, and lives in Wellington. But then who needs romance when they're trying to build a mini business up and everything is against it working?" she sighs. "Hey, off on a tangent here, did I tell you Leo read my palm the other day? He reckons there's some romance ahead for me; I just don't know how I would fit it all in," she laughs.

Clara knocks on the window and beckons them in. "Hey gals, I've just texted Martin. That wasn't a silly idea of yours – I'm going to meet him tomorrow. He's over here this weekend with his mates for some golf tournament and then drinkies up at the Mudbrick… do you know it Freya?"

"Yep, I do. We can drop you off there tomorrow on our way to the Saturday market. I thought he was out of bounds for you after hours? Oh well, I can't talk; rules are made to be broken. Look at the ones that have been broken this week by the council, the bank, and that bastard Church…"

The girls go back inside where they continue to gossip and drink, but they slow down the pace as they want to do lots on Saturday. The weather forecast is looking good and Freya has said a swim at Palm Beach is compulsory.

They head upstairs to Freya's room, where they continue talking about their love lives and their future aspirations, into the wee hours of the morning. Eventually they drift off to their own rooms to sleep.

Chapter 12

Skinny Dip and into the Deep

Saturday is a hot sticky December Waiheke day with high humidity. The beaches are packed with locals, tourists and weekenders coming over from Auckland. The narrow roads are jammed with four-wheel drives, tourist buses, cyclists and pedestrians, as there are no pavements. Sven drops Clara off to see Martin at Mudbrick winery.

"God knows what Jack must be thinking. I wonder if he's clicked yet that he's now no longer in the frame – well, the mainframe, so to speak," Sven comments to Freya. "Wow, I'm shocked, Flat White is normally the seriously responsible one and here she is risking her reputation that is so important to her in the public service arena, by sleeping with some guy that's old enough to be her father. Anyhow, bugger that, let's head for the market and see what we can find. Are you still on the hunt for quirky things for Portobello? You might find a painting or an Art Deco something..."

They cruise on to the market and have to park miles away as every man and their dog is there this weekend with the build-up for Christmas.

They buy fruit and veggies but nothing for Portobello – all the goodies have been seriously picked over by the time they arrive. They pull into the local supermarket and push down the narrow aisles past the tourists to get their provisions, even if it's just for one night and one day. They buy hot barbeque sausages wrapped in bread from the local Girl Guide troop raising money for their next jamboree, then head for Palm Beach. Freya sends a text to Flat White, but gets no reply.

"She has a habit of ignoring us when we're doing something she's not interested in," Freya remarks.

"So much easier to ignore us than be honest and say, 'No, that's beneath me'. I can't imagine Flat White exposing her porcelain white bleached skin for a swim in a heated pool, let alone in the ocean," Sven replies.

Freya laughs. "No, that would muck up her hair, and god forbid if she were to expose herself completely by jumping in naked at a nudist beach!"

"Well call me old-fashioned, but I would prefer to expose my body at a naked beach where I don't know anyone than risk exposing my name and reputation in the *Capital News* for breaking up the marriage of the most popular 'rock star' judge this country has ever seen. Hell, that's risky business. Look, you know I love adventure, but this is playing with fire... Rather her than me," replies Sven as she looks out for a car park.

They end up parking miles away from the beach due to the backlog of cars everywhere and walk on down. It's so hot that they just drop their towels and head for the surf. It's high tide, the surf is up, and it's fabulous to see golden sandy east coast beaches again after living in Wellington and frequenting the Kāpiti Coast's grey sand and rocky beaches.

The temperatures soar and it gets hotter as they approach the sea. Palm Beach gets more and more crowded as families pour on to the sand with screaming kids. Freya and Sven look at each other. "Come on then, Sven," says Freya. "Have you plucked up enough courage yet? You've ripped your clothes off before, skinny dipping with Charlie, so come on, let's lose the crowd and head down to Little Palm Beach. The regulars around here are a friendly bunch and besides, they're not interested in perving at little old you or me. Come on, we haven't got our little handbrake with us, so now's the time. Tomorrow we'll be off."

Sven agrees and they walk the short distance between the two beaches, through the rocks and high tide waves to a slightly less-packed Little Palm, but with less screaming kids – just a whole lot of couples and singles lying under umbrellas. Sven and Freya, fully clothed, stand out as they walk the length of the beach. They carry on all the way to the end and plant themselves down by two men with polka dot umbrellas and matching polka dot baseball caps. Freya chuckles to herself thinking of the polka dot handkerchief she bought from this very island for Zac and wonders if the gay boys bought their polka dot attire from the same Waiheke market stand.

"Okay Sven, are you ready?"

"Yep, ready as I'll ever be, Freya."

They both strip off and run for the waves. Twenty minutes later, after body surfing and catching every wave possible, they come back to their little possie. The two men have moved on and the space is empty, making Sven feel more comfortable.

"Wow Freya, that was awesome. I really enjoyed that. I feel so invigorated and recharged. I feel like a whole load has been taken off my shoulders."

"Yep, I've been reading quite a bit of stuff lately about empaths, and evidently some of them use water to ground themselves, to clear their energies. I guess I've always known I was an empath as I always felt good in nature, and I've needed that over the years as my escape route when things like crowds and people get me down too much."

"Hey, can you explain a bit more about this empath stuff? I know about HSPs, highly sensitive people. But how do empaths fit into it?"

"Well, I'm still reading up on it all, but I think they're similar. It just means you're like an emotional sponge, you take in everyone else's energy, good or bad, and in the end, you can't work out where your boundaries or emotions finish and someone else's start. I used to wonder why I couldn't stay at parties for too long. And I used to think I was weird, but now I realise I'm just tuned into everything good and bad that's happening around me. It's so damn interesting. I even found a little assessment tool to do online and as a result, I reckon I'm all three types of empaths – the emotional empath, the physical empath and the inner empath."

Sven adds her knowledge from a work perspective. "Yes, I have noticed that some of the clients I see nowadays are highly sensitive. One I'm seeing right now at BS castle can't stand working in an office anymore. The artificial bright lighting does her head in, the fluorescent lighting overstimulates her brain and she gets horrendous headaches. She is right now trying to get her boss to allow her to be one of the many who are taking advantage of the new 'working from home policy'. I have another one who can't sit in meetings for too long with everyone sitting in such close proximity. She picks up the vibes of those sitting around her. It's quite fascinating – she'll pick up the vibes from the Sharks with Lipstick who are smiling sweetly on the outside but underneath seething, and this woman can feel what these women are really thinking and feeling."

"Wow, I'm similar; it's all about finding coping strategies, isn't it? Well of course, as you well know, it's about finding different ways of getting around the situation," Freya replies. "I've started to see how being an empath is a gift instead of a disorder. You know how much people love to turn it into yet another psychological and behavioural 'disorder', and all that does is makes you feel even more isolated and abnormal, versus gifted with a special talent. Please don't laugh, but I've started feeling things – for instance I've been sensing my grandfather around me. Now I know I'm working in his building, naturally I feel closer to him, but I've been getting signs."

"Freya, how exciting, do go on. I would love to be tuned into that extra sense so I could see things," Sven says excitedly. "It certainly would fast-forward a lot of the BS meetings I have to attend; I could cut through the BS and get to what is really happening."

"Well you can, we all have the potential to 'see, hear, feel'. You know that's a clairvoyant, clairaudient or clairsentient. It's just tapping into those latent potentials. That's why I loved Waiheke so much – I just met so many like-minded people. Anyhow, now I know why I'm so sensitive to noise, smells and crowded rooms, and why intuitively I always knew I needed my own escape route from parties. I'd often lay off the booze then I could take my own car – then I could leave when I'd had enough instead of staying on for hours listening to all that white noise they call conversation. There is nothing worse than listening to someone idly chatting about trivia for hours on end – you can never get that time back! I'm finding it easier and easier to just say 'No' now and not accept invitations or leave when I want. People believe they 'should' do this and 'should' do that, and then get all passive aggressive because they have to do something they don't want to do. Then they complain they don't have enough time, when in fact they brought it on themselves. People don't seem to realise they can turn down invitations, and ignore guilt trips and all the 'shoulds' one feels they must do as a mother, a daughter, a friend, acquaintance etc."

"Yep, I know what you mean, girl. You know, Freya, I have to say I always thought back in the day you were a little out there and on the edge, but now I get you were just more tuned in with yourself than any of us who were too busy ticking boxes and conforming to please society's 'worldview'."

"Yep, good old big brother and society and all the little clones dancing to that tune rather than getting in touch with their own feelings and breaking away. We can't have any little black sheep breaking free now. No, that certainly won't do!" adds Freya sarcastically. "We must all conform and be little robotic white sheep following the leader down the garden path of doom and despair," she finishes with a wink.

"Whoa, that got really heavy!" says Sven stretching

out on her towel. "Right, let's cap that for a while! It's interesting, but let's have some fun – we can't forget to have fun while we're on this planet. Let's get a bit of a tan and catch some rays. Besides, I need to digest and reflect on all of this."

They lie in the sun and soak up the Waiheke rays. People come and go and the vibe on the beach is relaxed and chilled. They both fall asleep until Sven's cell phone wakes them.

After several beeps Sven rolls over and checks it. "It's Flat White, she has been dispensed with and is back at the house looking for us. Okay Freya, I think that's our cue to get going. We don't want to leave her locked outside frying away in the sun. You know how much she hates the sun. She says that's why she loves Wellington as the weather is cooler."

Freya remembers the track back up the hill behind the beach leading up to the main road – within a short walk she can be back home within ten minutes.

"Look, Sven, if you don't mind, can you take the car back? I'll walk up the track when I'm ready. I just don't think I'm quite ready to hear chapter and verse of the married man and how it is all perfectly normal and that what they're doing is not hurting anyone. You know how Flat White gets – holier than the Pope, and we all know it is so hypocritical. I just want to think about Portobello and work out some finer details, a plan of attack so I'm all prepared for the week that lies ahead."

"Sure, no worries, see you back at the digs," Sven replies.

Sven gets dressed and walks back to the car, leaving Freya lost in her thoughts.

Freya, for the first time in ages, gets out her old trusty pad and pen and starts nutting out the finer details of Portobello. Looking out at the ocean she gets swept away thinking of her new life down in Wellywood and starts making notes, jotting down some of her favourite rhyming verse, a passion all the girls share.

PORTOBELLO

Portobello my little beauty

Dressed to kill, a real cutie

Blue windows and pink doors

Inside polished original kauri floors

She glows and stands out in the night

Like a lighthouse burning bright

Art Deco design through and through

With upcycled furnishings sparkling like new

Newish curtains and blinds to match

From a roll of material from a 'seconds' batch

Skirting boards, cornices and chandeliers

And the wrought-iron spiral stairs

Built-in shelves and drop-down tables

Beats all those furniture brands and their labels

High walls and impressive ceilings

Full of history and bygone feelings

Plenty of crannies and quirky nooks

A downstairs shelf full of vintage books

Hidey holes in all sorts of places
And views of big open spaces
An old-fashioned potter's shed
A chicken's shelter with straw bed
Therefore, free-range eggs out the back
To collect from that rustic shack

Chapter 13

Sven's Turn

S ven gets back to the house to find Clara sitting on the deck, pouting. "So, how did it go?" she asks tentatively.

"Seriously Sven, I spilled as much as I could last night. I just can't cope with the constant questions from you and Freya. Can you just not let it go? Besides, your love life is nothing to write home about. What's the story with you? Are you on or off or in that usual limbo stage? You know the best guy you ever had you let go, you didn't even fight for him. At least I fight for what I know is right," Clara snaps back.

Keeping her thoughts to herself, Sven counts to ten, afraid she might say something that she may later regret. She settles for talking to herself, *God that's rich coming from Flat White, fighting for what she knows is right. I would say Jack is the right one for her. He's funny, kind, intelligent, spiritual, caring, good looking and financially secure, not to mention puts up with Flat White. I just hope she works out that Jack is in fact the one that she's in love with, before it's too late. I would hate her to piss him off too much and go from having two in her life to a big fat zero.*

Sven, concentrating on keeping her mouth shut, unlocks the door. Perhaps it's too soon to be judging Clara, especially as they've only just persuaded her to open up about her love life. She doesn't want to go and undo the good work and the revelations from last night – it's hard enough getting Flat White to open up at the best of times, why ruin it now when she's starting to get real, thinks Sven. Besides, she needs her trusty ally Freya; best to have the two of them present before taking on this delicate matter, she decides.

Sven puts on the jug and flicks the stereo system on, carefully placing the vinyl LP of Carly Simon's greatest hits onto the turntable. 'You're so Vain' starts pumping out of the old seventies speakers. A bit too apt for right now, but nothing like a bit of upbeat nostalgic music to change the vibes and emotions in the house.

Sven gets on tidying the kitchen, and Clara, once she has dusted herself off in the bathroom, joins her and starts having a go again at Sven. One thing she does not appreciate is being ignored. Sven has held her tongue long enough and is about to unleash a tirade in response.

Freya opens the front door feeling refreshed and recharged as she's had time to write, soak up the rays and cleanse herself in the ocean. Unbeknown to her, her mates are on a different plane and she innocently walks into a minefield. Being an empath, she can sense the sudden change in atmosphere as she walks through the house.

By the time she steps into the kitchen the two girls

are going for gold. "Hey children, what's up, did I miss something exciting? We're not arguing over the superior sex as usual, are we? So, how's old Judge Boy? Was he in top form?"

"That's it! I'm off!" Clara bursts out, now in tears. "I don't need to listen to this crap! I'll let you two solve the world on your own as usual. I mean after all, look at your love lives that are just so exemplary – you Freya with both Zac and Simon eating out of your hand, and... and Sven you had Charlie and… and, AAHH!!" She runs upstairs to her room.

The door slams and the two girls look at each other, dumbfounded. "Well what did I miss? Was lover boy not in top form today? Did I just miss the tsunami of the century? Thanks for the warning."

The door opens upstairs and Clara screams out, "Oh, and before you two put your foot in it anymore, the ceiling and floor are like paper and I can hear everything you say! If you must talk behind my back as usual you may want to lower your voices so I don't have to suffer, or just come and say it to my face..." she adds, slamming the door again. This time the door handle flies off, hits the wall and rolls along the floor before bouncing down the stairs.

"Sven, just leave it," says Freya. "Let her calm down and stew in her own juices. But you know what? She does have a point; look at our love lives, they are a mess. We're no better than anyone else, bitching and solving everyone else's life instead of looking at our own first. Look, it's almost five o'clock."

"Wine o'clock!" they say in unison.

"Let's have a shower, get dinner ready and pop some wine," suggests Freya. "We haven't really been eating that well since getting here."

"Okay. I've unpacked the groceries, you jump into the shower first and I'll make a start down here," offers Sven.

By six o'clock the dinner preparation is complete, the bubbles are poured and Freya and Sven are sitting out on the deck.

"Okay Sven, you spill, you haven't had a turn taking the floor this weekend," says Freya. "So typical of you putting everyone else's needs first. Come on, you're off the BS Ministry's clock now, you don't have to coach us, that's what you do for a living. How about telling me what's happening with you. Let's reverse the roles, and I'll pretend to be you. Sven, you have the talking stick, take it away girl."

Sven laughs and takes the stick. After a big breath she begins. "Well, I've been thinking about what Flat White said before she headed upstairs, you know, about our love life, especially that crack about Charlie."

Seeing the emotion in Sven's face, Freya prompts, "Go on Sven, get it out…"

"I didn't think I still had such deep feelings for him, I mean it was so long ago… and it hurt so much… You know that's why I switched studies and then as soon as I graduated, I flew out on my OE," Sven confesses.

"Well, it was kinda obvious, you two were joined at the hip, and then… but Flat White should really be hearing this too," Freya replies. "Hold that thought while I go and get her," she says, heading inside.

Freya knocks on Clara's door. "Hey doll, are you ready for dinner and drinks?"

There's no answer so she tries again, attempting to tailor the invitation to suit, putting on her best upper-class

English accent. "Clara, your presence is requested with an invitation for some alfresco fine wining and dining downstairs…"

The door opens and a red-eyed Clara peeks out. "What sort of fine wining and dining?"

"Ha, got you babe, come here," says Freya, giving Clara a big hug. "But seriously, only the best, we went to the supermarket today and checked out some fine cuts of meat, a delicious array of salads, and your favourite bubbles, Piper Heidsieck. None of that cheap Kiwi stuff you dislike with a passion."

"Piper? Okay then, I'll just wash my face and be down in a minute," Clara perks up.

"Good girl, be quick, Sven is about to spill…"

"About bloody time!" Clara says, wiping her face, softening. "Thanks for the hug, I really needed that, Fin."

*****

"Is she coming down?" asks Sven.

"The 'Piper' is calling her," Freya winks. "I told you that was a good choice. Now let's just go a bit easy on her as she was still crying – I suspect there's a bit more going on than we thought. Now it's probably best…"

"Probably best what, Freya?" Clara asks as she bounces out onto the deck.

Pouring the drinks Sven replies, "Probably best we all get one of these down the hatch as it's my turn to spill, thanks to your crack about Charlie, Flat White. By the way, sorry if I set you off babe, but I'm not sure I'll be thanking you for hitting that particular raw nerve."

"I bloody well knew it!" Clara exclaims. "You have

been holding a torch for him all these years!"

"Have not," Sven shoots back, then remembering her rules of being honest from last night, "Well… maybe I have." She pauses for a moment. "If I'm really honest with myself, and you two of course, then I always knew he was the one…"

"Even back then?" Freya asks.

"I mean you were engaged," Clara adds.

"Yep, even back then…" she says with a far-away look in her eyes. "There was just nothing else like being held in his arms, feeling so safe from the world."

"You two did make the most adorable couple," Clara states. "I always thought you hit the jackpot with Charlie. Sven, tell me truly, how close were you?"

"Well, I just thought that we would finish police college, start our careers and then get hitched, buy a home in the country – you know, that sort of thing," Sven replies. "The life we saw modelled by our parents."

"Wow, now that's what I call in L O V E!" Clara says, winking at Freya.

"Hmm, I still do fancy him. I just don't know about being married to a copper…" Sven daydreams.

"What did you just say?" Freya nearly spits out her wine. "Did you just say the M word? Married… Holy crap Sven, you *have* got it bad for him! *Marriage?*"

Sven falls silent and realises what she has just said. She is just as surprised as her friends. "Hell Freya, I have no idea where that came from. That's given me more food for thought. I need to do some serious thinking. Hey, do you think I should go and visit your palmist mate Leo? Will he be able to point me in the right direction?"

"Woah, back up the bus, bro. Who said Charlie still

wants to be with you, let alone marry you?" Freya asks.

"Well, there is the small matter of him cheating on me, which is why I left him in the first place. There's a lot of water under the bridge that has to be cleared up. Like that Māori female copper I saw him with that night many moons ago."

"Oh, for god's sake Sven, practise what you preach; you do have to let bygones be bygones sometimes. We've all made mistakes and ended up with the wrong people. If anyone knows that, it's me," Clara exclaims. "Besides, we're much older and wiser now, aren't we?"

"Sven, I know he hurt you back then, but you know he's been the only true man for you. If you find him, don't you dare let him slip through your fingers again!" Freya says.

"Not much chance of tracking him down, but yeah, if I do, I will see if I can work my feminine wiles on him," Sven laughs. "Anyhow, now you have my love life sorted, shouldn't we get onto yours, Freya?"

"Thanks for being real, Sven," says Clara, giving her friend a hug. "Sorry for being a bitch before. Yes, now it's your turn, Freya."

"Just as well we haven't fired up the barbeque yet," Freya says. "How about another drink before I start?"

"A most excellent idea there, Freya. Can't get enough of this good stuff!" Clara announces, grabbing the Piper bottle and refilling the glasses. "Here's to the Trinity Trio, *salute!*"

Chapter 14

Freya (Opens Up)

Clara leans back on the balcony rail. "Okay Freya, let's hear it from you. I mean, what's really going on with you and Zac? Why does he need to go down to Wellington two weekends in a row, especially when public servants don't work over the weekend? What does he expect to achieve in just two days? Shouldn't he be the one showing us around the island since he's been working here?"

Freya raises her glass again. "Yes. Long story, but for now I propose a toast: here's to Waiheke and deep and meaningful discussions and getting REAL!!"

Sven joins in and toasts, "Here's to endings and new beginnings."

Clara, still sensitive from the day's events, asks, "What do you mean by endings?"

"I just mean that for a new beginning, something has to end. And Freya and I have had a number of endings. What about you, Flat White? Why do you ask?" Sven replies coyly.

"I thought you were referring to Martin and me, because we are not ending, we are just beginning. To address the potential elephant in the room, today was about 'timing', that's all it was. It was meant to be a boys' weekend, and then not long after I arrived, Martin's wife Margot, of all people, turned up. There were a few fireworks, but we managed to get through it," Clara sighs, before continuing. "No one knew who I was – they just thought I was some floozie that Martin had got talking to at the bar. There was a wedding going on up there as well as the post golf tournament leer-up, it was swarming with people, too easy to mingle and blend so to speak. Everyone was as high as kites, talking to the different groups and intermingling. Margot couldn't let a trip to Waiheke pass her by, so she'd come over on the car ferry and just driven up with one of her mates. Martin had come over earlier on the passenger ferry with his golf buddies, but she thought she would surprise him. Anyhow, I was promptly told to disappear, although I took my time. I tell you girls, if you are on the look-out for some new fresh talent, they are up there at Mudbrick by the Mercedes-load!" Clara looks at her mates expectantly, hoping she can entice them to abandon drinks at home and return to Mudbrick for a bit of a nosey.

Freya is quick to respond. "Thanks for the invite, Clara, but I think we might already be over the limit, and besides, it would be too noisy if there's a wedding going on and the drinks have been flowing all day. We're in the middle of a deep and meaningful – well, about to be. You spilled last night and did such a good job, we thought we would follow suit today. I don't know if we'll be able to do as good as you, though. You really upped the stakes last night with your revelation. Sven, can you up the ante and do better in the 'affairs' department?"

"Not recently," Sven replies with a wink. Then the penny drops. "Why, are you having an affair, Freya? Oh my god, you are, aren't you? That's why you can't commit to all those men who are flapping around your feet – Simon, Zac… Come on, spill, who is it?"

Clara pipes up, "Yeah Freya, come on, it's an even playing field here. I've exposed myself – well obviously not as much as you two did today down at Little Palm for all to see. What's with your love life?"

Freya takes a moment to compose herself before replying. "Well fair play, my dear. Yep, nothing like calling the kettle black. A bit has happened lately, and truth be told, I'm in a bit of mess…" Her voice trails off and suddenly she breaks down and cries.

Both girls are taken aback at Freya's sudden reaction. Sven comes to the rescue, grabbing the tissues from the coffee table, while Clara comforts Freya and promptly tops up her glass.

"It's okay guys, these tears have been welling up for ages and they're well overdue. I need them to come out before my dam bursts from holding it all in for so fucking long."

"It's alright Freya, start where you need to and take as long as you want. Time is not an issue on this island. Remember, we're on island time here, so just go for it when *you* are ready."

"Well I know you guys think I'm a bit of a wastrel, a bit of an airy fairy and I appear as if I just drift from one job, one place, one relationship to another, and you're probably right. But I've actually been planning my future in great detail. I'm a free spirit – I like house and farm sitting, looking after animals, being out in nature. This feeds my soul and I know it all sounds very hippie-ish, but it's not. I'm just not like you guys – I don't get off on this 'climbing the corporate ladder' lark and 'adding value' or whatever you call it today in corporate speak. Sitting in on meetings, navel-gazing, and all that BS. I just want to be Freya. I'm not normal like you guys."

It's now Clara and Sven's turn to look at each in sheer shock and dismay. Is this really their independent carefree mate Freya talking? Where has she gone?

Clara is the first to talk for a change. "Hey Freya, what are you on about? We love how you're a free spirit, and don't feel you have to conform and fit in with the crowd. That's what makes you special, unique, groovy. Since when have you felt the need to be a clone and be like us? You're taking the piss, aren't you? What happened to you on that Inward Bound expedition you've just come back from? Have you had a lobotomy?"

Freya laughs at Clara's forthright words. She really is refreshing after a couple of glasses. "Funny you should say 'Inward Bound', it's actually Outward Bound, but you definitely go inward a lot on that hīkoi. Sorry, journey. I found out a lot about myself while I was down there. Stuff I didn't even know about myself, or maybe I did know once, but it was so well parked beneath all my layers."

"Okay, Outward Bound, whatever you call it, retreat, physical work camp, some type of Fluro activewear hell?" Clara asks.

"It's confusing," Freya continues. "I can't explain myself, especially when I'm in this state of mind, but I like being who I am – essentially the free spirit, the animal lover, the plant lover, the moon worshipper, the stargazer, the non-conformist, the potential activist. But it comes at a cost. It's hard seeing everything outside the square and being in the triangle or whatever you want to call it and being highly sensitive to it all. People don't take you seriously."

"Which people don't take you seriously?" asks Clara.

"Like you two, you have never taken me seriously. You always think I'm the flighty one, without my feet on the ground, with these airy-fairy ideas, like me getting my granddad's place up and running."

Sven is a little taken aback. "That's bullshit, sheer bullshit, Freya," she mutters, then carries on. "It's a brilliant idea, it's admirable, it's out there. Who but you would follow a dream like that? Just you, you are the one bold and brave enough to do that. Only you. Us two wouldn't. Right now, we're clinging on like every other public servant to the fragile safety net of four government department walls, and we all know they're constantly crumbling, waiting for the next earthquake or change of government. Freya, you have balls, following your dreams, and we really admire you for that."

Clara goes a little silent, and then takes a big breath. "Freya, I would love to jack in my job and follow my heart and take off overseas. I wish I could be more like you, instead of the safe, boring, conservative Clara."

"Are you serious? You don't think I'm some fey flighty fairy just trying to fight against those corrupt, big-shot 'Snakes in Suits'?"

"No, we don't," Clara replies, adding after some reflection, "In fact, Freya, when we're sober I want you to give me more details on what all this court injunction is about, as I'd like to have a word with Martin or one of his cronies about it. The only perks of my job besides the pay and keeping me off the street is I do know a lot of people high up in the courts who'll know about your case and the people involved. You can be rest assured I will get to the bottom of this, even if it costs me my job. No friend of mine, especially my best friend, gets fucked over the way you have been recently."

Sven and Freya look at each other aghast, then back at Clara. "Wow, Flat White," says Sven, "you really do come up with some pearlers, and this conversation is no exception!"

"What can I say?" says Freya, humbled that Clara would do that for her. "I really would appreciate that, as long as you don't get into trouble. I hate it when people get into trouble for trying to do a good thing for someone."

"Yay! That's one thing solved. So, go on Freya," prompts Sven. "What else has you feeling so overwhelmed besides trying to survive let alone thrive in this twenty-first-century world of chaos?"

"Well, like I said, all I'm trying to do is let my granddad's legacy live on. You know, he worked hard for his clients; while all the others today charge like wounded bulls, he did so much pro bono. I just wish I'd been born earlier so I could have helped him out with his accounts. I could have kept a running tally of his hours and sent out bills for all his work, time and ideas. Then he wouldn't have died more or less broke. And half this shit wouldn't be happening now with all the bankers and the so-called big shots wouldn't be coming in threatening to take Portobello away from me."

"Hasn't Simon and your lawyer got on the case with

that?" asks Sven. "Didn't he work out an interest-only loan for you, with no penalties if you pay it off earlier? And hasn't Dimitri given you the hourly rate you've deserved for ages so you can manage repayments?"

"Yes, but Simon's head office is giving him grief, and you know the job with Dimitri is only for another three months. We know government can never commit to anything longer, no matter how good you are. And yes, Zac is on the case playing project manager, trying to work out my budget with expenses that seem to be going through the roof to get the place up and running. He recommended I get an accountant in."

"Well guess whose old man is an accountant?" says Sven triumphantly. "I know he may be a bit out of date with some stuff, but he's one of those old-fashioned ethical professionals like your granddad. I'll ask Dad if he'd mind looking through your books, I know he'd love to do that for you."

"Really Sven? Oh, that would be wonderful," Freya says relieved. "Okay, tick that one off. Now girl, what else is troubling you?"

"Well I guess I've just got overwhelmed with everything that needs to be done to get Portobello open and paying her own way by Christmas. Zac is meant to be up here on the island doing his project management but he's now down at Portobello for the second weekend in a row. He has his own life up here now and I can't be relying on him to look after me all the time, can I?"

Sven and Clara exchange looks. "Well don't take this the wrong way," Clara laughs, "but do you want Zac to be looking after you, do you want him to be your knight in shining armour? Do you want to be his damsel in distress, or his equal?"

A silence ensues, and then Freya lets it all out. "Well, I guess that's the point, I'm not sure. I'm so fucking nervous. We've been mates forever. My godmother's son. My childhood school mate, someone I grew up with in Lowry Bay. He's been married. I haven't. He's gone off and been successful. I haven't. I just think he looks at me like a little sister who's always in trouble and needs help all the time. Besides, I'm just not his type. Look at his ex. And even if I *did* stand a chance, I've tried long-distance relationships and they just don't work. As much as I love Waiheke, I've moved on and my home is now in Wellington at Portobello. What I'm trying to say is my days of being free and easy in a relationship are over. I want to have a fixed abode, I want to have roots, I want to be running Portobello. No more house sitting, short-term government contracts, commuting. No more blind dates; I want certainty in my life. And man, was Outward Bound a huge wake-up call for me. There's no going back after that hīkoi of a lifetime!"

The others listen in silence as Freya gets her words out. It's been a long time coming.

"I really had to confront a lot of fears on that three-week leg of a bender. Everything pushed me to the limit. Getting up early, starting the day with running, climbing cliffs blindfolded, steering a cutter past the bloody ferries in the pouring rain, rowing a waka across Lake Takapō, sleeping outdoors in wet smelly rotten clothes. Getting up at the marae and doing my pepeha. I didn't even know what pepeha meant before I went!"

"I don't want to sound too ignorant," interrupts Clara, "but what is a pepper ha?"

Sven and Freya laugh good-naturedly, and then Sven explains. "It's your intro, bro, you tell everyone where you're from, your mountain, river, your marae, your tribe, ancestors, whānau..."

Freya continues, "It's kinda like asking what school you went to or what your job is when you're at a party; it's all about connections, finding a link between you and the people of the land (tangata whenua) at the marae."

"Man, it can get really heavy," says Sven, "especially when you say your ancestors' names who have passed, it just makes me cry. Hell, I wouldn't be here today if it wasn't for them."

"Oh, give us a demo, Freya. I haven't heard you speak Māori before. Come on, just a couple of lines, any old lines, let me hear your Te Reo pronunciation," Clara asks, thinking this will be good for Freya's confidence.

"Maybe another time," Freya stalls.

"No, now, Freya," Sven insists.

"Okay… just a few…" Freya takes a deep breath and psyches herself up.

"Ko Aoraki te maunga

Ko Waitaki te awa

Ko Takitimu te waka

Ko Ngāi Tahu te iwi

Ko Tahu Pōtiki te tupuna

Ko Freya tōku ingoa."

"Wow Freya, that was dead impressive," Clara says genuinely. "Sorry for getting us off track, please continue your revelations from Outward – or should we call it

'Inward' Bound now?" she giggles.

"Yeah, a lot happened. I was so out of my comfort zone – the early starts, the lack of sleep, the healthy food, not being able to be in contact with anyone on the outside world. They take your phone off you, so no devices. And you know how addicted we are today to texts, emails, the internet – it's one big messy addiction from the time you wake up until you go to bed at night. Anyhow, while I was away, especially the day-in-day-out walking through the valleys following in our ancestors' footsteps, I realised that one day you feel like so much is in front of you and then suddenly you feel you've lived maybe half your life and you have nothing to show for it. You know how society puts those expectations on us – by now we should be married, or up to at least our second marriage, have mortgages, kids, high-flying careers. Man, it was a real turning point, it just got me thinking of all those serious things in life that you don't worry about when you're footloose and fancy-free, like, 'What do I want? Who am I?'."

"Heavy stuff indeed!" Clara replies, topping everyone's glasses up. "So who are you really, Freya Isobel Nilson?"

"I am an incredibly kind, caring, generous, wanderlust free spirit who wants to do good. I want to give back to the community, look after and enhance my little patch of the planet," announces Freya, as her two best friends nod their heads approvingly. "I know it's ambitious, so starting with giving back to the community is enough. I want to run a joint where all my business partners have true values that they really believe in, not your usual corporate BS. They must care about people and want to offer them great experiences, whether it be through food, wine, accommodation, a lesson, whatever. They need to be able to make ethical decisions... And yes, of course, make a buck on the side, as that is the currency in today's world, isn't it? I mean let's face it – we're not on a commune where we can barter a cow for a roll of loo paper."

The girls all laugh; Freya is funny even when she's being deadly serious.

Wiping her eyes with the back of her hand, Freya continues. "What I'm saying is that I have all the right intentions; it's not just for my granddad, it's for me and it's for the greater good of the community, the planet, the whole deal."

Sven asks gently, "I thought your dream was to live off the land in the country, Freya?"

"It was, babe, but that's not where Wolfe built Portobello. Having plenty of time to think things through while I was hiking down south, I realised that even though Portobello is in the middle of Petone, my dream of a cooperative community can still become a reality. It's near the area where I grew up, my tūrangawaewae, so I'm familiar with it. And I have a great network of friends, like you guys."

Sven butts in, "But why can't you still follow your 'living off the land' dream one day? It's not all about following just ONE dream, you can have the whole lot and Portobello can be just one part of the whole dream. Do you remember old Hans's loft apartment in Stockholm? He had that great rooftop balcony area in the heart of the city where we had a couple of parties – remember his greenhouse up there and those raised gardens and potted citrus? We were grabbing fresh limes off the tree for our drinks. It was so high up in the sky and full of greenery you didn't even know you were bang in the middle of a large European city. Why can't you do that at Portobello? Have your own inner sanctuary in the city and when you become rich and famous you leave it to others to continue to run, once you retire to the country to start up your next dream plot."

"Yeah, exactly," says Freya wistfully. "But I'm not a typical developer or entrepreneur. I don't want to do big – I just want to do something that makes my heart sing," she explains.

"Oh, I know what you mean," Clara interrupts, "I just hate those developers who knock down historic buildings and put up ugly steel and glass monstrosities!"

"Yeah, just like that Church bastard who's been trying to get hold of Portobello just so he can pull it down and build a row of sterile apartments!" Freya spits out vehemently. "I'm going to preserve history and attempt to restore Portobello back to its former glory and share it with others."

"And make enough money so you don't have to go out and work for Dimitri?" Sven asks.

"Well I certainly haven't bought into the 'Happiness Trap' where I'm waiting for some man to sweep me off my feet and save the day, have his children, grow old and live happily ever after," remarks Freya.

"All power to you girl, I love it!" Clara exclaims.

"That reminds me, Flat White," says Freya, "you so have to read *The Happiness Trap* by Russ Harris. It explores that fairy-tale principle that everyone expects – they'll live happily ever after once they meet their knight in shining armour. Guess what? Life just doesn't pan out that way, so everyone's expectations fall short of the reality and then we all crash and burn and wonder why we end up self-medicating on alcohol, drugs, sex and overcomplicating stuff by taking the doctor's prescriptions of Prozac and the like."

"I love how you're so passionate about your dream," responds Sven. "You're very determined, no matter what shit gets in the way, to continue on your path, your Yellow Brick Road. Ha, just like Dorothy in *The Wizard of Oz*. That's commendable. My dream was always to live off the land as well, be self-sustainable, and I would love to have a plot of land in the country."

Clara adds, "Well girls, be careful what you ask for, because remember that *Law of Attraction* – 'Ask, Believe, and Receive' with the right intention and you get it."

"Yep, ain't that the truth," agrees Sven. "Okay, where to now, my girl? What's happening in two days' time for Freya when she's back in the capital city? What are your contingency plans?"

"Well, find myself a great lawyer," Freya replies, looking at Clara hopefully, "or get Mr Tombe some information he can use, and a great accountant, and…" Freya looks at Sven.

"And a great man?" finishes Clara.

"Yes – Zachary Tyler MacLean-Smith, Simon the bank manager, or Mr X?" Sven hints. "Is there room in your life for one, or all three of these men?"

Freya decides to come clean, "I haven't told you Flat White what happened last Sunday. After Zac and I finished getting some more materials and fittings for the renovations at Portobello, we stopped in to get the council report, and found a dead man at the bottom of the stairs."

"What!" Clara exclaims.

"You never told me all the details. Do you know who it was? asks Sven incredulously.

"I still don't know, Detective Croft…"

"Ah ha! I knew there was a third man in your life, a.k.a. Mr X, and he is Detective Croft eh?" Sven interrupts.

"Hardly Sven, policemen are more your type," Clara winks.

"As I was saying, Detective Croft won't tell me anything and has closed Portobello off so I can't make any headway, of course as it's a potential homicide I'm not meant to say anything," Freya clarifies.

"Yeah, that would be right, holding off releasing details so the cops can catch the killer," Clara comments.

"So how does this fit with your love life Freya?" Sven asks.

"I saw Zac completely differently, so assertive, he really took charge, stopped me from seeing the body, dealt with the police, made sure I was okay and then drove me home," Freya explains.

"A side you hadn't seen before Fin?" Clara asks.

"Exactly Flat White, since then I've kinda felt differently towards him, like I couldn't imagine my life without him. He's changed over the years – he used to be a gangly teenager, but now he's filled out in all the right places, and he's really quite handsome. I get butterflies when I look at him now," she admits.

"How do you know he's filled out in all the right places, Freya? Are you sharing the bunker with him?" Clara whistles.

"Ha, ha. No, we went swimming the other day at Lowry Bay and man did he look hot. I was watching him through my sunglasses, and he was completely oblivious. I made out I was looking up at the sky, at the planes, but I wasn't," she giggles.

"You naughty, naughty girl!" Sven teases. "Go on, explain, give us more detail – especially on his body."

"Well, he's got this great tan after his trip to Samoa this year with his mates, and an incredible hairy chest which trails down past his abs to his speedo line."

"Yeah, and past the speedo line I would say…" Clara sighs dreamily.

"Well I don't know about that!" Freya gasps.

"And does he 'fill' his speedos, Freya?" Sven teases.

Going a bright shade of red, Freya continues, "Anyhow, he has strong, hairy arms and when he's in his singlet and Hi-Viz onsite he just looks the bomb, like those Māori guys that work on the roads, muscles to die for. And now that he's out of the boring stuffy council offices and out onsite, his hair's a bit longer and wilder. He has a natural curl… Anyhow, you know all that, you saw him the other night. Mind you, he was in his suit then but still looking hot. So, why am I telling you stuff you already know?"

"Exactly, Freya," teases Sven. "Anyhow, what about the small detail that his mum Zita really wants you guys to get together? You don't think he and his mum have talked about you, do you? You don't think she may know more about his feelings than you do?"

"They say a mother's intuition is usually on the money," adds Clara. "Zita would have seen the way he looks at you, the way his pupils dilate when you come into the conversation…"

"Do you want to be Miss Spinster for the rest of your life? Do you want to run Portobello all on your own, just you and maybe a cat? Maybe it's time to have a serious think about that," Sven points out.

Freya thinks for a while, sipping her wine. "Well,

there's Simon the banker, Micco the coffee cart franchiser who I know fancies me, or Zac the hot, reliable dude who has known me forever, knows my moods, my weaknesses, but still gives up his weekends for me…"

"Come on Freya, when do you get to see Zac next? You know he's the one you really want," Clara says gently.

"Good question. I don't know. He'll be flying back up here on Monday morning; I guess we could write messages on the plane windows to each other as we fly past at thirty-thousand feet above Wellington…"

"Yeah, or you could stay behind and greet him on the island?" suggests Sven.

"Nice one Sven, but I do need to get back, earn some money to pay the interest…" Freya replies.

"Okay, your call. But you know what I think?" asks Sven. "We deserve dinner and another drink after solving all the trials and tribulations of the world. Do you feel better now?"

"Yes, I do actually, thanks a lot, gals," Freya replies

Sven throws the marinated steaks onto the barbeque, cooks them to perfection and dishes them out.

They sit down for dinner. "Well, we've revealed a bit this weekend. It's amazing what we can do on a relaxing weekend away." Clara comments.

"Okay, tuck in girls. I didn't make the marinade too spicy…" Sven advises.

Deep in their own thoughts, the girls tuck in and look out the window, admiring the ocean views and the jagged rocks in the bay below.

Chapter 15

Crossing Paths

The next day they tidy up, check out and catch the Waiheke passenger ferry back over to Auckland, stopping at their favourite inner-city golden sand paradise, Kohimarama Beach. All three, even Clara, jump into the tide and enjoy a high-tide swim; Freya swims out to her two white buoys and back to shore again.

They stay the night at a B&B in nearby Mission Bay where they take it easy. They walk around the bays and get takeaway fish and chips to eat on the beach, although Freya ends up feeding most of them to the resident seagulls.

Noticing Clara is not too upbeat, Freya asks, "What's up Flat White? You have been very quiet today."

"I'm torn Freya, on the one hand Martin lives so close by, but he's out of bounds, and on the other hand I've really been thinking about Sven and your words," Clara explains.

Sven turns and looks at their friend, "Which words were those Flat White?"

"About how an affair could mean I lose the best man I've ever had," Clara clarifies.

"You know we are only looking out for you, but what ever you choose Flat White, we will be there for you," Freya makes clear.

"Damn right there! We just don't want to see you hurt Flat White," Sven supports.

"I've still got a lot of thinking to do, but thanks, you two are the best," Clara says with a tear in her eye.

"Come on, lets get back as we have an early start!" Sven urges.

They order a taxi for their early start on the 'red-eye' domestic flight from Auckland back to Wellington Airport, when they get back to the B&B.

*****

Monday comes soon enough, and the plane touches down in Wellington just before 7.30am. As the trio emerge from the concourse, they see Zac striding towards his plane's departure gate.

"Well fancy seeing you here, Zac," Freya says, a little too casually.

"Hey Fin, hey girls! How was Waiheke? No doubt you all got up to a ton of mischief, I can't wait to hear the tales!" Zac replies as he hugs and kisses each of the girls in turn.

Sven bats her eyelashes. "Who, us innocent wee things? Why, what sort of girls do you think we are, Zac?" she says, feigning innocence.

Clara squeezes Zac's biceps. "Hmm big boy, we could have got up to all sorts of trouble if you were on the island..." she teases, in a deep husky voice.

"Oh, I can believe that, Flat White!" Zac replies, enjoying the girls' banter. "Come on, quit horsing around and I'll buy you all a coffee and catch you up on Portobello before you race off to your high-powered government positions."

Zac's plane is delayed, and Sven and Clara wait for the coffees while Freya takes advantage of the delay to chat with Zac. They take a seat around a high table near the window looking across the tarmac towards the main runway. "Good news, Fin," says Zac. "I've managed to get the council's earthquake red sticker removed."

"Wow! That's fabulous news," Freya says excitedly, tempted to hug 3im again, "How did you wangle this, especially as we know council bureaucrats don't work over the weekend?"

"Ahh, now that's for me to know and for you to find out," replies Zac, tapping his finger on his nose. "All I can say is I did my due diligence with the engineer's report and your archives on how solid the building was. It all helped, plus Dad knowing people in high places. But you know what? Even with what proof we had, the reports, the archives, the council contacts, I somehow think it was swayed by someone a lot higher than us mere mortals."

"Zac, I don't know anyone in high places," Freya replies bewilderedly.

"Yes you do, you're in touch with the big guns up there," he laughs, pointing up to the sky. "That's who's helping you; Wolfe your granddad, your guardian angel, and your tupuna," he tells her, as he gazes into her eyes.

"Yeah, well I know, and I am eternally grateful for that. But on this earthly plane I don't know anyone in high places," Freya continues.

"You don't have to. You're being watched over and looked after by higher beings than those in sterile offices. Besides, you've got me."

Freya thinks to herself, *Yes, that's true, who needs to win the Lotto when I've got those backers supporting me.*

As Sven and Clara arrive with the coffees, Zac looks at Clara intensely. "And your mate knows people in high places. Don't you, Flat White?"

"Who, me? But I'm just a mere public servant," she replies innocently, before breaking into the *Hogan's Heroes'* Sergeant Shultz character, and in a poor German accent adds, "I know noth-zink, noth-zinkkkk!"

"Yeah right, Flat White. You may have High Court judges fooled, but not us. Anyhow, I'm not one to criticise. If you made some of this red tape go away, then I'd be eternally grateful. So please thank whoever needs to be thanked," Freya winks, "and the next bottle of bubbles is on me."

"Now you're talking my language, Freya!" Clara grins.

Sven looks at her watch. "Hey, I hate to break up the party, but we really need to floor it into town. Shall I go and grab a taxi?"

"Yep, sure. Hey Zac, we had the best time ever," Freya says. "You are so lucky hanging out at Waiheke again. We had a fabulous time at Palm Beach."

"Yeah, and the rest," Zac smiles wickedly.

"What do you mean?" asks Freya.

"Now don't you act all innocent, it's all over the social media, you and Sven doing your nude bathing stint on *Little* Palm," Zac teases.

"What? It's on Facebook?" shrieks Freya, turning red with embarrassment.

"Ha, I caught you out!" Zac says. "No, just jiving mate. Relax, your secret is safe with me."

"But how did you know we went to Little Palm?" Freya asks.

"Come on Fin, it's not rocket science, is it? You, a nature-loving free spirit, being *au naturel* so to speak – of course you're going to take advantage of a naturalist beach. I must admit, it is pretty quiet during the week when I'm there, so I don't get to see it through the same colourful lens as you would have."

Their conversation is interrupted by the intercom announcement. "Flight to Auckland please board now… apologies for the delay…"

"Gotta go, Fin. So glad we're all on track. Now I just need to get this assignment sorted on Waiheke and then I can come back down and help you. You seem to have a habit of taking on more than you can chew – the minute my back is turned, something new arrives," Zac says as he leans over and gives Freya a kiss on the cheek.

"Hmm, well that's the structural part sorted. Just a couple more chapters to close; here's to a successful week. See you when we see you," says Freya, hoping that it's soon.

They hug each other and Zac races off to his gate as his name is called out. "Would Zachary MacLean-Smith please board…"

Freya looks back at him as he races through the sliding doors and suddenly feels a huge hole in her heart. She wonders how long it will be before she sees him again, and hopes it's not another week from hell.

"Come on Freya, Sven is out with the taxi waiting patiently," Clara says. "You know, you look really flat, but

I'm not surprised when you farewell that hunk of a man. Are you sure you're not interested…"

They climb into the taxi bound for their respective jobs, and look out at the fog rolling in over the grey city. The girls sit in silence, the thought of going back into the concrete jungle after spending a blissful weekend on a tropical island hanging over them, their chatty trip to the airport on Friday a distant memory.

Freya is lost in her thoughts. If it wasn't for Portobello, she would race back to Waiheke without a moment's thought. She wonders if Wolfe wanted her down here for some reason.

Clara, on the other hand, is wondering about Martin, unsure if he's going to be that rapt to see her, as he didn't seem overly pleased at Mudbrick the other night. She has a feeling she may have got him into deep shit with his missus. Oh well, nothing she can't handle; just business as usual. She looks to the day ahead, anticipating great surprises.

Sven looks at her Fitbit anxiously, and realises with alarm that her first coaching session is in five minutes. There's no way they're going to get through the tunnel and through town in that time in this rush hour.

It's eight-thirty and the working week is well underway as their phones go off like synchronised alarms as each of them get notifications on their little twenty-first-century digital devices.

Ping, ping, ping. The girls struggle to hide their irritation. Sven is the first to break the silence.

"Hey girls, welcome to another working week. Aren't we lucky to all have jobs to go to? Nothing like being a wage slave and lining other people's pockets. Oh well, not for much longer I hope!"

"Hmm, I don't know how I'm going to be able to wear a bra for the rest of the day – that bloody sunburn around my tits doesn't half hurt," replies Freya. "I knew I shouldn't have stayed on the nudie beach for as long as we did."

The taxi drops the three of them off on Lambton Quay where they hug and kiss before parting ways.

"Okay gals, it was a blast, catch you soon," Clara says, as they all disappear in their bright-coloured clothes, not blending in at all amongst the grey and black suits marching down the street to their home away from home for the next eight hours.

Chapter 16

Zac Returns

"No way, give me a break, Dimitri!" Freya exclaims good-naturedly. "I can't believe you're still that flexible! Look, do us a favour and grab me a coffee and I'll have that proposal you want for the Minister ready in fifteen minutes."

"Oh, you don't believe I'm still that flexible? I'll have young Kostas call you and tell you *all* the messy details…" Dimitri threatens as he leaves the office.

Dismissing the screen saver, Freya turns back to the latest mad proposal she's currently trying to turn into 'ministerial speak', when her smart phone rings. *That's the last thing I need, Dimitri's lover confirming their latest outrageous activities,* she thinks to herself.

"Fin, it's Zac. Guess what great news I've got for you!" an excited voice says.

"Zac, thank god it's you and not Kostas!" Freya replies, relieved.

"Who's Kostas? A relative of Micco's?" Zac asks. "Do I have some competition?"

"Well, not unless you bat for the other side, Zac. Kostas is Dimitri's flexible young lover, and this afternoon I've had the joy of hearing *all* about their luncheon activities."

"Far out, you poor girl!" Zac commiserates. "Okay, now you have to guess what the good news is…"

"Thanks Zac, you know how I love guessing games," Freya replies, "but right now I'm up to my eyeballs in turning the next madcap idea of Dimitri's into a coherent proposal for the Education Minister. I'll have to cheat and ask you to cut to the chase. What *is* the good news?"

"Well, here's a clue," Zac says, lifting his phone up and catching the intercom, *"…gate seven is now open for flight NZ1679 for Wellington…"*

"What the…" Freya asks.

"I'm heading home, Fin. You've got me full-time for the foreseeable future. Well, until after the New Year's break at least," Zac informs her.

"Oh Zac! That's not great news, but fantastic news!" Freya replies, "but how…?"

"Long story short, it seems there's a major dispute between what Mr Hose-skin wants his en suite to look like and what is physically possible in the budget he is prepared to pay," Zac explains. "But all my Waiheke work is on hold until my boss works it out with Hose-skin. I'll tell you in more detail when I get in, sugar plum, which will be just over an hour. See you soon, Fin!"

"Bye Zac." Freya hangs up and breathes a sigh of relief that he's coming back. She'll get her work done and then meet him at the airport… *Wait a minute, did he just call me sugar plum?*

*****

After fielding a call from Mr Tombe advising Freya that he's been called into an arbitration meeting with both Mr Church's lawyer and the bank's legal team by a High Court Judge, an agitated Freya paces the arrivals hall at Wellington Airport.

She wonders what Sven would be doing if she were in her position. She'd probably be asking her usual probing questions, getting right down into the murky depths and dragging the truth, kicking and screaming, into daylight. Flat White, on the other hand… She wonders which High Court Judge they're meeting with… *She wouldn't have, would she?*

Breaking out of her thoughts, she spies a beaming Zac emerging from the arrival doors with a carry-on suitcase in one hand and laptop bag in the other. Her stomach is suddenly overcome with butterflies as she makes a beeline for him. Wondering why her eyes are misting over, Freya jokes, "Zac, we must stop meeting like this, people will start talking…"

"Fancy meeting you here," Zac replies, a massive smile on his face. Dropping his cases to the floor, he leans forward to kiss Freya on the cheek as she goes in for a hug. As Zac steps back, he trips over his cases, nearly falling over.

"Careful there doofus, or you'll have the Health and Safety police coning you off behind a safety barrier," Freya laughs.

Red-faced, Zac replies, "Doofus? Really?"

"Come on doofus, let's catch the airporter to Petone," Freya winks.

*****

"Hey Fin," Zac asks Freya as they walk up Jackson Street towards Portobello, "as you're using my room at the moment, how would you feel if I moved into Portobello? Would you mind?"

"Why Portobello? Wouldn't Zita's be more comfortable?" Freya asks.

"Well, of course Mum's would be more comfortable, but I was thinking if I'm living onsite and playing the new full-time security-guy-cum-house-manager/painter or whatever, I can really rip into the painting and renovations. Just call me one-stop-shop Zachary... what do you reckon?"

"Okay, that would be a great solution; do you think you could handle some of the B&B bookings too? That would mean I can stay at Ed House and get more hours in to pay off that mortgage."

"Deal, as soon as the police let us open for business," Zac says as he points at the police tape blocking the front entrance.

"Look, Micco is still open, let's catch up with him," suggests Freya.

Micco looks up, noticing them walking rather closely to each other. He whistles and says, "Welcome home, Zac. How about a celebratory baklava and raki or ouzo?"

Then he calls out to a police officer standing by the rear entrance, "Hey Rex! Your cappuccino is ready!"

"... some excellent prints on the stair rail... Yeah they are with forensics'... Roger that Charlie, gotta go," Rex finishes his phone call as he walks towards the group.

"So, your liquor licence got approved then, Micco?" Zac asks.

"Sure did, Zac. The Hutt Council is much easier to deal with, especially in the Petone ward when I told them I'd be specialising in authentic Turkish cuisine and liquor," Micco explains. "Now, don't tell me, you told your JAFA boss where to stick his job as you had to return to the best little city in NZ?"

"What's this about JAFAs?" the police officer asks. "Sorry. Hi, I'm Rex, the lead investigating detective."

"Hi Rex, this is Zac, my business partner and I'm Freya, the owner of the building. Can you tell me when we can get control of the building back?"

"Hi Zac, back again so soon?" Rex enquires with a smile.

"Sure am Rex," Zac smiles as he shakes the detective's hand, turning to Freya he explains, "we met over the weekend and Rex let me have access to the upper floors."

"Apologies Freya, to answer your question, this is great timing, I've been asked to help out in the investigation. Normally my partner Charlie and I are based up in Palmy, but they're a bit short-staffed down here; Charlie is still up in Palmy holding the fort. But hey, to answer your question, not long now. You have access to the upper floors via the rear entrance, but we still have some forensics to do at the front door and the stairwell down to the basement. Unfortunately they'll be here all this week, at least."

"So you wouldn't mind some people staying onsite?" Freya asks, smiling sweetly.

"Well, it's normally against regulations, but in this case… Okay then," Rex concedes.

"Are you off shift yet, Rex?" Micco asks. "Can I tempt you with an ouzo?"

"I can see I may have to stay down here for the whole

week," Rex replies, winking, "just to make sure the forensics are wrapped up early. Now let me tell you a story about this JAFA detective that came down…"

*****

After a couple of ouzos and friendly banter with Micco and Rex, Zac takes Freya by the hand. "Well Fin, let me be the NZ tour guide and take you on a Grand Design Tour inside the main building."

Freya looks at Zac as if he's lost it. "What are you up to? I've only been away for a couple of days. And what with the council, the lawyers, the banks, police, murder, how would you have had time to actually do some real work, especially when you had all that red tape at each corner to cut through?"

"Ahh, never underestimate a MacLean-Smith, Ms Nilson, you know we didn't get where we are today by just our good looks and charm…" he drawls, leading Freya inside.

Freya gasps and stands aghast, her mouth wide open. Zac's not sure if it's a good sign or a sigh of disappointment. "Is it… I mean, are you okay Freya?"

She walks from room to room in utter astonishment. She touches the new beds, recycled retro fittings, the Art Deco basins, and rubs her hands over them as if they're a genie bottle that needs polishing. Her eyes well up with tears.

"Are you okay Fin? Have I gone too far this time? Is this not what you wanted?" Zac asks, concerned.

She walks over to him and gives him the biggest hug ever. "How could you ever go too far? This is perfect. You did exactly what we'd planned, I just never thought you would be able to get it done this weekend. Zac, I love it, I truly love it." She continues to walk around touching everything with a look of disbelief on her face.

"But surely you couldn't have done this without some help?" she asks incredulously.

"I had a lot of help from friends," he admits. "Put it this way, I called in a lot of favours this weekend. We had a whole working bee going on. Everyone mucked in and Micco was a star as usual, dishing out pizzas, falafels, coffees, cokes, whatever the lads needed. Everyone worked around the clock. To be honest I don't think they were much good for their own clients back at work today after what they put in here. But we needed to get it out. I'm so glad I was here and able to share it with you."

She gives him another hug and leans in to kiss him on the cheek, but they both turn and end up kissing each other on the lips instead.

Both flustered, they look at each other, Freya blushing and as usual the first to cover up any awkwardness. Pretending it never happened, Freya pipes up, "Zac, thank you, thank you, thank you. You know what this means now, don't you? It means we can start hiring out the rooms this week. As soon as I dress them up with linen and flowers, they're all ready to go. We can now genuinely take bookings."

Zac, still trying to compose himself, finds his voice. "Well, I forgot to tell you, Fin. I've already been accepting bookings. In fact, the first one is tomorrow. I just thought we need to get this show on the road and paying its own way. With Rex being kind enough to let us re-open just the upstairs, and with a whole lot of interest from *CSI* fans curious about a real murder investigation, why not make hay while the sun is shining?"

"Our first booking! But How?" Freya questions.

"The marvels of the internet," Zac replies.

"That is so exciting! Oh no, are we even ready for guests?" Freya asks.

"Pretty much, but I think a feminine touch of pizzazz is needed," Zac concedes, "Tell me what you think of the painting?"

"Oh Zac, this all looks gorgeous." They both look around at the paintwork the boys have done over the weekend, and all the nick-nacks that are sprawled out over the beds under cover sheets, ready to be displayed on the shelves and in the glass Art Deco cabinets Freya has scored from the local charity shops. "Man you have got so much done! Right, I'll clean up and make the beds, put the towels out, pick some flowers from the garden and tart the rooms up."

With a frantic whirl of activity, they get the rooms ready; even Zac has a bed in the corner of one of the unfinished rooms. Freya is impressed with the amount of work Zac has miraculously managed to achieve while she was on Waiheke.

"Now when are you telling Zita that you're home but staying here?" Freya asks. "I don't want any awkwardness that *I'm* staying with her, rather than her son."

"I already told her before I left Auckland that I was heading home, and that I was going to ask if I could stay at Portobello to continue the renos, so no drama there," Zac replies, putting her mind at ease.

"Thank goodness for that, now partner, tell me more about this booking…"

*****

"Hello… Hi Marama," Rex answers.

"Kia ora Rex, hey those prints on the stair rail match a known associate of the deceased," Marama informs.

"Marama, don't keep me in suspense, who is it?" Rex pleads.

"Thomas Harris, has form for breaking and entering amongst others and a known lockpick…" Marama replies.

"… and a member of the 'Choir Boys' along with the deceased Damien," Rex interjects.

"One problem Rex before you go off half cocked, Thomas' prints aren't on the pipe," Marama advises.

"Bugga, ah well a bit more work to do then, I might need Charlie down here," Rex sighs.

"Let me know if you find anything else Rex, ka kite anō," Marama rings off.

*****

The days fly by in a blur of activity, with hard work and very little play. Zac renovates Portobello and takes bookings from the crime voyeurs, with some only wanting to book a room for an hour at a time, while Freya juggles long hours at Education House with helping Zac out.

Towards the end of the week, Freya receives a call from Mr Tombe regarding the arbitration meetings.

"It's looking good Freya, the new judge has really put Mr Church's lawyer on the ropes and the bank's legal team are frantically trying to distance themselves from their part in the debacle. I'm hoping we will have a decision tomorrow," Mr Tombe explains.

"Well, thanks again Mr Tombe, fingers crossed you can finally get a decision from the judge tomorrow. By the way, who is the judge again?" Freya asks. "Oh of course, you can't say. Well here's hoping," she replies as she hangs up.

Micco hands over a fresh coffee. "Any news, Boss?"

"Not yet Micco, and I'm not your boss but your… well I guess your partner in crime," Freya says good–naturedly, liking the new title.

"What about 'Guvnor'? It sounds so good on those British TV shows, I've always wanted to see how that sounds," Micco winks.

"Hmm, Guv or Guvnor?" Freya turns to Zac for his opinion. "What do you reckon?"

"Guvnor," laughs Zac, "as you're the one paying the bills. But Guv will do at a pinch. Right, I'm back into it, 'Guvnor'," he teases as he heads back inside.

"Well, I guess either sounds way better than Boss!" Freya exclaims. "Okay guys, I need some decompression time, so I'll start planning another project. I might check out the shed and see what needs to be done to turn it into a summer house – maybe a little garden around it would work too, although not sure when it will make the priority list."

Freya hasn't been out there since returning from Waiheke, and as she turns the corner of the shed to follow the weed-filled garden path, to her amazement the path is clear and the garden suddenly in order. She walks a little further and there on the windowsill is a gorgeous home-made wooden flower box filled with flowers, along with two little wrought-iron chairs and table sitting beneath the window, bathed in sunshine. She marvels at the private peaceful haven, strategically positioned in the sun, away from the bustling road and foot traffic.

She puts her coffee, pad and pen down and walks back to the caravan. "I don't suppose you had anything to do with this, did you Micco? Zac? Where has he got to? This is the sort of thing you two would do."

Micco laughs. "We have been waiting to see how long it would take you to notice. Zac and I have been counting down the days since you returned from your girlie retreat."

"So, it was you who did this?" she asks again.

"I can't possibly comment, I guess you will have to take a leaf out of Rex's detective book in there and do some more thorough investigations." Micco returns to serving the next punters who walk in off the street.

She laughs, and retreats to the back of the shed to text Zac. 'I don't suppose you have anything to do with upgrading the garden shed into a 'summer house'?'

The cute little rustic house reminds her of the gorgeous summer houses she admired so much in Sweden. She had planned to do it up just like a Swedish summer house when she had the time, but it looks like someone may have beaten her to it, or at least made a healthy start.

She tries the door to the summer house but it's locked and a piece of material hanging up over the window prevents her from looking inside. She assumes Zac has the key, as he's now working on the finishing touches to the bathrooms and bedrooms and would need access to her precious fixtures and fittings which are stored inside.

She sits down on the summer house door step to wait for a reply, and begins to write more of her poetry.

MY GRAND-DAD (GD)

My GD the kindest man you could ever meet

Designing classical houses, so hard to beat

Art Deco, colonial and Cape Cod

Just himself, all on his tod!

He only kept his favourite buildings, just the two

But charging for services, without a clue

People took advantage of this much to my disgust

And as a result, he went bust

This was revealed in his recent will

And the mortgage and outstanding bill

It's now time for me to turn this all around

I'm off now back inside, Portobello-bound

.....

She starts going through her project list and looks at the work they've completed and what there is left to do. It's quite an overwhelming list and now that the police have opened up the upstairs floors, she wants to get that finished as quickly as possible so it can be open for Christmas and the summer holidays.

She puts on her headphones to listen to some inspirational music and flicks through some of her journal entries, mostly written in her favourite rhyming verse.

TO-DO LIST

Oh my god, there's so much to do, where to start?

A coffee and slice at the coffee cart

Get my brain into gear
Prioritise, oh what to wear?
Oh, bugger that with deadlines to meet
Who cares what shoes I put on my feet?

....

A logo and some simple branding
The walls in the bathroom are ready for sanding
The rest of the curtains to be hung
Who was it Zac you said had rung?
Which night and room do they want to book?
Can you grab the schedule and take a look?
A slap of paint just one more coat
How much money is in the float?

*****

She puts down her book and looks at her watch to see she's been out there for an hour. With downtime over she walks back inside, feeling uplifted after her time out in the sunshine. She still has her headphones on and is oblivious to the people coming and going, and doesn't hear Zac sneak up behind her. Seeing a shadow looming, she spins around, startled.

Seeing Zac, she sighs with relief. "What are you up to? Did you not get my text?" she asks, taking her headphones off.

"You know me, Fin, I never check my texts when I'm in the zone. Not when we've got a show to get on the road. We have so many bookings coming in I've had to turn potential punters away. Anyhow, what do you think of your new little outdoor area and summer house?" he asks, smiling. "I was wondering how long it would take you to notice."

"So it *was* you! Just when did you get time to clear the pathway, plant up the garden and make that cute little outdoor space?"

"It was a worthy cause, so I made the time. Besides, I've heard you go on enough about the cutesy red summer houses in Sweden so I thought I'd take on your little shed out there and transform it. I thought I'd start with the outside area first as I really have no idea about Swedish houses. Hmm... maybe you could take me to Scandi one day and I could see for myself?"

"Well, as Wolfe would say, 'be careful what you ask for – you just don't know how it may manifest'." She imagines going back to Sweden and knows Sven would be up for it. Although there's always the danger of her never coming back to NZ, as she loved her job over there and connecting with her father's side of the family.

"Freya, seriously, I've never been to Sweden. I would love you to show me around, maybe someday?"

"Well it sounds like a great idea in theory, but we've just taken on a house much larger than a small shed – we've taken on this," she says, pointing towards the huge Art Deco building she is now the proud owner of. "Man, it looks even bigger from the back here than it does from the front. Well, one day when we have reliable people running this show and we have all our tenants in place and word has got out about us, *then* I will be your Scandinavian tour guide. Now I assume you're holding onto the key to the shed so I can't get in?"

Zac produces a rusty old key out of his pocket and dangles it in front of her. "Yes I do."

She reaches for it, but Zac snatches the key behind his back. "Hey, I want to get inside," protests Freya.

"Not so fast, Fin. Inside the shed is out of bounds right now. I want it to be a surprise."

"But I want to grab the rest of the Art Deco bathroom gear."

"And why do you think it would be in there?"

"Because it was when I went up to Waiheke. And with all these bookings coming we need to – as they say in Swedish – 'full fart' this process and steam ahead with getting the bathrooms sorted."

"Well they might just be in a couple of cardboard boxes… can you guess?" Zac teases.

"Hmm, let me see," Freya replies, trying not to notice how hot he is in just a pair of black shorts and singlet. Heading back indoors, she says, "Knowing you, they're probably propping up your bed."

"Fin, just how the heck do you do that? Is that women's intuition or something?" Zac asks incredulously, while following her up the stairs.

"Something like that, doofus. It keeps you men on the back foot," Freya winks.

Just then Leo walks up the stairs and saves the day. Freya wants to have a chat with Zac, but not right now with everything to do.

"Ah, there you are young lady," Leo interrupts. "Greetings my darling," and he pecks Freya on both cheeks. "What excellent timing to catch my favourite couple at the same time."

"Hi Leo. What brings you here at this hour?" Freya asks.

"I have a small group gathering soon, up in the turret that your good man Zac has been kind enough to rent out to me at a very reasonable rate," Leo replies enthusiastically.

"That's great news, Leo!"

"Now, you must excuse my brevity, but I must away upstairs and set up for the five soon-to-be trainee palmists!" Leo says.

"Let me know if you need a hand, Leo," Zac insists. "Now please excuse us; I have a surprise for Freya, and I want to show her what I've been up to over the weekend since she ran out on us to return to Jafaland."

"Of course, if I had such a gorgeous woman on my arm, I would want to whisk her away to some place more discreet too," Leo teases.

Freya can't help herself. "Hmm, some place more discreet. Now that's given me an idea... we could branch out and run a discreet dating agency here too."

Leo pipes up, "Now that's an idea – how about we set up a speed dating coffee-type event out in the courtyard? I can just see Micco running it – something like The *Love Boat* but a 'Love Garden', getting people together over baklava and coffee."

"What a fantastic idea, Leo. I'll go and have a word with Micco now," Zac says enthusiastically.

"Oh no you don't, Zac. You're not wriggling out of this, let's get those cardboard boxes," Freya says.

"Ha ha, yes you two, what a splendid idea. As Rod Stewart would sing, 'Upstairs before the night's too old...'" sings Leo before darting upstairs towards the turret.

When Leo is out of earshot Freya turns to Zac. "What

have you been saying since I've been away?"

"Do you want those Art Deco handles or not?" Zac asks, trying to divert the conversation. "Well, come on then…"

*****

Rex makes a call, asking his friend, "Charlie, I'm going to need a bit of help down here mate, any chance you can get released from Palmy?"

"I'll check with the boss, but I should be free by the end of the week mate, why Bro?" Charlie replies.

"Mate, I'm getting all sorts of interference from upstairs which is weird as you would think that when we finally get a lead on Church and his gang the Choir Boys, that we would get the green light," Rex explains.

"Hmmm… not from the Police Commissioner himself is it?" Charlie enquires.

"It certainly looks that way, but if it is, he's covering his tracks."

"Best I talk with the boss and get down there pronto, keep me in the loop Bro," Charlie says as he rings off.

Chapter 17

Roof Top Transformation

Later that week, Freya is back in the office and rings Zac. "Zac, I've just seen an ad for Portobello on Facebook. Just when did you get time to do that?"

"Last night, Fin. I woke up around 2am and couldn't get back to sleep," explains Zac, "so I looked at my Facebook messages on my phone, saw an ad for accommodation up the coast at Waitarere Beach, and thought why can't we do that? So, I spent the next couple of hours nutting it out."

"Well a big thank you, my clever nutter, it works!" Freya answers gratefully.

"Great! Now I've called in a couple of mates again from the gym who are at a loose end, to help get the next couple of rooms ready by tonight, because the bookings are going crazy Fin! Look, do you think Dimitri might let you off a little earlier, as I know you'll want to see the rooms before the guests arrive?"

"I'll see if I can twist his arm and grab an earlier train,"

Freya smiles.

"Have you seen the papers Fin?" Zac inquires.

"No, I've been flat tack here, why?" Freya asks.

"The Capital News is reporting that the body we found was an associate of Mr Church," Zac replies.

"What! Wow, I'm blown away… what were they doing?" Freya ponders.

"I'll see if I can get anything out of Rex next time I see him, see you soon," Zac farewells.

*****

The police don't look like they're moving on any time soon, which is a huge inconvenience as they're holding up the basement and the restaurant renovations. In the meantime, Zac has been promoting the website and social media pages, taking a few photos and uploading with a quick comment to create more interest. He's also downloaded and re-posted all the online news articles speculating about the property developer Mr Church and the suspicious death of his right-hand man Damien. The re-posted headlines read: 'Death of the Deal', 'Shady Basement Killing' and 'Art Deco Downfall'.

The mysterious death has set tongues wagging and everyone wants to come and stay, get in on the action and see it for themselves. There hasn't been a mysterious death in the High Street for ages, especially not one involving a prominent property developer.

As he heads out to see Micco for a morning coffee, Zac bumps into Detective Rex, who's on a call. The detective covers his phone mic and whispers, "Hey Zac, I'll join you in a moment, order a latte for me please…" Then he turns away and continues speaking into the phone; "Yeah, yeah Charlie, pull the other one, I know you're itching to get back down to Wellywood… didn't you have an attractive blonde down here back in the day? Is she still available? Any chance I may meet her?"

Zac approaches the coffee caravan. "Micco, could I have two lattes, mate. Hey, I've got some of my Samoan gym buddies turning up soon. Could you please give me a ring when they arrive? And as they're doing me a favour, could you order some Vailima beer in? I know that'll put a smile on their faces when we've finished the work."

"Sure thing, Zac. Blue or green label?" Micco asks.

"Blue label every time!" Rex interjects. "Now Zachary, we need a quiet word, young man."

"This sounds very official, Rex," says Zac, "should I call my lawyer?"

"Only if you plan on confessing to a crime you didn't commit, Zachary," Rex jibes. "Look, the up and ups in HQ are starting to get a bit tetchy about some of the articles online, not to mention the number of people onsite while we're continuing our investigation."

"Well, Sir, I can't do anything about the online articles as I'm only re-posting what's already out there in cyberspace," Zac explains, "and I'm not showing any police faces or using any names on the photos that I'm posting, so what's the problem?"

"I guess what I'm trying to say is, and this is strictly off the record," Rex quickly comments, "Mr Church has friends in high places who are putting pressure on my bosses to hush this up and keep his name out of anything to do with this investigation."

"What do you mean, 'high places', Rex?" Zac asks

innocently.

"Bloody politicians who can make our public servant lives a living nightmare. I'm already sending a daily briefing report to my boss to keep him in the loop," Rex mutters. "I'm sure some of that information is going straight to Mr Church's lawyers."

"But how can that be?" asks Zac.

"Don't be too naive, Zac. You know how these property developers work, when there's big money involved like there always is with land sales, then a few palms are greased in the council for consents and in political circles through 'donations' for influence or to hush things up, as in this case," Rex explains.

"FFS, that just makes me so mad!" Zac explodes. Then he takes a few deep breaths and says calmly, "Well, what can I do to help nail this bastard? Because I do know a few people around town."

"Okay, I've been taking some direction from my partner Charlie who's winding up a case in Palmy; he could be down here in the next couple of days. He reckons if we could prove that Damien was having an argument with Mr Church on other sites, then we could build a case against him."

Thinking on his feet, Zac asks, "Do you have a list of the building sites?"

"I can get that list, why, what are you thinking Zac?" Rex asks.

"Oh, I know a stack of tradies and contractors around the Hutt, who may have done some work on those sites, do you have some photos of the people involved?" Zac requests.

"Sure, this is highly irregular, but so is the interference, okay let's see what we can do…"

*****

"Talofa lava Zac! Phew-we, flash place you've got here, my man," a large hulking man calls to Zac as he eases himself out of the driver's door of a Mini Clubman.

"Hey Isaia! Glad you could make it. Sweet drive mate!" Zac calls back.

"Ha, he drives like an old lady, eh," calls out a second large imposing figure as he emerges from the passenger's side of the car. "O ā mai 'oe Zac?"

"Manuia, fa'afetai Paulo," Zac replies, "did I get that right?"

"Phew, not bad for a palagi, eh Paulo?" says Isaia. "Have you been schooling him up while he's been spotting for you on the weights?"

"Yeah bro, he's quick eh," Paulo replies. "So where do you need these muscles, Zac?" Paulo asks as he flexes his pumped biceps.

"Gentlemen, can I interest you in a fresh orange juice or a protein smoothie, perhaps?" Micco asks.

"Is there no stopping your entrepreneurial spirit, Micco?" laughs Zac.

"I like this man, Zac. I'll have two protein smoothies, thanks," Paulo says.

"Better put them on my tab, Micco," Zac offers. "Okay guys, when you've finished, I need a hand up on the roof. The plan is to get the railing up to standard, then work on securing these marquees so they won't fly off in a gentle Wellywood breeze."

"Seki a, sweet as bro," Isaia replies. "Let's get up them

stairs, Paulo."

"I've got a surprise for you both when the work is done," Zac winks at Paulo, "but I think the missus better pick up the car, what do you reckon, Paulo?"

"Brother, you are the man! Where do we start!" Paulo replies enthusiastically.

*****

The boys work hard to transform the roof into a safe and spacious space, with strong modern marquees and four gas braziers strategically placed beside the four newly-built extended wooden picnic tables to create an open-air bar-cum-alfresco dining area. They secure the marquees with some innovative brackets bolted to the concrete rooftop.

"Wow! Just wow Zac!" Freya exclaims as she walks out onto the new rooftop in the afternoon sun. "What a difference a day makes!"

"Hey, I know that song," Paulo says, before breaking into song; "Twenty-four little hours, the sun and the flowers…"

"Oh no, not another one Paulo," Isaia cries, "give our poor ears a rest!"

"We're just doing the finishing touches, Fin, then stopping for a well-earned beer," says Zac, breaking into a big smile.

"Where are your manners, Zachary?" Freya asks. "Aren't you going to introduce me to your big handsome friends?" she teases.

"Well, Paulo is the songbird – Paulo, Isaia, this is my friend Freya," introduces Zac.

"Malo, pleased to meet you, Freya," Isaia says, then

turning to Zac, "What do you mean 'friend?' Zac? You better be quick, or Paulo will sweep her off her feet!"

Paulo stops singing, does a dramatic bow, and kisses the back of Freya's hand. "Hmm, Freya, we could be so good together. Shall we leave these two to do the work and let's go dancing?" he suggests.

"Is that a wedding band, Paulo?" Freya replies quick-wittedly. "Oh, you are naughty!"

"She got you there, mate," Zac laughs, firing off a quick text. "Come on, let's show Freya what we've been up to."

After a quick tour, reassuring Freya the wild Wellington winds won't whisk the marquees off the rooftop, Micco arrives with a chilly bin in one hand and a basket in the other.

"My first rooftop delivery!" Micco exclaims, setting the basket on the nearby table-top. He starts spreading out hummus and snacks, and then opens the chilly bin. "Okay, who gets the first Vailima?" he says, brandishing a blue labelled brown bottle.

Paulo and Isaia chorus, "Bro! You the man!"

"You two make a start, I just need a quick word with Zac," says Freya.

She pulls him away from the celebrations, heading down the stairs and checks in with Zac. "Hey you, how's it going? Looks like thanks to you, another space has been transformed. The roof is looking fabulous. Does everything you touch turn to gold?"

Zac laughs. "It would appear that way. I think I'm just on a winning streak at the moment. It feels like since I returned to Wellington, everything is just falling into place. I mean who would have thought losing a job just before Christmas would actually turn into a great stroke of luck? I do feel like the starter gun has gone off and I'm part of a race to get to the finishing line. But hey, I'm not complaining. I've needed to get my teeth into something like this for a while."

"Yep, I know what you mean. The office gig does suck your soul dry, doesn't it? I can't wait until I can finish contracting once and for all in town. My boss is a laugh, such a DQ, but really, if it wasn't for him and his highly flamboyant temper tantrums it would just be so dull and boring. Right, I was just checking in to say I'm doing some work in the turret tonight; do you have the booking sheet for that room, so I know my deadline and what I need to set up for? Also, have I been grown-up enough yet to get the one and only key back to the shed?"

"Maybe, but on one condition," Zac replies.

"And what is that?"

"That you stop calling it a shed. It really is so much more than a standard shed. I think you could give it a more suitable name, like the 'hideaway retreat', the 'rustic retreat', the 'summer house', the 'potting shed' – anything but the 'shed'."

"I'm hearing you. I'll see what I can come up with. When I was little Wolfe let me use it as my very own secret club house."

"Hmm… 'Club House', sounds good. I know – we could do a bit of a spruce up in there as well, couldn't we, and have yet another celebration, an opening, but just the selected few on the invite list?"

"Now there's an idea. Hey, how about you hold onto the key for now and I'll concentrate on the turret, and then we can do the Club House together?"

"Roger that! Sounds like a plan."

"Oh, and Zac, do you mind if I skip out this weekend? The girls and I are heading up to Waitarere. Flat White has had a real hard time this week."

"Not a problem, Fin, the boys and I will just crack on," Zac smiles.

Zac heads back upstairs onto the roof to join the boys in a job-well-done drink, while Freya walks over to the turret, remembering that Leo was the last to use the space. She takes a breath, and opens the red door, entering her very own lighthouse. Straight away she feels like she has just walked through a portal, into another world, leaving the mundane and everyone else behind her.

Every time she walks into this room she's reminded of the wardrobe in *The Lion, the Witch and the Wardrobe*. She feels as if she's entering a different world where time and space no longer matter. She wonders what it is about this space that makes her feel like she's operating from a different dimension.

The room is incredibly hot as the sun has been shining in through the windows all day, so she opens the door and side window for fresh air. She remembers her grandfather using this room a long time ago and tunes into him and feels his energy, strong and bright like the sun streaming in. Something catches her eye near one of the windows, and she looks up to see a crystal hanging there. As it catches the light a rainbow spreads across the room. She goes through the cardboard box of goodies she picked up at a charity shop, finding all sorts of treasures; a hanging lighthouse chime in colours that will reflect nicely, a packet of incense, matches, duster, and a couple of incense holders. There's even a Tibetan singing bowl.

She sets to work cleaning the room with her broom and

duster and allows the fresh air to sweep through. She lights her candle and leaves it burning in each corner. Then she lights the incense and waves it around carefully, in all the corners, ceiling, floor, and all the nooks and crannies. With sheets of scrunched-up newspaper she cleans the windows inside and out and places her crystals strategically around the room, along with ornaments to represent each element: air, water, fire and earth.

She turns her iPhone on to play some cleansing music. She finds her favourite Tibetan singing bowl tune, synchronises it with her own singing bowl and immediately feels uplifted. Once she is done with the cleansing, she leaves the music on and the door wide open and heads outside, feeling a difference in energy as she walks through the door and back into the outside world.

She decides she would benefit from spending more time in there, as it's a great way of recharging and feeding her soul. She vows to make time to meditate up there each night after work for an escape, before starting work on Portobello. It could be her 'recharger' – a state change from one office in town to another out here, changing the energies before working with a new audience.

*****

Zac is having a laugh with the Samoan boys, some of his mates he's met at the local gym over the last few years. They're a great bunch of guys and they always meet for a protein shake after their workouts. Lifting all those weights at the gym has paid off and they're proving to be a great help around Portobello.

"Hey Zac, you're one lucky man. She's one good-looking palagi chick, what do you reckon?"

"Yeah, I know she is."

"Hmm, does she know you think she is pretty hot?" Paulo asks.

"Ahh, let's not go there mate, don't want to tip up the apple cart."

"I see, but you are happy for someone else to tip it up and try their luck?" Paulo grins. "I reckon I nearly had her there."

"Ha, ha, good one, Paulo," Zac laughs nervously. "But if you put it that way, then no, I don't want anyone going there."

"So, what are you going to do about it then, mate?" Isaia asks. "Wait and watch some good-looking Samoan muscle in? Chicks like that don't stay on the shelf forever."

"You know, you're right guys, good call. I will see what I can do."

"Well don't take too long mate, or you may regret it," Paulo smiles, flexing his biceps again. "She won't resist these beauties for long."

"Oh my god, so many people have been speaking along the same lines lately," Zac replies, realising he'll need to make a move soon. He thinks about the accidental kiss the other day.

"Yeah, well sometimes you need a great big shakeup to make you see the light," says Isaia.

"Hmm, less of the shakeups – you know we live on a massive earthquake fault here, so we could go off at any time, especially after that small shake the other day." Zac advises.

"Yeah, I know, and it's going around town that the BIG one is coming soon," says Paulo. "Man, I hate them. I mean, you know, coming from Samoa we had our own big shakeup a few years back with that tsunami that took out my village; we were on the part of the island that suffered the most. Anyways, they say when we get the mother of all earthquakes we will then get a tsunami to follow. So lucky we are far away from the beach and up high enough, eh?"

"My missus told me that her Auntie reckons there's a big one going to hit in a week, give or take a couple of days," Isaia says.

"Auntie Sefina? The one that reads tea leaves?" Paulo asks.

"Yeah, Auntie Sefina felt that big one coming in Samoa, and got lots of the village kids up the hill before the waves came," Isaia says.

"Okay boys, well on that positive note, I think we should change the subject and enjoy the afternoon sun and this nice cold beer," Zac laughs nervously.

His mind wanders, thinking about Freya and the fact that he needs to talk to her soon, but when is a good time? No time seems to be a good time for him. Even his mum has been telling him to stop 'shagging around'. He makes a mental note to take the plunge and talk with Freya about his feelings at the next possible opportunity.

Chapter 18

Waitarere Weekend

Boarding the train, Freya and Clara take a seat at the back of the carriage.

"I'll get the first round in; can you save the seats please, Flat White?" Freya asks.

"Don't worry Freya, I'll guard the table with these talons," Clara answers, flashing her newly manicured bright red nails.

Clara spreads her bag and jacket over the two opposite seats, then takes the aisle seat and sets up her laptop on the table, pointedly ignoring people when they stop to ask if the seats are taken.

Freya returns with a four-pack of small 200ml bottles of bubbles and three plastic wine glasses. "Here we go. Any trouble, Flat White?"

"The usual couple of persistent commuters, but I saw them off with my 'Don't fuck with me' frown," Clara laughs, and points to a woman taking a seat at the other end of the carriage. "Oh look, here comes my new workmate, Claudia."

"Wow, a new job starting Monday," Freya comments. "You must feel good, especially after this week from hell."

"Like you wouldn't believe! Cheers!" Clara toasts before taking a large mouthful of wine.

"One heck of a roller coaster for us both; I'm just so glad Zac was able to carry on with the work at Portobello," Freya says. "Sorry Flat White, this project is just so all-consuming, I must sound really boring."

"Freya, I'm really proud of you for persevering through all the hurdles you've faced, I'm not sure I could have done what you have," Clara says, straight-faced.

"Really?" Freya asks, shocked at her friend's honesty. "That's high praise indeed from Clara James!"

"Drink up Freya, I think we've both deserved this girly weekend up the coast," declares Clara, as she pours herself another glass and tops up Freya's.

"Skål!" they chorus.

*****

"That woman's voice is dreadful!" Clara comments. "How do you put up with it, Sven?"

"I know, right?" Sven replies, taking a seat. "Thanks for getting the first round in, sorry I was late."

"Drink up Sven, I'm just off for the next round – you've got some catching up to do!" Clara says, staggering slightly as she slides out of her seat and winds her way through the passengers towards the buffet car.

Sven picks up her glass, takes a swig and leans towards Freya. "What have I missed? Flat White looks determined to tie one on tonight!"

"I think everything is starting to catch up with her," Freya replies with concern.

"Our steady, reliable Clara has certainly been thrown a few curve balls this week," Sven nods.

"Okay, let's be a bit gentle this weekend at the bach," suggests Freya.

"I'm looking forward to giving the Capri a good run; shall we take her to Palmy via the Foxton Straights?" Sven asks.

"Why not, you petrol head!" Freya laughs.

*****

"Hey Robert! Can a girl get a drink around here?" Clara asks, leaning between two hulking young men talking rugby.

The barman sees Clara and walks over to her end of the bar. "No wonder I didn't see you. Gentlemen, please move away from the bar so the other customers can get a drink."

The rugby boys look surprised and move off towards the front of the train, a flash of purple momentarily catching Clara's eye. Turning to have a closer look, she admires an older woman in a pinstriped purple jacket. *What an interesting jacket... that woman looks like Margaret...* her attention snaps back as the barman addresses her.

"Now, what can I get you?" Robert asks. "Sorry, I can't remember your name."

"A four-pack of bubbles please, Robert," Clara replies. "It's Clara, and I'm not surprised you can't remember everyone's name, there are a lot of people on the Kiwi Con."

"Here you go, Clara. I normally recognise the face and the drink that goes with it," Robert explains, smiling. "Enjoy."

"Thanks Robert, this should keep us going for a while," Clara replies, before weaving her way back to the girls.

Stopping next to the rowdy table in their carriage, Clara takes a deep breath and asks, "Excuse me for interrupting your conversation… ah Claudia, a quick question, does Margaret Johnson normally catch this train? I think I just saw her down by the buffet car."

Looking down her nose at Clara, Cathryn asks, "And you are…?"

Claudia replies quickly, "I think that is highly unlikely… Clara, isn't it? I actually saw her drive off to her bach up the coast about two hours ago."

"Sorry, my mistake," Clara apologises and heads back to her friends.

"What was that about, Flat White?" Freya asks as Clara slips back into her seat.

"Yeah, fraternising with the enemy," Sven laughs. "Did you tell Cat to keep her voice down?"

Clara drops the four-pack down on the table. "Do I look like I don't want to start my new job on Monday, Sven? I thought I saw Margaret and was just asking Claudia about it… I've seen that jacket somewhere… but she left work early today, so my mistake."

"Come on you two, let's chill and plan our weekend," Freya intervenes.

"Sorry if I came off a bit strong, Flat White. Come on, you propose the next toast," Sven suggests.

Taking a deep breath, Clara raises her topped-up glass. "Here's to my two best friends, without whom I'd never have made it through this week."

"Skål!" they chorus.

*****

Freya puts the rusty old key into the rusty old-fashioned lock and wiggles it about until it finally clicks open.

"Wow, everything looks the same. Just like back in the day. Ooh, I can't wait to get inside. When did we come here last, the three of us?" Clara wonders.

"Was it that long weekend, a few months before we headed off on our OE?" Freya asks.

"No way! That was yonks ago! Come on, let's get these goodies inside," Sven exclaims as they enter the bach.

"Geez, you know, I think Freya's right," Clara muses. "Hey, do you mind if I skip on the nesting and settling-in routine and go for a walk? I'll do dishes all weekend to make up for it."

"Sounds like a deal to me," Sven says, as she unpacks the groceries.

"Take your phone with you and I'll text you when dinner and drinks are ready," Freya says.

"Thanks," Clara replies as she heads out the door towards the beach, deep in thought.

Kicking off her slides as she leaves the bach path, Clara walks barefoot, enjoying the warm sand between her toes. Weaving her way through the wildly strewn driftwood, she meanders to the edge of the tide, watching the softly lapping waves throw the odd piece of driftwood or shell up onto the beach. Walking mindfully, she collects her favourite brown olive seashells, inspecting them to make sure they haven't got any fish inside. Losing track of time, she wanders far down the beach, pictures crowd her mind, fancy dinners in restaurants with Judge Martin Jacobsen. As she thinks of all the promises he made, now broken, tears stream down her face, blurring her vision. Taking a seat on a nearby driftwood log, she asks herself how she could have been such a fool to believe all his sweet talk. She lets the tears flow, sobbing into the westerly wind, wrapping her arms around herself, allowing the hurt and pain to wash over her.

*****

"Have you been for a swim, Flat White?" Freya asks as Clara arrives back at the bach, then answering her own question, "No, your clothes are dry."

"Clara James, you dark horse, you've been skinny dipping, haven't you?" Sven teases.

"Not likely with those bogans doing donuts and drifting their cars on the beach," Clara replies. "I just washed my face… to sober up a bit."

"Come on and take a seat, dinner's up in two," Sven says.

Noticing how red Clara's eyes are, a concerned Freya rushes over and throws her arms around her friend. "Hey Clara, you've been crying. What's up?"

This sets Clara off again. "How could I have believed him… all those lies… damn it, here I go again," she sobs.

Sven joins her friends in a three-way embrace. "Darl, I so wish we were wrong."

"And then I get this text," Clara says, pulling out her phone to show her friends.

'Clara, where are you? I was expecting you to take

me to the restaurant for dinner tonight. You are such a disappointment. Poor Fred was looking forward to seeing you. I expect to see you tomorrow for morning tea. Mother.'

"God she's a bitch!" Sven says, shaking her head.

"Who's Fred?" Freya asks.

"I'm going to need a drink to tell this story," Clara replies. "My shrink has said sometimes poetry can help my recovery, so I have a poem to share that explains some of this…"

"No, not another poet?" says Sven. "Our crusty old English teacher Miss Burnell would be very proud of us after all!"

*****

As they leave Foxton, Sven puts her foot down on the accelerator. "Keep an eye open for the cops, girls, I'm about to open the ol' girl up."

"There's something about riding in a classic car as its engine winds up. I'm glad I'm riding shotgun," Clara comments from the passenger's seat.

"Why's that, Flat White?" Freya asks from the back seat.

"You'll find out on the trip home," Clara replies cryptically, then comments, "A bit of a washout in Foxton, here's hoping Palmy has better pickings."

"Yeah, only a couple of Art Deco pieces for Portobello," Freya agrees. "I hope Zac is okay with me leaving him for the second weekend in a row. I feel kinda bad on that score."

"I think he's a keeper, Freya. You should make a move before someone else does," advises Sven, easing off the accelerator. "Damn, a slow tractor up ahead."

Clara jumps in, "Why, Sven? Are you thinking of making a move on the hunky Zac?"

Sven, recognising the game Clara is playing, joins in to tease Freya. "Oh, his muscly arms and hairy chest, couldn't you just melt into his embrace?"

"What…" says Freya, shocked.

"And his deep brown eyes, oh you just get lost in them…" Clara continues.

"Ah, and that tight bum, doesn't it get you all hot and bothered?" Sven adds.

"Oh yes, yes, YES!!" Clara exaggerates.

All the girls burst out laughing.

When Freya gets her breath back, she says, "You had me going there for a while… but seriously, do you think he's on the lookout for a girlfriend?"

"Come on Freya, when isn't a man on the prowl?" Clara asks.

"Are you serious?" Freya looks genuinely surprised.

"All I'm saying Freya, is that you should have a good hard think about it before he gets a wandering eye," Sven points out.

"He's only got eyes for you at the moment, girl," Clara confirms, then suggests, "Maybe we should keep an eye out for some sexy outfits for you, just to help Zac notice what's under his nose."

"Now you're talking, Flat White. That's our new mission in Palmy – hot new fashion for Freya," Sven agrees, putting her foot down to pass the tractor.

*****

"Okay, are you ready?" Freya calls from the bedroom.

"Yep, we're sitting on the couch, waiting for the fashion show," Sven yells back. "Cheers Flat White."

"Skål!" Clara replies, clinking her glass against Sven's, then she lets out a wolf whistle. "Look at you!"

Freya does her best fashion runway stroll from the bedroom out to the lounge. She stops halfway to put one hand on her hip, pout and look left and right before continuing on towards the couch and her friends.

"Wow, rocking it babe! I think if Zac were here, you'd be in serious trouble!" Sven laughs.

"He'd have you back in that bedroom in a flash!" adds Clara.

"Settle Gretels!" Freya replies. "Thanks for pushing me to get these cute ankle boots though, they're really comfy."

"And they sure do set your calves off," Sven adds.

"That sundress is just so you, Freya. I love the leather-jacket-over-the-shoulder look too – a hint of intimidation and spice," admires Clara. "Poor Zac won't know what's hit him!"

Grabbing a glass of bubbles and joining the girls on the couch, Freya admits, "Okay, okay, I get the hint, Zac is the one. I promise I'll talk with him on Monday."

"Sooner rather than later, Freya! I'll expect details hot off the press," Sven demands, "or else you'll have me to contend with!"

Taking a sip of her wine, Freya glares at Sven. "So if I'm sorted on the boyfriend front, where does that leave you two?"

"Well, I'm certainly hopeful, but have you seen my work colleagues at BS? There's no talent there," Sven replies.

"And I'm off the market for a while," Clara says adamantly.

"Now don't bite my head off, Flat White, but what about Jack?" Sven asks gently.

"He does put on the 'action man, I'm bullet proof' act really well, but you can see his tender side in the little things he does," Clara replies.

"He's been pretty reliable over the last few years," Freya adds.

"Yeah, but he's in Nepal mountain biking and I've cheated on him. He won't want me anymore," Clara replies.

"You don't know that for sure," reasons Freya.

"Show me anyone who takes back a cheating partner, and I'll show you a door mat," says Clara.

"I wouldn't exactly call Hilary Clinton a door mat," remarks Sven. "Just hypothesising here – if you did try to get him back, you would have to lay everything on the line and be completely honest with him."

"Geez, Sven, I'm only just starting to get honest with myself! I'm not sure if I could," Clara replies.

"You've been honest with us, Flat White, and if there's one thing I know about Clara James, it's that if she puts her mind to something, she will achieve it," declares Freya.

"Here's to the three amigos finding love," Sven proposes, raising her glass.

"Skål!"

Chapter 19

Confessions and Quakes

Monday morning as she walks from the station to Ed House, Freya is deep in thought over the revelations from her second girls' weekend. She had fun blowing off steam on the Kiwi Con with her besties, but her feelings for Zac are becoming clearer. With the progress at Portobello she sometimes feels as if Zac is taking over and she's intruding on his schedule. Steeling herself, she phones Zac. "Hey good looking, how was your weekend?"

"More to the point, how was yours?" Zac asks. "Need a few painkillers for the hangover, perhaps?" he teases.

"Ha ha, thanks for asking, but I'm fine," Freya replies. "I think it had something to do with Flat White overseeing buying quality bubbles. But we did pick up a couple of Art Deco lamps that I'm sure will work a treat in the restaurant, once we get clearance from your policeman friend Rex."

"I'll follow him up once we've finished our call – he's

just arrived and having a coffee with Micco."

"Ah Zac, I'm not sure how to say this, but am I cramping your style coming out there every night? I sometimes feel like I'm intruding," asks Freya tentatively.

"Don't be ridiculous Fin, that is so not the case. I'm sorry if you get that impression," Zac flounders. "I just get so in the zone when I'm on a mission, I get tunnel vision and forget about everything else. Sorry if it looks like I've been ignoring you."

"Well it's just a bit weird since you've been down in Wellington permanently. I'm staying at your mum's house and you're staying in my house. It's meant to be my baby, but I'm stuck in town working and you're there at Portobello permanently; this is now your work, your digs, your life. Sometimes I forget how I fit into it all," says Freya dejectedly.

"Hey Fin, sometimes you're so insecure, I don't know where it comes from. How could you even think that?" Zac asks, before reassuring her yet again. "This is one hundred per cent your place, through and through. Well, for one, you own it – there's that small detail – and then all the décor, ideas, etcetera, they are all yours. And it's been *you* chasing the punters. I'm just the gofer – you can see that, can't you? I should be the one feeling like a spare prick at a party," Zac confesses.

"Don't be ridiculous. How can you feel like that?" asks Freya. "You had the brainwave about the booking website and the crime voyeurs! You're doing most of the renovations." She stops for a moment and sighs. "You know what? We are both being ridiculous; shall we just forget we ever had this conversation?"

"Fin, I have to say you have been acting really weird

lately. Is there something going on that you want to share with me?" Freya can almost feel Zac's eyes looking intensely at her through the phone. "Come on girl, I know you better than you think I do. So come on, now is the time."

There is a deathly silence while Zac waits for Freya to open up. Freya freezes; she can't think, no words will come out. She feels an anxiety attack coming on and starts taking slow breaths, looking out at the calm harbour water. She finally finds the words.

"Nothing Zac, I think you're overanalysing things. All is good. Everything is on schedule." She instantly regrets not taking the opportunity to come clean, but it just doesn't feel like the right time. "I'm just a bit nervous with this lead-up to Christmas – there are only two weeks to go. Look, I'm nearly at work. I'm going to ask for some time off work, but need to square it with Dimitri first, so I'll be out a bit later."

Zac stares at the phone in disbelief. "Sure, if that's what you want, Freya. Look, while we're being honest here," he says with a hint of sarcasm, "I haven't had a break from here for a while. Don't get me wrong, I love what I'm doing, it's just – you know, all work makes Zac a dull boy. Some of the lads are going out tonight and I thought I'd join them. Would you mind filling in for me and being the security-cum-receptionist dude for the night?"

"What, all night?"

"Yep. Well, you know I haven't been out for a while and I think I'll be staying over at one of the lad's places – I can't drink and drive."

Freya feels her stomach do a somersault, and can't help but wonder where he's going and why he needs to stay out for the whole night.

"Sure, I can stay on. You'll have to show me the ropes. What's the room like? Have you cleaned the sheets lately, or is it a typical bachelor pad?"

"The sheets are clean, but you could always make them dirty with me," replies Zac, without thinking. He instantly regrets it. "Oh my god, I am so sorry Freya, that was so out of order. I was just joking. Ah, can we just pretend I didn't say that?"

Freya tries to laugh it off, not quite able to believe he just said that. Had she imagined it? Her emotions are all over the place, and she really needs to get in to work. "Okay Zac, text me later when you're leaving, and I can come over. Ciao for now." She rings off, more confused than ever.

*****

Zac hangs up at the other end and can't believe he just said that to Freya. Sometimes he feels she's really into him and other times he thinks she's just taking him for granted and thinks of him as just the labourer. She seems so fragile lately though, and he doesn't want to rock the boat by taking the risk of letting her know how he feels. Surely he's made it obvious enough now, by leaving Auckland to come down here and spend 24/7 getting this show on the road. He decides to back off now, despite his mother urging him to tell her how he feels.

Each time he thinks he's taken a step forward with Freya, he feels as if he's taken two quantum leaps backwards. All he knows is he's going out on the town tonight and getting seriously trashed.

*****

Freya walks into the office feeling out of sorts. She had the opportunity to tell Zac how she feels, but somehow she got tongue-tied. What on earth just happened? She's rehearsed what to say hundreds of times in her head, but she blew her chance. Deciding she seriously needs some counselling, she calls Sven in the hope that she can squeeze her in this morning.

"Hey mate, what's up?" answers Sven.

"You at work?" asks Freya, relieved she managed to get hold of her so quickly.

"Yep, just the usual meeting after meeting, around in circles. Same theme, just a different day," Sven replies automatically, then thinking about it, adds, "Well I did overhear the strangest conversation as we were leaving the Kiwi Con this morning, but that's another story. What's up with you?"

"Well I just had the most bizarre conversation with Zac. We were both acting weird. I think he just made a pass at me, but in a really tacky un-Zac-like way. He said something about helping to make the bed sheets dirty together."

"Oh my god, Fin!" Sven exclaims. "That is so unlike Zac, you're so right. Man, sounds to me like he's been giving you the signs and you just haven't taken them. He's obviously trying to make it more than subtle now, so that you get it. And you have. Have you still not told him how you feel?"

"No, of course I haven't. I'm great at giving others advice, but when it comes to me it's a different story. I'm out to lunch. He wants a break tonight and plans to go out on an all-night bender with the boys. I feel bad because he hasn't had a break from the place since he moved back down."

"Look girlie, I think you should try and see him face to face, before he goes out, and just tell him how you feel. You can't have this hanging over your head, especially with the silly season approaching. You know how some girls get at this time of year after a few too many vinos, they see who they can pull for the night," Sven points out. "But if you've got his vibe wrong, which I don't think you have, it's better to find out now before you go and ruin a fabulous friendship. Have you guys gone into partnership yet, business-wise?"

"Kind of, but we haven't signed anything yet," Freya replies. "Do you think he really would sleep with some scrubber?"

"Oh Freya, wake up. The fact is that Zac is one hunk of a man, and with a few too many inside him and feeling rejected, who knows what he could end up doing by mistake," warns Sven. "I'm sorry, part of me wants to laugh – you're normally the independent, strong-willed one and now you're a complete mess. It's just not like you. You've clearly got it bad. I mean all of us for years have thought you two were so well-suited, the only problem is you two never saw it. And now it's got to a point where it's do or die. So baby, you know what you need to do. I'm not talking to you again until you've done the business," she adds sternly.

"What do you mean?" Freya asks, shocked at Sven's frankness. "Get down and dirty with him before someone else does?"

"Well if that's what it takes, Freya!" Sven says sharply,

before softening her tone. "But you've got to tell him, or show him how you really feel by the close of business today, before he goes out tonight and gets horribly pissed and does something that you and he may regret. Freya, in case you hadn't noticed, Zac is an incredibly good-looking guy, he's a fantastic catch. He can hold a conversation, he has great morals, values, an incredible sense of humour, and he's a reliable person to go into business with. So, no more excuses, honey. Look, I have to go, the next boring meeting is calling me in neon lights, an HR Stand-up, looks like a biggy. Gotta go, good luck and let me know when you've spoken to Zac!"

Unsure if she feels any better after talking to Sven, Freya puts in a few hours' work, getting the approval from Dimitri to have the rest of the day off and work from home for the rest of the week. She ferries back to Lowry Bay, relieved to see Zita is out. She sits in the bunker and contemplates, and finally sends Zac a text asking him to catch up with her before he goes out.

She tarts herself up, but not too much as she doesn't want to draw attention to the fact that she's made the effort. Perfume, lippie, tight jeans and her new ankle boots with her favourite white camisole top to show off her tan. She grabs her jean jacket in case it gets cold and flies out the door. In her mind's eye, she pictures sitting on the rooftop having a drink and confessing, just before he goes out.

This time, my girl, you will say it, and nothing will get in your way, she tells herself. She sings at the top of her voice, 'It's now or never' as she roars down the parade. She turns the radio up and sighs, letting go of her nervous energy.

The traffic slows down as she gets closer to Petone; it's

rush hour, just before 5pm, and everyone is crawling. The traffic coming out of Wellington is bad as usual, although nothing like Auckland. She tries to turn right to get across the oncoming traffic and onto Jackson. Just then she hears a dog howling, then more dogs join in.

The air feels dry and electric, like the calm before a storm. She notices the residents on the four-storeyed building nearby holding on to the balustrade tightly, and hears their screams. Something the woman is holding in her hand goes flying over the veranda and comes crashing to the ground near her.

Wow, are they having an argument? An alarm goes off, and someone else comes flying out of their house. The music on her car radio stops and the DJ interrupts. "Hey Henry, what was that? Feels like the tenants above us are doing kung fu fighting!" They're on the tenth floor of Radio Towers in town. His colleague responds, "No it's an…"

Freya manages to get across the traffic and fly down Jackson Street, panicked thoughts racing through her head. *Not again, that shake the other day was bad enough, fuck is this the big one … I need to get to Portobello; I can't let this happen again. Not my building, not my Zac…*

She swings into the car park behind the old building and watches in dismay as Portobello rocks and rolls. It's like watching someone drowning right in front of her eyes. She knows it's going to happen, but she can't do anything about it, except sit back in horror and watch. She remembers her grandfather always built his sturdy buildings on rollers and knows theoretically that it should be safe, but still, just seeing it move is alarming.

She watches as things not tied down come flying off the roof into the courtyard. She watches Micco's caravan move and rattle, some of the tables and chairs go flying. *Shit, this is a good one, she ain't going to take no prisoners.*

She's about to get out of the car when she remembers her incident management training, so she holds on to the steering wheel and leans back into her seat, — there's no room in the car to do the 'Drop, Cover, Hold' move that all public servants know off by heart. She waits it out as the seconds turn into minutes. After seven minutes of serious shaking she slowly emerges from her car, unsure if the end has passed. She flies over to Micco's caravan.

"Micco, are you okay mate?" She crouches down between the kitchen benches where an array of pots and pans are scattered throughout the caravan. Micco still has his hands over his head.

"Oh Freya, that one was huge, I didn't think it was going to stop," Micco replies. "I think I'm okay. Shit that scared the blazing daylights out of me. They just get worse. Where were you when it took off?"

"I was in the Beetle, cruising down the parade. I heard these weird noises and then saw things come flying off the apartment block down the road. Shit, where's Zac? He's not still up the ladder inside, is he? Have you seen him?" Freya asks, panicked.

"No, I haven't seen him for a couple of hours," Micco replies. "Last I saw him was earlier today when Rex told him he was called to another investigation in town. Zac's been upstairs ever since." He stands up. "Let's go find him and check out the damage, looks like Portobello is okay from the outside."

He looks at his watch, still in a state of shock, and starts to babble away nervously. "It's bang on five o'clock. Oh man, all those commuters will be on the motorways and heading for the trains and buses, or worse still, some may already be on those electric trains halfway home. I hope there haven't been the usual landslides – those high cliffs the trains follow to get out of Wellington don't look that safe at the best of times. Just one big rumble like that and it's anyone's guess where the trains could have ended up. You know they never maintain those tracks, let alone the power lines that run them. Remember the last time the electrical wires collapsed and that created a huge backlog of trains going nowhere."

"Come on, let's get upstairs and deal with the aftermath of the commuters later. I need to find my Zac," Freya says urgently.

They race up the stairs and find Zac sitting on the floor in a doorway, dazed.

"Zac, are you okay?" asks Freya, relieved.

"Well I almost wasn't," says Zac, standing up. "I was about to go up the ladder again to hook up the curtains and then something just didn't feel right. Everything went silent, you know that eerie calm before the storm feeling? The dog next door started barking its head off and I knew something was up. Then it started to rock and roll, and I jumped in the doorway over here and sat it out. It sure was a good one!"

"Well as long as you're okay?" Freya sighs.

"Well I am, but I'm sorry Freya, there's been a bit of damage. Some of your lovely Art Deco lights smashed. I can't have secured them tight enough and this one, as you can see, smashed into a hundred pieces. I'm really sorry," Zac apologises.

"You doofus, it's only a glass object. It's not you. Just as long as you're okay." She turns to Micco who gets the hint straight away.

"Hey, I have a kitchen to clean up before the crowds arrive tonight," he says quickly. "I'm out of here, don't let me get in your way," he adds, and runs off down the stairs.

Zac watches Micco retreat down the stairs and then looks at Freya, slightly bemused. "Look, I don't think I'll be heading out tonight with the boys," he says, clearly still dazed from the earthquake. "Besides, you wanted to catch up…" then with a look of clarity and hope, he ventures, "sugar plum?"

Still afraid to make the first move, Freya asks tentatively, "Shall we look at the other rooms?"

"Okay Fin," Zac replies as he puts on his 'engineer hat', inspecting the walls and door frames. "So much for being structurally unsound; come on through here." They look for any damage in the rooms. "I think we got let off pretty lightly actually, but I'm not so sure about our neighbours."

They check all the rooms and end up on the Romeo and Juliet balcony overlooking Jackson Street. They stand side by side assessing the surrounding buildings, and then turn towards each other at the same time.

Mustering all her courage, Freya looks intensely into Zac's eyes. "I was afraid I was going to lose you this time. I've been such a fool. This is not how I'd planned it. I've rehearsed this moment a million times but I could never find the words."

Zac takes a step back from the window into the safety of the room in case another shake begins, besides the one stirring in his body. He puts his arms around her and says softly, "Fin, I've been afraid of losing you ever since I met you. But especially in the last few weeks since we've gone into partnership together; I've just felt you distancing yourself more and more."

"Yes, but…" He puts his finger on her lips to silence her.

"Fin, I have loved being with you forever. You make everything so god damn exciting. I love working on this with you," he points to the rooms before continuing, "I love our deep and meaningful chats. I love your sense of adventure and humour. In fact, I love everything about you." Zac pauses momentarily then takes a deep breath and plunges onwards. "What I'm trying to tell you is that… I LOVE YOU Freya Isobel Nilson!" Taking her elfin-pointed chin into his hands he plants the most passionate kiss Freya has ever had on her perfect lips.

There's another little shake, but Zac pulls her in even tighter and doesn't let go.

Eventually they come up for air. Freya's hair is dishevelled and her face has softened. "Zac, oh my god, I've been trying to tell you the same, but the words just wouldn't come out of my mouth."

"Well I guess I'm a little old-fashioned, thinking that the man should make the move first. Sometimes I thought you were giving me signs, and other times I just thought I was your lackey, your live-in Jack of all trades."

"Well I would like you to continue to be my Jack of all trades, but I would also like us to change a few conditions in the contract we haven't finalised or signed yet. I think there's still room for some negotiation," says Freya.

"You don't like the changes I made to our business contract?" replies Zac, perplexed. "What clauses do you want me to change?"

Freya laughs. "The one about you being the sole live-in business partner. I want to live here too, with you."

Zac laughs with relief. "Damn it sugar plum, you sure know how to make a man happy."

"We will need a bigger room though," Freya smiles.

"Well you just happen to have an engineer here who can approve which walls need to be moved, knocked down, and I think I know how we can extend the security man's accommodation," he says, pointing to the wall. "This one has to go, that will make it a little more spacious but still with that 'cosy' feeling you love. I don't even think I'll need approval from the council for that."

"And why's that?"

Zac sheepishly confesses, "Because I got approval from them last week, that in the off chance we would be expanding that I could pull down this wall."

"Oh Zac, you're too good," Freya replies.

"Well, I kinda felt bad holding out on you, Fin," he admits.

"Zac, I think we've both been holding out on each other." She grabs the front of his T-shirt and pulls him in close. "Come here doofus," she whispers, and kisses him tenderly on the lips.

Zac responds passionately, then coming up for air yet again, he murmurs, "Oh Fin, I've made such a hash of trying to tell you..."

"Shut up, doofus," Freya says as she pulls him back for more.

As they find comfort in each other's arms, from the open window they can hear Micco's radio: "The biggest earthquake Wellington has ever had has just broken out across the city. It is a... centred in... and... deep. Wellington commuters were heading home.

The city is in absolute chaos. The BS Ministry in charge of incident management is trying to…"

Chapter 20

Community Beacon

Taking Zac by the hand, Freya leads Zac from the room towards the stairs. "Come on babe, let's go and see if Micco needs some help."

"And anyone else for that matter, sugar plum," Zac teases, reaching for his phone, texting. "I hope Mum's alright."

"I'll try the girls," Freya adds, as they start dialling and heading down the stairs. "Damn, sounds like the phone systems are down."

"Try texting, sometimes they go through easier than phone calls if the system is overloaded," Zac offers.

As they exit the stairs, Micco calls from the kitchen, "Can I get you guys to tidy up in here please, while I sort out the caravan?"

"Sure thing, mate," Zac replies.

Freya looks around the kitchen in amazement. "When did all this happen? The kitchen was still closed this morning by the police investigation."

"Rex let us in first thing, when he was called away for another job," Zac explains, "so Micco and I washed the place down and Micco stocked the fridge, freezer and cupboards."

"Yes, that's right, I want to start the restaurant up as soon as possible, Freya," Micco confirms. "I was hoping for a Wednesday night opening."

"Fine by me Micco, but it might be sooner than you think," Freya replies. "I'm just thinking we could get a few lost people needing warm food and a bed after that earthquake."

"You're right, Fin, can you get cracking here and I'll just check a few of the neighbours to see if they're okay?" Zac adds, leaning over to give her a kiss before leaving. The sound of sirens can be heard as a fire engine tears down Jackson Street.

Freya busies herself in the kitchen, putting packets and tins back into the cupboards and cleaning up the small mess on the stainless-steel benchtops and floor.

Zac returns half an hour later, "It's bedlam out there, the place is a mess. The road is covered in smashed glass, further down where the high-rise buildings are. You were lucky, Fin, as the road is blocked and traffic can't get through," he explains. "Fortunately no one around us was injured."

"Wow, the earthquake was just starting when I flew past that building – stuff had started flying off the balcony. It must have got worse as she continued to roll."

"Evidently town is a lot worse off because of all those apartments and office buildings. Hopefully a lot of the workers got out of their buildings in time, but those who were there until five wouldn't have been so lucky," says Zac. His phone beeps and he checks the text, sighing with relief. "Thank god, Mum's okay and is heading our way with the dog and dropping off one of her yoga friends."

"Shit, Sven, Flat White, Dimitri… I still haven't heard from them," panics Freya, dialling through to Sven's phone again. "Come on Sven, pick up babe, you can't still be in a meeting, it's well after five now. Come on, answer…"

The phone goes to answer machine and she leaves a message. "Hey Sven, it's your buddy. How are you, are you okay? Of course you are, I know you, you're burning the midnight oil and still in a meeting. Hey, guess what happened, you'll be impressed with what I've done since you stuck a rocket up me only a few hours ago. I finally spilled. Ring me back, I need to tell you what happened with Zac; you won't believe it. The earthquake did me a favour – it's kind of fast-tracked it all. Okay, ciao bella."

Next she tries ringing Flat White, but gets an automated message saying the network is temporarily down due to an overload and to only use the phone in an emergency. "Hell, it must be bad," she says to Zac, repeating the recording.

"It is, Fin, the power is out for most of Jackson Street. At least with the gas burners we can cook food and those solar panels I installed a few days back will keep the lights on – it might even power up the TV I moved into the bar."

"Good idea, let's see what the story is," says Freya, as they move into the bar and Zac turns the TV on. There are scenes of Wellington CBD and it is not looking good. Freya pours herself a glass of water and watches on as scenes around the Wellington area flash across the screen. Wellington is in a serious state of emergency and there are roadblocks, floods, and a reported possible tsunami.

Zac sees a mother and crying child outside the front door and brings them in for warmth and shelter. Looking at Fin, he says, "Babe, probably best if you stay indoors. It'll be safer in here and it looks like we may be opening up for trade early tonight. Even though it's a Monday and only five-thirty I think a lot of people will want to come in for warmth and shelter and a good hot coffee while they work out how they're all going to get home."

"Okay, I'll check with Micco and see if we can't get some hot soup on," Freya replies, motioning to the mother and child. "Come over here and take a seat. Would you like a cup of tea or something?"

"Oh, thank you both, I can't get through to my husband and there doesn't look to be any buses working to get home," the mother says.

"Just stay here and try texting, I'll be back soon," Freya says as she heads out to see Micco.

She nearly bumps into him as she walks out the back door. "I think we may need to put some hot drinks on, and some soup maybe for the kids. I have a feeling we may be playing 'soup kitchen' soon to half of Petone."

"Right you are, Guvnor," Micco replies, winking at her. "I've locked up the caravan, but I've got some good ingredients here," he informs her, as he heads towards the kitchen.

"It's going to be busy tonight. Can I help and focus on soup and hot beverages, if you want to put some of your famous kebabs and pizzas on and see how we go?" Freya asks.

Just then a bewildered Leo walks in, looking somewhat dishevelled. "Oh thank goodness, you are open. I was down the road when it hit. It's a nightmare out there," he says, then seeing the kitchen activity, offers, "Can I help in some small way, perhaps?"

"Leo, you are a star! It's so good to see you. Look, we're opening up the kitchen for soup and hot beverages – would you mind lending a hand? I'm just flying upstairs quickly to check a few things out," Freya replies.

She races upstairs to clean any damage and make sure all the rooms are in order in case people need to stay in town for the night, and finds all the beds are made up and ready to go. *Zac, you are a saint,* she thinks to herself. The bathrooms are looking good too. She gets out a couple of extra towels for one room and grabs some extra blankets before racing back downstairs.

Zac is like a traffic controller on a road site, ushering distressed people in off the street. "Come in and wait, no point staying out there in the confusion. Come in and take shelter here. Over that way," he advises, pointing towards the restaurant/bar area, where people are gathering around the TV to see the news feed. "There could be a brew on the go, don't worry, free coffees, tea and soup. Hey Isaia and Moana, good to see you and the whānau." Zac kneels down to Isaia's children. "Talofa Talia and Loto, do you guys mind going over and playing with that little boy over there? He and his mum are waiting for his dad, and he looks a little scared and lonely."

"Sure, Uncle Zac, toe feiloa'i," they answer.

Freya can't help but smile at people's comments as they enter Portobello. "Wow, we didn't even know this place existed." "This is truly gorgeous." "I love the turquoise. It is so retro." "How long has this been here for?"

She offers a blanket to the mother who is sipping on a cup of hot chocolate, watching her son play with Isaia's children.

"Freya, over here," Zac calls as he helps a woman through the front door, who Freya immediately recognises.

Freya thanks Zac, and greets Leo's friend. "Welcome Evelyn, come with me and take a seat."

"Freya, you are a darling, but have you seen Leo?" Evelyn enquires worriedly.

"He's currently helping in the kitchen – shall we check on him?"

"The kitchen?!" Evelyn exclaims. "Lead me there straight away please! Why, he could be poisoning your guests!"

Leo is in full swing playing sous-chef to Micco, both of them laughing as they chop ingredients and stir bubbling pots on the gas range.

"Leo, what on earth are you doing in here? I've been looking all over for you," Evelyn admonishes. "Besides, I didn't know you had culinary talents," she adds, with a wink.

"My dear, what a pleasant surprise, the chef here is Micco, lovely chap by the way. You just missed me; I had just finished my usual coffee and last reading in the café for the day when all the upheaval in the street occurred, and I found myself naturally gravitating here," Leo replies, coming over to give Evelyn a warm hug. "I'm so glad you are here. Look, I know this is a frightfully presumptuous thing to ask, but would you mind giving us a hand? It looks like we could be the fastest emergency response in the area, and this wonderful establishment is standing out like a beacon by the looks of the crowds now gathering out there.

Evelyn asks, "Where is Timmy?"

"Thank you for asking Evelyn, I have checked on him, he and the dog sitter are just fine."

Evelyn, with a determined look, grabs an apron from the back of the door. "Leo, Micco, let's get cracking."

"That's the spirit, Evelyn," Micco replies, turning to Leo. "I can see what you mean, Leo – a feisty wee rocket," he laughs as he pours more soup into cups on a tray. "Here you go, Guvnor."

Casting a sidewise look at Leo, Evelyn asks Micco, "What nonsense has this rogue been spouting?"

"Thanks guys, what a team!" Freya says as she heads back out into the crowd with the tray of soup.

*****

Early evening turns into late evening and Portobello is full. People are in a combination of fine spirits and anxiousness as some cannot get hold of their loved ones. Everyone is glued to the TV for updates as the phones and internet are only working spasmodically.

Freya is in her element helping everyone. She too is concerned as she can't get hold of Sven or Flat White, but she soldiers on. She has this warm feeling inside; she is so blissfully happy about her and Zac and feels guilty for feeling like this amongst all the turmoil, but it's what's keeping her going.

Zac directs some of the locals to her, such as the local book shop manager Steven Cooper, who seems impressed with Portobello. "Hi Freya. What a fabulous venue for a book launch. Which to be honest, I'm in desperate need of since the collapse of the back of my shop. Fortunately no one was injured. I see you have a street frontage display area I could use as a temporary shop, if it's still available. Can I place a booking for the restaurant please?"

"Of course, Steven," Freya replies. "Let's look at the diary, but can I ask who the author is?"

"Well, I have three – a couple of up-and-coming locals, and the poet Sam Hunt," Steven replies.

Freya marvels at how often there is a silver lining to the grey clouds in life, tonight being no exception.

Zac walks past and pinches her bum subtly. "Hey sugar plum, who would have thought this was going to be the way you market your little enterprise?"

"Remember one thing, Zac: it is *ours* now. Portobello was never just mine – it was always ours and it always will be. Come on, help me with these soups. I don't think we can take anyone else in now. It's a pity we can't have people up on the roof."

"Why can't we? The marquees are all sorted and before you ask, yes, it is all compliant. Not that anyone is going to care too much about that right now. Besides, it's all relative – what's safest? Standing out in that war zone," he points towards the street, "or upstairs away from the falling debris?" Zac asks.

"True. Okay, there's a slight chill in the air, I think I'll put the braziers on?" Freya asks.

Then the local bottle shop proprietor approaches them. "Look, I feel funny asking at a time like this, but I need some bulk storage and was wondering if your cellar was underutilised? Do you think we could have wine tastings down there, if I bring our monthly wine promos over?"

"Of course you can," replies Freya enthusiastically. "Look, just write down your contact details and we'll get back to you tomorrow or when things settle down and we can work out the details."

Something has suddenly caught Zac's attention, and he races off towards the door. "Mum!" he shouts, sweeping his mother into a big hug as Harry barks excitedly at his heels.

Freya joins them. "Oh, we were so worried! Where have you both been?"

"Well, some roads are blocked, there are detours everywhere, bless the police they're trying their best, but they must be overloaded," Zita replies.

"That's Mum for you, always thinking of others," Zac says with a tear in his eye, disengaging from the hug.

"So that's where you get it from, Zac?" Freya teases.

"Come here, daughter-in-law-to-be," Zita says with her arms opening to welcome Freya into an embrace.

Tears spring from Freya's eyes as she hugs Zita tightly. "Oh Zita! Or..." Freya hesitates, "it's a bit early to be calling you Mum, isn't it? But how do you know?"

"A little birdie sent me a text earlier," Zita replies, smiling. "Amongst all this chaos, you two are my little rays of sunshine."

"Well, come on in Zita," says Freya warmly. Turning to Zac she asks, "Tell me we have a spare room for Zita and Harry?"

"Fortunately we had some cancellations and only have two bookings left for tonight, so when I got some coverage an hour ago, I blocked out the other rooms just in case Evelyn, Leo and Micco were staying, so that leaves a spare room for Mum, and of course a dog!" laughs Zac.

"What would I do without you, Zac?" Freya says.

"Settle down you two," interrupts Zita. "Now, can I smell soup?"

Freya leads Zita over towards the bar, where Evelyn is helping to serve refills of soup and beverages to the crowd. "Aren't Evelyn and Leo stars? I love the way they just turned up and mucked in. We couldn't have done all of this on our own."

Zac starts talking to some people and leading them up the stairs to the rooftop to free up some space downstairs.

"Now Freya, have you eaten?" Evelyn asks. "Here, have a small cup of soup, there's some bread over there. I think you need a little break."

Freya and Zita thank Evelyn and take a seat to catch up and replenish some energy.

"Now Zita, tell me, where were you at five o'clock?" asks Freya. "It reminds me of when Princess Diana died in that horrific car crash in the Pont de l'Alma tunnel in Paris. For weeks afterwards people would share what they'd been doing at the exact time of her accident."

"Well, I was just coming out of yoga. It was quite good timing in some ways. I was going to head for home, but then it happened. Harry started barking so we both stood still by a tree. It was pretty bad. I'm just so glad I wasn't in town shopping, and so glad I hadn't left Harry at home on his own. What about you?"

"I was driving here in your Beetle…" Freya catches Zita up on the news.

*****

After showing Zita and Harry to their room, Freya walks back downstairs to find Zac in the entranceway ushering a few new people towards the bar. His empathy and humour, not to mention his good looks and charm, do him wonders and the visitors are lapping it up. She is so proud; he is her man. He looks up and suddenly sees her standing there staring at him.

"You are quite the natural, aren't you, Mr McLean-Smith? I think you could have a whole new career in hospitality," Freya says admiringly.

Zac takes her in his arms, looking into her eyes. "Well, I find this much more natural," he whispers as he kisses her deeply. Both of them are so distracted with each other they don't hear the front door open behind them. Coming up for air, Zac asks, "How's my sugar plum this evening?"

A loud voice interjects. "I wondered when you two would get together!" Rex turns to his companions. "Charlie and Sven, this is the place I was telling you about, where I've got a room booked. Zac and Freya's."

"Freya!" Sven exclaims.

Tearing herself from Zac, Freya rushes to her friend. "Oh Sven! Look at you!" The two friends hug each other gently, then Freya gingerly touches Sven's forehead. "What the hell happened to you?"

Zac shakes Charlie's hand. "It's been a while, mate."

"What? Do you guys know each other?" Rex asks quizzically.

"Hey, Wellington's really a village, Rex – if you've spent any time here, you soon get to know the people," Charlie replies. "Sven and Freya go way back," he says, turning to Zac. "We would have met at one of the many bars back when I was engaged to Sven, no doubt."

Sven and Freya, oblivious to the men, walk towards the bar. However, Freya is in a state of shock seeing Charlie after all these years but keeps her composure.

"Come and have some hot soup, Sven, and tell me

what happened. Obviously a bit to catch up on, such as CHARLIE."

"Well, I've been helping Charlie and Rex investigate the Kiwi Con murder of Cat…" Sven starts.

"What! Whoa, hang on a minute, lets get a seat and you can tell me all about it!" Freya replies shocked.

The men all look at each other, shaking their heads, before following the girls.

"Hopefully Micco has some of that ouzo left, I think we all need a good drink after today," suggests Rex.

"Hell, you guys are doing a great job here, Zac," Charlie comments looking around at the crowd. "How have you got power?"

"Some solar panels on the north side of the building I installed a few days back," Zac replies, "just enough juice in the battery for TV and lights, the kitchen is running on LPG gas bottles. So sorry Rex, probably no hot shower in the morning, but we'll see what we can manage."

"You wouldn't have a spare room for Sven would you, Zac?" Charlie asks, adding quickly, "I'm thinking Rex and I could bunk down together."

"Hey, I'm sure we can work something out," Zac replies, as they gather next to the table Freya and Sven are sitting at.

"And Flat White?" Freya asks Sven.

"Well I haven't seen or heard from her all day except for a text saying…"

"The funny thing is," Zac interjects, "I was sure earlier on in the day I saw Flat White marching down the street here on Jackson at a brisk pace. But Freya, you told me she was starting her job in Wellington today, so I thought it can't have been her – what would she be doing out here in Petone?"

"Weird, Zac. But Freya," she says, turning back to her friend, "what do you make of this text? 'Hey bud, you'll never guess where I am and what I'm up to! I know you love guessing, oh psychic one – you have three guesses.' Sven raises her eyebrows. "That doesn't sound like the straightedge Clara we know…"

"Well after that knock to the head, Sven, I'd be surprised if you could pick up any psychic messages," Freya points out.

"Then I got this one: 'Sven, this is not funny, where the fuck are you?' So either she's out of sorts hitting the bubbles again, or she's in trouble," Sven replies.

"What are the time signatures on the texts, Sven?" Charlie asks.

"Look, two real life detectives to help us out on this mystery!" Freya laughs. "This is almost Enid Blyton-ish!"

They all have a good laugh. "Hey, I'm off the clock, so I'm off to chat up Micco. Back soon," Rex says.

"For 'lashings of ginger beer' or something a bit stronger perhaps?" Charlie jibes.

"Well, can I suggest that in the spirit of Enid Blyton, let's head up onto the rooftop where it's a bit quieter and see if we can't contact Flat White," Freya suggests, "or at least work out where she is, what she's up to and if she's safe."

*****

As they gather around one of the outdoor tables on the rooftop, Freya raises a glass. "Well, here's to surviving the biggest shake down in living memory," she announces, taking a sip. "Wow, this is strong stuff!"

"Some seriously authentic 'raki'," Rex comments.

"No wonder you were a bit slow on the case today, mate," Charlie ribs, laughing. Then he turns serious. "Did you know that when the network goes down, like it has on and off this evening, not all the texts and messages will come through in the order they were sent?"

"Yeah, that threw us after the Christchurch quakes a few years back," Rex comments. "We had that briefing from the IT boys – did you follow all of it, Charlie?"

"Too much techo stuff for me, but the gist was that one, sometimes you don't get the texts; two, the texts sometimes don't come in the order they were sent; and three, sometimes the texts can take up to a week after the event to come through, even though you've been receiving messages as usual after the system crash," Charlie summarises.

"So looking at the time signatures won't help?" Zac asks.

"Well, let's see… Clara's first text was sent before the earthquake, so that one should be accurate," states Charlie. "The frantic text appears to have been sent at 5.25pm."

"Okay, so everything is fine and dandy, then she went through the earthquake and gets her urgent text away when she can afterwards?" Zac sums up.

"Are you trying for a third career, Zac?" Freya teases, then looking at the others, "Sorry, an inside joke. I'm just winding him up, trying to keep it light."

"I think we seriously need to keep things light, otherwise we'll just stress out over things that are out of our control," Sven says.

Chapter 21

The Lighthouse Keepers

Freya walks through the dining room and it seems to be a bit busier. Some of the punters from outside have come indoors due to the drop in temperature.

Evelyn and Leo have had a ball conversing with everyone, but Freya can see they have now taken leave and Zac is leading them upstairs. She decides to check in on the dinner guests and see where everyone is at.

"Good evening, how are you two?" she asks a couple seated at one of the tables. "What's the latest? I haven't tuned in with the news for an hour. Any positive developments?"

"Still a real mess downtown, the army has been dispatched from Linton and the engineers are on their way from Waiouru," the man says, his eyes glued to the screen. "That tosser of a prime minister still hasn't made an appearance; hopefully he didn't make it out of the Beehive," he adds angrily.

"Dwayne! That's a horrible thing to say!" his partner

cries.

"Sorry Darleen, you know how much of a loser he is and how angry he makes me." He turns to Freya and apologises. "Sorry, my better half is quite right, that was a horrible thing to wish on anyone. Have you heard from your loved ones?"

"Thanks for asking, we've heard from most, but still can't locate one of our friends," Freya replies, "but believe me you are not alone in your political thoughts. It sounds like the right people are making the right decisions, if the army has been called in. I think us Wellingtonians are going to need all the help we can get for a while."

A distraught young man wearing a Hi-Viz vest enters the dining room, looking around frantically. "Bronnie? Tommy?" he calls out.

The young mother that Freya had first brought into Portobello waves out to him. "Over here, Gary!" Tears of relief stream down her face as she gently wakes the young child. "Look Tommy, Daddy is here, I told you he would find us."

Gary rushes to her side, kissing her and kneeling next to his family. "I'm sorry I took so long, they're only letting a few people at a time through the Haywards. God, it's such a mess out there."

"Daddy!" Tommy cries, wide-eyed. "You're alive! The whole world shook, Daddy."

"Yes, little Tommy, I'm sure you were very scared," Gary says, picking up his boy from Bronnie's arms, hugging him close. "Lucky you had your brave Mummy."

"And my new friends Talia and Loto," Tommy answers excitedly.

Smiling, with a few tears escaping, Freya walks over

towards the family, noticing from the surrounding tables that she isn't alone – a few other patrons are wiping their eyes at the touching scene.

"Hi there. Have you had anything to eat? I'm sure we still have a little soup and bread left," Freya offers.

"Ah thanks, and thank you for looking after my family," Gary replies, with little Tommy perched on his hip.

"You sit down, dear," Bronnie says, "I'll sort you out. Freya here and her staff have been wonderful."

"How much does it cost?" Gary asks Freya. "I only have a card and no cash," he explains.

"It's on the house. Don't worry, it's not every day we have an earthquake." Freya reassures him.

Freya looks at her watch, suddenly feeling exhausted. 'My god, it's still only Monday. It seems a lifetime ago I caught the train into town.'

Before she heads for the stairs, Freya checks on Micco in the kitchen and finds him cleaning up. "Last one standing, Micco? How were your staff?"

"Hey Guvnor!" Micco replies with a smile on his face. "I loved those two; Leo and Evelyn were pulling each other's legs all night and had me in stitches."

"They do make a good team," Freya agrees.

"Just tidying up and getting ready for the breakfast trade; I'll be sleeping in my van tonight."

"Don't be silly, I'm sure we'll have space inside somewhere, let me find Zac."

"Don't worry Freya, I do have a proper mattress and bed that folds down," replies Micco. "I'll be fine, now you go find that man of yours and get into bed yourself."

As she climbs the stairs, she notices a crack of light coming from the door of Zac's room. She peeps inside to see Evelyn fast asleep on the bed. Leo has fallen asleep in Zac's red chair, and Timmy is faithfully sleeping on the mat. Sneaking inside she pulls the curtains gently and shuts the door quietly. She can still hear faint voices from up above and makes her way to the rooftop to find Zac talking to some of the guests.

The night is clear and a little windy, but the marquees are doing their job well. The glowing turret looks like a lighthouse against the dark sky. Zac is standing in the red marquee beside a brazier talking to some of the guests who are having a nightcap before retiring. She can smell the remains of a pizza, and feeling famished helps herself to a couple of slices.

Zac says good night to the remaining punters and comes over to join her. "Well sugar plum, what a night," he says, putting his arm around her. "Who would have thought our first night in business would be so surreal and so successful. I think we can say that was a one hundred per cent success rate."

"Thanks so much for being my partner in life, my partner in crime, I couldn't have done this without you," Freya replies.

"Oh yes you could have, Freya, I saw you in your element with all those people," insists Zac. "You don't think I'm watching, but I am. You were a hit, a natural conversationalist, just like your buddies who are asleep in our room."

"Yes, I saw that, so cute. Let them sleep there tonight, they deserve it," Freya replies. "But where does that leave us?"

"Well, good question. We have a choice – there's the rustic summer house downstairs, or the lighthouse up here?

Take your pick, my fair lady," he says gallantly.

"Oh, decisions, decisions. A Swedish summer house or a lighthouse? Now for a change, that is an offer I can't refuse, but both sound equally as delightful. I'm too tired – you choose, babe," Freya replies.

"Look, I'll just go and check on the stragglers downstairs and give you time to decide," says Zac. "I'll be back soon."

Zac slips away and Freya pops into the lighthouse to check it out. She lies down on a yoga mat on the floor and pulls a blanket over herself to stargaze, and before she has had time to think, she falls asleep.

Finding her fast asleep, Zac snuggles up next to her. "Oh, my little lighthouse keeper, looks like the decision has been made. Good night my sweet one," he whispers as he plants a kiss on both her cheeks.

Chapter 22

Business as Usual?

Struggling through the mists of her dreams, Freya is finally woken by the light streaming through the window. Opening her eyelids a crack, she shades her eyes with her hand and blearily tries to work out where she is. She sees the curved windows of the turret and realises she must have fallen asleep when she came to check out the room last night. She wonders where Zac is.

Shrugging off the blanket, she sits up to see Zac's curly mop of hair as he appears with a tray of toast and coffee. "Good morning my darling, did you sleep well?"

"Yes, surprisingly enough I did. But I do feel I slept on a slab of concrete last night," she replies sleepily.

"Well that's probably because you did," says Zac. "I left you for five minutes and when I came back you were out like a light and still that way when I got up a couple of hours ago."

"What *is* the time?" Freya asks. "Have you been up all

this time?"

"Well someone had to make sure none of the guests did a runner without saying goodbye, not to mention give them the breakfast they paid for downstairs," Zac teases.

"That is so you, Zac. So what's the status? The guests, Wellington, your mum, Evelyn, Leo?" Freya asks.

"Well how about you eat and drink up and I'll give you a quick rundown," Zac says as he passes Freya the breakfast tray. "We have guests coming down for breakfast and I don't want to leave them on their own for too long. Micco has laid out a buffet breakfast so it's all organised, but I'm on coffees and chatting."

"Oh thanks, Zac. What would I do without you?"

"Well we don't have to think about that, do we, as it's not going to happen. So, Evelyn and Leo are up and they're outside in the sunny part of the courtyard having breakfast. Mum and Harry have just left – she was insistent as she wanted to check on the house and give Harry his proper dog food. I've asked her to text me if she needs a hand, but I'll pop around once the guests have left. It really is quite surreal out there. It's a fine gorgeous sunny day – one of those Wellington days you just can't beat. Come out here and have a look at the harbour."

They both walk out onto the roof and between the buildings they can see the blue glistening water. Everything is calm and still.

"Now I have something funny to tell you. You will never guess who is downstairs," Zac quizzes.

"Who?" Freya asks.

"A couple of Sven's work mates, Lloyd and…"

"Not Lloyd and Carmen!" Freya exclaims.

Zac's face breaks into a grin. "Shall we go down and

get front row seats to see Sven's face when she gets up?" he suggests mischievously.

"You are so naughty, Zac!" laughs Freya. "So Lloyd the mailman who I think ran off with the mutton-dressed-as-lamb Carmen? She has blonde bleached hair, and even at this time of the morning her false eyelashes are probably neatly glued on and standing up to attention."

"No doubt that's not the only thing that's been at attention this morning," Zac comments.

Freya laughs. "He's probably never seen her without her fake eyelashes on. Has she got her full face of make-up on? Fishnets or just bright stockings? Any traces of leopard skin?"

"Funny you should say that," replies Zac, "but pretty much yes to all of the above. You know they stayed the night last night?"

"Really? How come I never saw them?"

"Because you were so busy being the charming hostess talking to all and sundry in the restaurant. I got the impression they wanted to be discreet, so I escorted them to their room as soon as they arrived."

"Oh, are they not an official couple yet?"

"Don't know, don't care. They paid good money for the best room and they've booked it for a second night as well. You know Freya, sometimes it's best just to leave people to their own devices; they are pretty low maintenance. Anyhow, they were up early this morning and they're in the restaurant now if you want to talk to them."

"How do I look? I should have a shower first," Freya says. "Oh, I had a text from Dimitri – Ed House is closed until further notice, so I can work from here when we have a quiet moment."

"Our room is free again, so go for it now, you just never know where this day is going to take us," Zac advises. "If it's anything as unpredictable and exciting as yesterday, I would take the chance now."

After a quick cold shower Freya heads down the stairs to the restaurant. There are a few couples having breakfast and the sun is pouring in from the courtyard, creating a very different atmosphere to last night.

Freya stops by the front door to look out at the street; there are people walking around the designated cones and a couple of guys are out on the street in their Hi-Viz vests sweeping up the broken glass. Some of the shops are opening up for business, but most of them look like they won't be opening any time soon. There are a couple of locals out walking their dogs.

She recognises Lloyd and Carmen instantly at one table and Rex sitting by himself at another. "Morena Rex, how did you sleep?" she asks as she approaches his table.

Rex looks up from his phone. "Good morning Freya, very well thanks. I was just thanking Zac a bit earlier; you know installing those solar panels was a stroke of genius. I've managed to keep our police comms and phones fully charged; it's a double-edged sword, as I've been contacted by the Commissioner three times already this morning."

"Morning Guvnor, and here you are, Sir," Micco says with a smile as he arrives with a large cappuccino. "Oh, I mean Mr Rex," he adds, with a wink.

Confused, Freya asks, "Did I miss something?"

Rex explains with a smile on his face, "It's a bit of an inside joke in the forces that Micco has picked up on."

"But it would be too hard to explain at this time of the morning, eh bro," Charlie interjects. "Ata mārie Freya,

Sven is on her way down shortly. Ah Micco, could you please grab me a couple of those coffees as well?"

"How's the patient, Charlie?" Rex asks. Freya, about to say the same thing, looks at him expectantly.

"The bruising looks worse, but Sven's a feisty one; a bump to the head won't keep her down," Charlie says admiringly.

"Excuse me Freya, but I need a word with Charlie," Rex says as he turns towards his colleague. "Mate, I've just got another text from the Commissioner – that fraud case we were talking about seems to be tied to the basement body. We've had a tip-off from an informant and I'm off in a minute to have a word so we can get the warrants."

"Geez, that's fantastic news, Rex," Charlie congratulates his friend. "Let me know if I can help. I'll just get Sven organised and then I'm available."

"Not *our* 'basement body' is it, Rex?" Zac asks as he arrives with two coffees.

Rex gives Zac a wink, replying, "I couldn't possibly comment, but I think we'll be needing the rooms again tonight. Oh, and ask Micco to make sure the bar is stocked, I can feel a celebration coming on."

"How many celebrating bobbies should we expect?" Zac asks.

"Now if that's an invitation, you can expect half the local station to turn up," Charlie grins, and starts counting off on his fingers. "Let's see – Central, Forensics, Fraud, Comms, Financial Crime Group, and if they hear about it, then the Special Tactics Group and the Diplomatic Protection units won't be far behind."

Finishing his coffee, Rex adds, "Well there won't be a party if I don't get going. They have a car for me at the local station, so I'll see you later!"

Feeling a wave of emotion, Freya asks with tears in her eyes, "Charlie, does that mean this nightmare over the ownership of Portobello is over?"

"Let's all sit down and I'll run you through what will likely happen, all strictly off the record of course," Charlie replies. "But perhaps you should check in with your lawyer, just to keep the legal paperwork in line. So…"

*****

Rex pulls his mufti car into the Percy Scenic Reserve car park, scanning the area for the short man in a dark suit. Not seeing him, Rex gets out of the car and starts walking up the path towards the entrance. As he rounds the corner, he sees a man fitting the description, standing by a greenhouse door inside the gardeners' closed-off area. Rex discreetly changes direction and enters through the plastic barrier, ignoring the 'no public access' sign.

"Mr Croft, I presume?" the smaller man enquires as Rex approaches him.

"That is correct, Thomas Harris," Rex replies, nodding his head towards the greenhouse. "Now shall we have a little chat inside?"

"First up, I do get full protection?" Thomas asks. "Church is an unforgiving man, if he knew I was talking…"

"I get it; then you would end up like your mate Damien," Rex answers. "Look Thomas, we only found your fingerprints on the handrail upstairs, so I don't think it was you, but you'll have to step me through what actually happened. Then I'll make a call to the Commissioner to get your witness protection status confirmed, and we can make the formal statement."

"Not that crook! What about the Assistant Commissioner, does he have the authority?" Thomas asks.

"Ah yes, he does," replies Rex. "Why, what's wrong with the Commissioner?"

"If I'm going to sing, you better be prepared, because there are a few skeletons in a few closets," Thomas states.

"Like who?" Rex asks, intrigued.

"Like a High Court Judge, a couple of Queens Councils, your current Commissioner and a couple of cabinet ministers and Heads of Government departments," Thomas starts. "You better have plenty of straight copper mates if we're going to pull this one off."

"Okay then Thomas, you have my full attention…"

*****

As Charlie and Zac catch up over coffee, Freya heads back upstairs to check on Sven. Knocking on the door, she calls out, "Hey, you in there, your breakfast is getting cold."

"Freya!" Sven exclaims, as she opens the door and immediately gives her friend a big hug. "Sorry, I was just checking my laptop for any word from Flat White."

"I haven't heard a thing yet either, and I'm starting to get worried," Freya replies.

"Nothing in my inbox, no texts, no messages or activity through any of her social media accounts," Sven recounts. "It's like she's just disappeared."

"Do you think we should contact her family?" Freya asks.

"After last weekend's revelations at Waitarere Beach,

I don't think that would be welcome," Sven replies. "But I'm thinking of asking Charlie if he can do anything."

"Great idea Sven," says Freya. She looks at her friend fondly. "I'm so happy you and Charlie have worked things out. How's your head?"

"Thanks Freya. My head is spinning in a good way, if you know what I mean," Sven replies, smiling. "Yeah, what a couple of dipsticks, wasting all those years apart. Come on, let's go see our boys."

*****

As the girls head downstairs, a cacophony of trilling mobile phones suddenly fills the room. People stare at their devices in a mix of horror and surprise.

Standing up, Charlie announces to the room, "Don't panic people, it's just the Civil Defence emergency beacon."

"A bit late don't you think, Charlie? Did they get some cheap foreign software that sends the alert fifteen hours late?" Sven asks.

"Hey, you gorgeous comedienne, about time you came down! Ah, your coffee was cold so I've ordered you another," Charlie replies.

"Yeah, right," Zac laughs, "A good save though mate, after you scoffed both drinks."

"Samantha?" A blonde asks from a far table.

Looking over towards the vision in leopard skin print Sven replies, "Carmen! Lloyd! It's so good to see you're both injury free after yesterday."

"Yes, well we left work a bit early for a... date," Carmen replies.

"One H – O – T, hot date at that," Lloyd adds.

As Carmen blushes a deep shade of red, Sven takes in her bright turquoise blue eye shadow and matching stockings. She has a matching blue top with a leopard skin jacket and matching leopard skin boots and handbag. She really does look quite the character. "Carmen, I just love your outfits, you wear them well."

"Thank you, Sven. So you stayed here last night as well?" asks Carmen.

"Yes, she did," interjects Freya, "and it looks like you're both here again tonight. We should have a little party, if you're up for it?"

As Charlie's phone rings, Sven asks Freya, "Did Charlie book us in?"

"Yes, it sounds like he's down here for the duration," Freya replies.

"What's up? Uh huh… oh, you are kidding me… you can't be serious! Okay, okay mate, settle down… alright… let me make a few calls… well if you could swing by and pick me up, I'll be ready in five… Roger that."

"Work calling, or have I got some competition?" Sven fires at Charlie.

"Well that bump to the head certainly hasn't slowed you down, now has it gorgeous?" Charlie laughs. "Sorry Sven, looks like Rex needs a hand with his investigation. Freya and Zac, there'll be quite a few of the lads coming by tonight for a drink if we pull this one off."

"Okay, we'll start planning," Zac replies.

"Ah, Charlie, can I have a quick word… in private?" Freya asks. "Come on Sven, Charlie, let's head outside."

"Come on, lover boy," Sven says, taking Charlie by the arm and leading him outside.

Once they're out of earshot of the other guests, Sven asks, "Charlie, what do we do about Flat White?"

"Neither of us have heard from her since yesterday," adds Freya, "Sven's checked and there's nothing happening on any of her social media accounts either. I guess we're asking if there's anything you can do 'officially' or 'unofficially'." She raises her eyebrows hopefully.

"Well, strictly speaking, we need to wait twenty-four hours before filling in a missing person's report," then seeing the concern on their faces he adds, "leave it with me and I'll see what I can find out, but give me a little more info…"

*****

As they head back inside after waving Charlie and Rex off, both Sven and Carmen's phones ping at the same time. Glancing at the message, Carmen says excitedly, "That's BS castle closed until further notice, working from home if you can log in! So we're on holiday, Lloyd!"

"Fantastic, Carmen! Come on, let's go for a walk and do a bit of sightseeing," Lloyd replies.

"Woo hoo!" Sven says to Freya. "That means I can help you guys out here."

"Yay! Come on out to the courtyard, let's have a proper breakfast with Micco and make some plans," Freya says excitedly. "The day is definitely looking up."

Chapter 23

The Case Gets a Break

Jackson Street is slowly returning to normal as shop owners and volunteers help to tidy up the mess. Most of the older buildings have survived the quake intact, while a few of the newer buildings are looking worse for wear. Hi-Viz-clad people abound, with contractors and council staff laying out cones and 'Restricted area' tape around the worst-hit buildings. Freya and Zac take in their neighbourhood as they walk to the bank to see Simon.

"Wow, we did get off lightly, when I see all this," Freya comments, pointing at a new apartment building that has slid into the side street, completely blocking the road.

"Yes, we sure did," agrees Zac. "I'm just amazed there were so few casualties. I guess the timing was perfect as most people had left their workplaces and most retailers were closing."

They find Simon outside the bank, putting a sign up on the cashpoint machine and apologising to a customer.

"Sorry ma'am, but the machine is empty and we don't anticipate it being refilled for a few days, but please come inside and see one of our tellers."

"Good morning Mr Brown," Freya calls out.

"Why, it's my favourite new businesswoman. Hello Freya and Zac, please come in." Simon leads them inside the bank to his office. "Now, to what do I owe the pleasure of this visit?"

Freya gestures to Zac to open his leather shoulder bag. "Well, I had to bring the muscle to carry the takings from last night. We were really surprised at the result."

"We thought we'd best drop off the week's takings from the accommodation, as it was getting a bit much to hold onsite," Zac informs him.

"Okay, so what are we talking here…" Simon starts, peering into the bag. "Oh my goodness!"

"Yes Simon, as I was saying, we were really surprised," Freya continues, while Zac counts out the money into piles. "The accommodation takings are up due to Zac being onsite last week meant our business plan was seriously underestimated."

"Who knew there was such a big market of 'crime voyeurs' wanting to watch a police crime scene investigation," Zac adds shaking his head.

"Well, that's a good job you brought that haul in today! We're a bit short of cash due to the sudden demand!" Simon exclaims. "And at this rate you won't have a mortgage for long."

"And then there's this lot from the restaurant last night," Freya says as she pulls out a plastic bag full of notes and coins and places it on Simon's desk.

"I didn't think the restaurant was opening until the end

of the week?" Simon says, shaking his head at all the cash.

"We had so many people come through the restaurant last night after the quake, and we just kept them calm, feeding them soup and helping them contact loved ones," Freya explains.

"All I did was put a box on the bar for donations," Zac continues. "I reckon we must have had close to two hundred people through the place over the course of the night."

"That is seriously impressive, you two," says Simon, smiling. "I will duly note this. It will be interesting to see how you go over the next month as December is a strange month – a lot of action for the retailers pre-Christmas, and then everyone off on holiday and the place is pretty much deserted. I mean Petone is hardly a holiday destination, is it? With its long golden sandy beaches, palm trees and Gin palaces lining up along the wharf."

Freya and Zac look at each other, then burst into laughter, never having heard Simon talk like this before. Usually he's so awfully serious and business-like.

"You crack me up. Where did our calm, well-tempered, brown-suited, strait-laced, conservative banker go?" Freya asks.

Simon smiles sweetly. "Well guys, it's like this: I have decided life is far too short to sit around stressing over 'compliance this' and 'best practice that', with all the robust twenty-first century systems that we know clearly don't work. All of which has been clearly demonstrated with those head office and developer shysters coupled with the murder at Portobello. This has left me really thinking about my career. I have put the best part of my life into this bank. As you know, I was a trainee here back in the day when your grandfather used to bank with us, and with all due respect that is going back further than I wish to care about."

"So what are your plans, Simon?" Freya asks.

"Well, it does involve Portobello, and after hearing how many people went through her yesterday, it has confirmed my thinking," Simon replies.

"Portobello? What do you mean?" Zac asks, bewildered.

"Let me explain. Freya, your determination and drive is contagious, I absolutely love all your ideas to turn Portobello into a community hub, and seeing the patronage and innovation has inspired me to try my own hand at a project I've had in the back of my mind."

"But where does Portobello come in to this, Simon?" Freya asks.

"I'm hoping to rent the ground floor office space – that is if it's still available?" Simon asks, adding, "At commercial rates, of course."

"Yes, you sure can, Simon, but what are you going to do with the office?"

"I want to start a business mentoring service. Do you know that most small businesses in New Zealand go bust in their first two years of operation? I want to change that by helping locals to make the right decisions, put them in contact with good quality lawyers, accountants, trades people. Team them up with people who have some experience to share, like you two, to inspire them to succeed. With my years of experience, I've seen the financial cost to people, their families and the local community when their good ideas fail, and I want to turn that around."

"Wow, now that's inspiring!" Zac replies, clearly impressed.

"Can you imagine what would happen to Petone, then Alicetown, Seaview, Moera, if local businesses thrive?" Simon continues passionately. "Instead of the money leaving the country when it's being spent in chain stores, most of which are owned by Australians, the money stays in the local community. You may not know this, but for every dollar spent locally, it is spent another three times."

"That sounds great! Are there any other benefits?" asks Freya, intrigued.

"This is called the 'local multiplier effect'. There are overseas studies proving the concept; they also show an increase in local employment with between three to five jobs created for every new business start-up," Simon says.

"Now that is exciting!" Zac replies.

"Simon, can you swing by this afternoon? I'd love to talk more about this with you and Zac," Freya says.

"Gladly," replies Simon. "Have some lease paperwork ready for me please. I'll just write up a receipt for this deposit, and I'll bring over the revised mortgage balance this afternoon."

"How about coming for a drink before dinner?" suggests Freya. "A few who stayed last night are staying for a second night. With most of the office buildings in town being red-stickered, the 'working from home' policy is now in full force and most people will be pretending to work from home for the next few days leading up to the Christmas rush. There could be a good crowd tonight. Now that will make your bank happy, won't it? I'll be able to continue as the very reliable mortgage holder with my regular payments."

"Frankly, my dear, I couldn't give a toss about what the bank thinks. It's not like the old days when we actually lived by their values and ethics. Today the new flashy branded mission statements and visions aren't worth the paper or the screen they're written on. In your grandfather's time there were real gentlemen handshakes and that was as good as their word and clearly more honourable than these dodgy contracts today. I mean look what Zac picked up on your contract. Anyhow, let's not go there."

"Well, not yet, although once we have a few drinks under our belt who knows where our conversation will take us?" Freya winks wickedly.

*****

"Thanks Thomas. Look, do you mind continuing to talk with Constable Patel here?" asks Rex. "He will get your first statement written up while Detective Sergeant Rogers and I take a quick break and get some more trusted personnel involved."

"I told you this was big, Mr Croft," Thomas smiles, then looking at Charlie, "You must have some pull, Mr Rogers, a whole station at your fingertips."

"Thanks," Charlie replies as they exit the interview room.

"Damn it, Rex, this is a game changer!" Charlie says to his friend.

"Don't I know it, mate," Rex replies as they head into the 'Situation room'. "Inspector Burns, thanks again for your support," he says to the lead officer.

"I'm taking a big punt on this information of yours, Croft," Inspector Burns replies. "Both you and Rogers must have big kahunas to take on the Police Commissioner. If this intel is legit, I'm just glad I could help take that crook down."

"Do you mean to say you know the Commissioner is a crook?" Rex asks, somewhat surprised.

"He's a slimy bastard. I went through Police College with him, same intake; even then we knew he was being fast-tracked by his MP father," Burns replies. "I've contacted Inspector Moore in Upper Hutt, he's rounding up a team of trusted officers to assist with this afternoon's operation and I've contacted the Honourable Justice Harris and he's fast-tracking the warrants. He wanted to know, just how high does this rot go?"

"We're still working on that, Sir," Charlie replies, "but it involves at least one minister, a High Court Judge, and one QC that we know of so far, as well as that property developer Donald Church."

"Oh, the political fallout on this is going to be huge," says Inspector Burns, shaking his head in disbelief. "I suggest we take out Church and his associates first. If we focus on them for now, it shouldn't tip off the others. Then we can collect more evidence before we move in on the rest, probably by Thursday as any longer and some loose lips could sink the wider operation."

"Will we need more resources, Sir?" Rex asks.

"We will have to manage with what I've scrounged so far – most officers are still helping with traffic control and keeping the streets safe from looters after the quake," he explains, pausing momentarily. "But on the upside, I don't believe anyone will suspect we can mount an operation this size so quickly – they're likely to have their guard down, assuming we're busy elsewhere."

*****

As Freya and Zac walk back up Jackson Street, Zac smiles and comments, "You made that guy's day, do you know that? I've never seen him so alive and animated. You really know how to make a man feel good."

"Thanks darling, but there is only one man I want to be feeling good, and that's you," Freya smiles back naughtily.

"You know, Fin, that talk of Simon's about golden sand beaches with palm trees has got me thinking about a holiday," Zac says.

"What do you mean?"

"Well, when did you have a holiday last, I mean a *real* holiday, not Outward Bound?"

Freya thinks long and hard. "Well, there was last weekend with the girls at Waitarere Beach, and then the trip to Waiheke Island when you were down here," Freya replies.

"Yes, I know, but I mean a *real* holiday. Seriously Fin, now you have Micco well entrenched in the place and a few of your contracts signed up, we could get away. I have a little money put aside," Zac confesses.

"Okay, so who would oversee it and live onsite? Look, I love Micco, but I don't think it's fair asking him while he's just about to run the restaurant and bar on top of his coffee caravan," reasons Freya.

"Well, my darling, I wasn't going to bring it up so soon, but I've been talking with Mum," Zac replies, a glint in his eye.

"Are you sure you don't mean *Zita* was talking with *you?* But carry on," Freya winks.

"Well, this morning Mum told me that she would be happy to come in and look after the place if we decided to ever have a break. She had a ball last night with those punters downstairs. Besides, it would give her a break from Dad. You know how he is, always working and now Mum is kind of experiencing that... what do you call it? 'Empty nest syndrome'. I know she would love to get her teeth back into something again and we're only just around the corner from home. She could still tend to her garden and have her yoga and coffees with her mates, and just do the check-ins and check-outs. And besides, she can bring Harry along, so she wouldn't suffer separation anxiety from having to be away from her precious dog."

"I think I'm being hijacked here, lover boy," Freya laughs. "Yes, Zita and her beloved dog, they're so funny. I think she loves Harry more than she loves your dad. Does he ever get a complex?"

"No, he's used to it. As you know, she's always had animals – she's mad on them, like you. So, the holiday, are you up for it?" Zac persists.

"Well, not now babe, we've only just opened for business," Freya says realistically.

"But you know it will be relatively quiet over New Year's when all of Wellington empties out, just as Simon was saying earlier," Zac replies, clearly not wanting to give up.

"Let me think about it. Never say never. Now darling, on a serious note, I'm really concerned about Flat White. I still haven't heard from her.

"Well, let's give Charlie a chance, you know with the networks being down so often, her messages could have got lost, but then..." Zac searches his mind, "... you know I thought I saw her yesterday walking down Jackson."

"Yeah, you said that last night. So when exactly was this?" Freya enquires.

"It can't have been her, Fin, as she didn't turn up. Besides, wasn't she meant to be at her new job yesterday?" Zac points out.

"Yes, she was," Freya replies excitedly. "Let's check if Sven is still up; I've got an idea."

Chapter 24

Summer House and Raids

Freya and Zac race back to Portobello. Not finding Sven in the restaurant, they head out the back to the courtyard.

"Guvnor, looks like you have another staff member to look after!" Micco calls out as he clears used coffee mugs and plates from the courtyard tables.

"Hey, you two, look what I've found under these weeds!" Sven says excitedly, popping up from the courtyard garden.

"What, Sven?" Freya asks curiously.

"Some baby raspberry plants – look! There must be about twenty of them!"

"Your friends have some hidden talents, Fin," Zac says, as they kneel down and inspect Sven's discovery.

"I've picked quite a few already, just these last couple of plants to go and we should have enough," Sven says proudly.

"Enough for what?" Freya asks.

"For my world-famous Raspberry Tart," Micco replies, smiling. "I thought that would be dessert for the guests and hosts tonight."

"Well, we are expecting a crowd of happy police officers," Zac comments. "Micco, do you think we have enough stock for the bar?"

"I think we're safe. After all, police officers drink-driving could be career limiting," Micco laughs. "Besides, the wholesalers aren't open today – I've checked, and they lost a bit of stock in the shake and are still in clean-up mode. But if they get desperate, I have a bit of homebrew raki."

They head back inside, taking the raspberries to the kitchen. "Hey Sven," says Freya, "you know how we haven't heard from Flat White? Well…"

*****

"Hey, thanks Hemi. I owe you one," Charlie says into his phone, before disconnecting and hopping into the passenger seat.

"Not another one of your cuzzies is it, Charlie?" Rex asks from the driver's seat.

"Yes, Hemi is my second cousin on my mothers' side," Charlie replies. "I just asked if he could check if Clara's passport was used recently."

"You know you can get in a power of shite if you two get caught using government information for personal use," Rex admonishes.

"That's ripe coming from the man who disarmed a bomb by himself," Charlie laughs.

"Touché, bro," Rex agrees, laughing.

Then a crackle comes over the police radio in the car, followed by the deep baritone of Inspector Burns. "Right, ensure you all have the warrants. If you don't, let me know… okay, no reply means we are good to go. I want all cars in position within ten minutes, no sirens, and wait for my word before exiting. Operation Cathedral is on!"

*****

"Are you ready for your surprise, sugar plum?" Zac asks, taking Freya's hand. "Come on."

"Okay doofus, where are we going?" Freya asks.

He takes her down the garden path to her little rustic shed. The sun is shining brightly, giving the shed an almost mystical glow. He unlocks the door and motions Freya to enter.

"Oh wow, Zac, what have you done?" Freya asks, completely overwhelmed.

As she steps inside, she ooh's and aah's at the transformation of her little cabin. Zac has cleverly left the original features of Wolfe's design, but added a splash of paint here and there and some extra bookshelves for Freya's masses of books.

The loft upstairs has been transformed and she climbs up the now sturdier ladder to the top and sees the double bed. "Is this safe?"

"Of course it's safe; I'm not an engineer for nothing. Go on, knock yourself out. Well, not physically, we don't want you and Sven having matching bumps on the head, but jump on, try it out," Zac invites.

Freya throws herself from the ladder onto the mattress.

Finding it extra spongy, she lies down, sprawled out like a starfish. "This is heaven, so comfortable, I can't move. Where did you score this mattress from?"

"Well, the guy who dropped the beds off came in with two mattresses but no bases. He was sure it was part of our order, so I didn't want to argue with him, or he was threatening to take the whole order back, and we needed the beds for our guests. Besides, I could see where they could be used – here and in the turret," Zac replies.

"Oh my god, where was it last night when I really needed it?" remarks Freya.

"Sorry babe, it was out here. I gave you the option, but you fell asleep and I didn't want to wake you," Zac replies.

"No worries. Zac, this is absolutely adorable ⌐ and look," she gasps in delight, "you've even hung some of my paintings in here."

She looks at her little red summer house picture and the other with a lighthouse, admiringly.

"I love the colours as well – so bright, you've lifted and transported this little honey into the twenty-first century. You are a genius." Freya praises.

Zac, by this time, has climbed Rapunzel's stairs. "Can I join you?"

"Of course you can," Freya replies happily.

"I know there's not much head room," Zac says, joining her on the mattress. "You're right," he says in surprise, "this *is* super comfortable. I think I could sleep here all night."

"Zac, do you think Sven and Charlie would want to sleep here?" Freya asks.

"Well they could, but I was kind of hoping we could christen it and be the first to spend the night here," Zac hints.

Freya nudges him. "Don't be naughty. Remember, this is a secret club house, not a knocking shop."

"Who's talking about a knocking shop out here? That's what you've got going on inside. Look, if you help me, we can drag the spare mattress inside and put that in the turret; that can be for special guests. Or do you want to christen the turret as well?" he says playfully.

"Now I don't need to be that greedy; this will be fine," Freya replies, feeling safe and comfortable in his arms, she snuggles into his embrace and they both fall asleep.

*****

Inspector Burns confirms over the police radio, "Okay, that's everyone one in position… Operation Cathedral is GO, GO, GO…"

Charlie and Rex spring from the car. "Don't you just love it when the boss says that!" remarks Rex.

"Every single time, bro," Charlie replies, flashing his police badge at the approaching security guard as they enter the office building in Wakefield Street. "Back off mate, you don't get paid enough to tangle with us."

"Stop immediately or you will be arrested as an accessory," Rex commands the receptionist as she reaches for her phone. "I take it Mr Church is through there?"

The receptionist nods, looking nervously at the closed office door.

"Okay buddy, let's do this," says Charlie as he reaches for the door handle.

Rex pulls the search warrant from his suit jacket pocket, and nods at Charlie as they enter the office.

"Mr Donald Church?" Charlie asks as he approaches his startled quarry seated at his desk.

"Yes… w-what is the meaning of this?" Mr Church splutters.

"Donald Church, stand up please and put your hands behind your back," Charlie orders. "You are under arrest for suspicion of murder."

"Take your filthy brown hands off me, I'll not be spoken to by a hori like this," Mr Church replies pompously. He tries to push Charlie away as he wraps a handcuff around his wrist.

"Let's add resisting arrest to the charge sheet, shall we?" Rex says as he twists Mr Church around forcibly so that Charlie can secure the other handcuff.

"Anything you say, can and will be held against you in a court of law," Charlie continues professionally, as he bundles Mr Church out of his office towards the building entrance. "Rex, can you go ahead and open the rear car door?"

"Sure Charlie," Rex answers quizzically, as he opens the door.

"… and do you want to put the siren on now?"

"It will be my pleasure, Charlie." Rex smiles as he flicks the switch, attracting people from the neighbouring offices who crowd around to see Mr Church's fall from grace while he is slowly led to the police car.

"You can't do this to me," Mr Church pleads, "my reputation…"

"One down, two to go," Charlie comments to his partner. "Let's hope the other teams are as successful," he remarks, walking extra slowly to the car just to savour Mr Church's public humiliation a little longer.

*****

Freya opens the door to the 'Jardinière' room, overlooking the garden.

"This is cosy, isn't it? You can hardly swing a cat around in here. Reminds me of that tiny little apartment we ended up sharing in Stockholm that time. Remember our first one? It was like eighty square metres and a real bedsit, we had turns sleeping on the couch and then for something different, a sofa bed. Woohoo, real style," Sven reminisces with Freya.

"Well, you're welcome to stay the night in here; the rest of the place is booked but I want to show you the turret," Freya says excitedly. "A real sizzling suntrap, so cosy and warm, great stargazing, a glimpse of the harbour, and…" she swings open the little door and they walk on in.

There in the corner tucked away is the newly-laid mattress with duvet and comfy cushions. "And here awaits an alternative little love nest for you and Charlie."

They both laugh.

"Oh my god, a ship's cabin would be about the same size," exclaims Sven.

"Yes and like in a US Bachelor show – should you decide to forego your separate rooms – you and Charlie can have the key to the 'honeymoon suite'," Freya laughs.

"Ha ha, we only met up again yesterday," Sven reminds her.

"I know, spill – what is the status with you two? I just wish Ms Clara James was here, she would so like to be in on this goss as well!" replies Freya.

"You could write a book about this – two murders, an earthquake, a missing Flat White. Well what's next?"

remarks Sven.

The girls head down to the restaurant and order themselves coffee and cake from Micco. They settle down at one of the tables, so deep in conversation that they fail to notice Carmen and Lloyd walk into the entrance and then head upstairs to their room.

Chapter 25

Portobello Party Revelation

"This is highly irregular, Your Honour," Prendergast protests.

"Can he do that while I'm on some other trumped-up charges?" argues Donald Church, standing up.

"Your objection is overruled, Prendergast," Judge Martin Jacobson says as he bangs his gavel on the sound block. "I'll have order in my courtroom thank you very much, Mr Church. Now SIT DOWN, or would you like 'contempt of court' added to your long list of pending charges?"

The four defendants settle down and sit facing the judge, the look on their faces in various states of gloom.

"Your Honour, as you can see from the documents in exhibit 17," explains Mr Tombe, "there is clear evidence of an attempt to defraud my client, Ms Freya Nilson, of her rightful inheritance, the said building named 'Portobello'. That evidence, along with verified statements in exhibit

24 and 26, point to the two officers from the bank, QC Prendergast and Donald Church being the perpetrators of the conspiracy."

The Judge nods before speaking. "After reviewing the mounting evidence, I agree with your assessment, Mr Tombe. This is a despicable act on all your behalves, which the citizens of our country need to be protected against. While the normal sentence for this crime varies, I believe that the maximum sentence is appropriate in this case."

Nodding to the police officers standing behind the defendants, the court registrar stands. "Will the defendants, Donald Church, Malcolm Prendergast, Kevin Howard and John Rudd stand, to receive their sentence," he announces.

"As the Queen's representative for justice, I sentence each of you to serve seven years for conspiracy to commit fraud; this term will stand as a minimum and will be added consecutively to any further sentences that you may be facing. Officers, take them down. Court is dismissed," Judge Jacobson commands.

*****

Simon and Zac sit around one of the restaurant tables with the lease paperwork, waiting for Freya to finish her phone conversation.

"Yes… Oh that's fantastic news! Thank you, Mr Tombe. Look, call in if you can, we'll be having a few drinks here tonight… Oh okay, bye." Freya disconnects and turns to the table excitedly. "We won! We won!"

"Come on then Freya, let us know the details," smiles Simon.

"Well, long story short, all four of them got seven years

for fraud – Portobello is definitely all mine!" she replies triumphantly.

"Congratulations Freya!" Simon and Zac chorus.

"I feel a party coming on tonight!" says Freya, unable to contain her excitement.

"Well, back to business – what do you reckon, Simon," Zac asks, "shall we all sign and then celebrate with a drink?"

"Absolutely!" Simon replies, picking up his pen and signing the paperwork. "I'm so looking forward to getting started; it'll keep me busy in the afternoons."

"What, is there not enough work for you at the bank?" asks Freya.

"Another cost-cutting measure from head office and their Australian owners came through this morning," Simon explains. "As we've had a run on cash at the bank after the shake, we've been directed to close the doors at midday."

"But won't that stop people from being able to get cash to buy food? I mean most places are still without power and the eftpos system can't work," Zac asks.

"You can see why people get cynical about these overseas owned banks, can't you?" Simon comments. "That's why I want to help our local businesses and community, as there is only so much I can do in the bank."

Freya stands up and shakes Simon's hand. "Welcome aboard Simon. Zac, can you show Simon around and I'll go tell Sven the good news."

"And I'll get the bubbles open for you shortly," Zac winks, as Freya runs upstairs to find her friend.

"Now Zac," says Simon enthusiastically, "I've got this idea about a local currency…"

*****

"So, this is the place Carmen was raving about. Very bohemian, darling," a dapper young man comments as he enters the restaurant, scanning the room.

"Nigel! Ernest! Over here," Carmen calls out, waving at her friends.

"Sweetie!" Ernest cries, as he rushes over to give Carmen air kisses on each cheek.

"Lloyd, darling!" Ernest exclaims. "I hear that you literally swept our Carmen off her feet!"

Lloyd blushes slightly as Nigel explains to Ernest before turning to Lloyd, "It was such a stylish move, I didn't know you could dance, let alone tango!"

"Bravo! Bravo!" Ernest cries.

"Now we want all the details, but let us order some drinks first to celebrate," says Nigel.

As they order fancy cocktails from Micco, three police cars pull up with their sirens blaring. A multitude of police officers pile out of the cars onto the pavement, laughing and joking amongst themselves as the sirens are turned off and the cars pull back out into the traffic.

Freya, Sven and Zac rush downstairs to see what's happening, and meet a grinning Charlie and Rex as they open the front door, leading their workmates inside.

"Oh, you nearly had me worried there, Charlie," Freya laughs.

"Ha ha, a little irregular, but worth it to see your faces," Charlie replies, as he pulls Sven into a hug. "Hey Sven, how's the head this afternoon?"

"Much better now, *Big Boy*," Sven responds in a husky voice as she returns the hug.

Rex ushers the police officers through. "The bar is over there, boys," he says, before turning to Freya and Zac. "We're in the mood for a couple of quiets after today's success."

"I'd best give Micco a hand then," Zac replies, rushing over to help.

"So, did you catch your man, Charlie?" Sven asks.

"No, we caught Rex's man today," Charlie quickly replies, "but it looks like we've kicked the top off a wasp nest."

"Yes, my informant knows where the bodies are buried, so to speak," Rex says enthusiastically, "but heck, who knows what he'll let slip tomorrow."

"This operation is going to be huge," Charlie agrees.

"Well, you boys are talking very secretively," remarks Freya. "Grab a drink and come upstairs to the rooftop; we've just opened the bubbly as we're celebrating too."

*****

Portobello is in full swing, with a crowd enjoying the last of the sun in the courtyard, the restaurant half-full of patrons and the bar crowded with off-duty police celebrating the successful arrests in their case.

A separate roof party is well underway where a tipsy Lloyd is teaching some of the in-house guests and locals a few salsa moves. One lass from the roof is waving madly out to Micco in the courtyard below; clearly she has taken a liking to him and is trying hard to impress him with her cool moves across the roof, balancing in stilettos.

Many of the casual off-the-street patrons are enjoying the music, the punch, and the fresh air in the garden, making the most of a balmy Wellington evening.

Sven is having a good old laugh with Ernest and Nigel, finding them both a scream out of work.

Ernest has clearly had one too many cocktails and is starting to let slip a few home truths about working with government ministers, lawyers, judges and the lobbyists he usually rubs shoulders with.

"Scum, those bloody lobbyists are," Ernest mixes his words.

"Ernest, are you doing a Yoda impression?" Sven is highly amused and wickedly continues to encourage him to open up. "You are such a scream, but give us an example – what's a lobbyist?"

"My dear Sven, a lobbyist is the lowest form of life as we know it on this planet, if not the universe," replies Ernest, getting into his stride.

"Okay, but what do they do in Wellington?" Sven asks.

"They wine, dine, entice and entrap our politicians and senior government officials, to bend them to their will," Nigel explains. "Take the electricity industry as a classic example – the politicians get elected to promote environmentally friendly forms of producing electricity, right?" Freya and Sven nod their heads. "Okay," he says when he sees he has their full attention, "they say that they will subsidise solar panels for low income families, a supposed win-win proposition." He takes another sip from his cocktail – "Ah that's good," ¬ before continuing. "Then the lobbyist for the electricity company comes along and convinces the politicians that by subsidising the solar panels, the electricity companies won't make as much money and therefore they won't pay as much tax."

"But how do they convince the politicians? Aren't

they people elected to represent the people who voted for them?" Freya asks.

"Yes, they are Freya, but if a politician starts polling poorly, the lobbyist will prop them up with political donations and pay the media to start giving the politician 'good' coverage," Ernest explains.

"Don't we have laws to prevent that from happening?" Sven asks.

"Yes, we do, but if the Police Commissioner is on their payroll as well, and directs the police to do a 'road safety' blitz, then who will investigate the allegations?" Ernest replies.

"Ernest, I think you need to have a chat with my detective boyfriend, Charlie Rogers," Sven says, leading him by his arm. "Come and let me introduce you."

*****

"Sugar plum, these margaritas and cosmopolitans are going down a treat. Can you go and grab another dozen lemons for me?" Zac asks Freya.

"Sure thing, babe. How's the tequila holding out?"

"Yeah, best check if Micco has a spare bottle," Zac replies.

"Roger that, babe!" Freya replies as she leaves the temporary rooftop bar that Zac has set up.

Sven meets her on the stairs. "Hey Freya, how's the hostess with the most-ess?"

"I'm so rapt with the turnout, but where's Charlie? I thought you two would be inseparable."

"Hey, give a single girl a chance to get used to having a boyfriend! I've just had an interesting chat with Ernest and introduced him to Charlie as he may have some information to help the investigation," Sven replies. "I'm sure there is more to Cat's death than we discovered yesterday. OMG, was that only yesterday!"

"Geez, it sure was. We were coming back on the Kiwi Connection from that groovy weekend at the bach after charity shopping for more goodies," Freya remembers.

"And after all those talks with Flat White about her fucked family and love life," Sven recalls, "that seems like another lifetime ago."

"Did Charlie come up with any news from her?" Freya asks.

"Nothing yet. He tells me that he's put some feelers out that he's still waiting to hear back from," Sven replies. "Hey girl, we should grab a drink and sit down for a bit."

"Sounds like a plan. I'll just get some supplies for that drink," says Freya. "I didn't know Zac could mix cocktails."

"Another hidden talent – you struck the jackpot there big-time girl!" Sven replies. "Okay, see you soon."

*****

Paulo and Isaia are creating a vibrant atmosphere from the front corner of the rooftop, and everyone seems to be getting in the party mood.

"When they asked if they could DJ for us, I said only if you play for a wider audience," Zac tells Sven as he mixes her a cosmopolitan.

"Well, are you going to introduce me, Zac?" demands Sven.

"Faafatai Zac, this crowd is goin' off, brother!" shouts

Paulo.

"Paulo, this is Sven, one of Freya's best mates – Sven, this is Paulo, one of my gym buddies," Zac introduces, opening two bottles of Vailima. "And here comes Isaia, his brother from another mother."

"Seki a, sweet as bro! You da man!" beams Isaia. "Brother, this place is swayin'."

"It takes a master's touch to get this diverse crowd groovin', guys," Zac replies, "and that's down to you two soul brothers' talent at reading the party."

"Shaddap man, Paulo's head will get bigger than it already is," jokes Isaia.

"Hey, I know he appreciates us, with this," Paulo replies, raising his bottle in a salute. "Hey Isaia," he frowns, "that's doesn't sound like the extended play version. I better get back – nice to meet you Sven, come and make a request or two."

"Look out lady, he's gonna hit on you," warns Isaia.

"You two crack me up," Zac laughs, as the Samoans head back to their decks.

Nigel is bantering away with Carmen and Lloyd as they approach the bar to order another round of margaritas.

Sven sidles up next to Lloyd. "And how is the Latin dance instructor this evening? You have certainly got the party started," Sven gestures to the dancing rooftop crowd. "I hear you and Carmen were one of the first customers to stay last night. How did that go?"

"Great, it was our first night away," replies Lloyd. "We hadn't planned it; we were just in the area when the earthquake hit. It's a small world – I believe your friend runs it?"

"Yes, Freya and Zac have worked really hard to get

this up and running. How is Carmen? It's good to see her so happy – you two make a cute couple. You were lucky not being in BS Castle last night when the earthquake hit."

"Well, we made an early exit after her police interview into Cathryn Tennyson's murder yesterday," Lloyd replies. "You know it's only a matter of time before Carmen resigns. She is far too good to be working there. They don't seem to value what she does and what she can offer. I'm trying to persuade her to leave but she thinks it will all change, especially now that someone has done away with the HR Director. And not soon enough, if you ask me."

"That's a hell of a bold statement, Lloyd. Did you know Cat?" Sven asks.

"Yes, I know women like Cat, I have seen many Cats in my life. Fortunately I've never ventured to the dizzying heights of HR and the seventh floor, so I've never had to suffer bullying from her, but I've seen and heard enough. She had what was coming to her. Or do you believe that crap that she died from natural causes?" asks Lloyd.

"Well I thought it was possible, but I wouldn't want to say anything until I knew a bit more," Sven replies.

"You can't tell me that the Cat of nine lives died of natural causes. She had the whole building wanting to terminate her, especially with what she had planned for the likes of my Carmen, and Nigel's recruiting team. In fact it was no secret that most teams in the BS were to have staff cuts just before Christmas. Aren't you involved with the young detective investigating Cat's murder?"

"We're old friends who have just reconnected, Lloyd," Sven answers. "But if it was murder, what have they missed?"

"Maybe I've been watching too much *CSI*, but didn't

the autopsy come through yesterday?" Lloyd asks.

"Lloyd, like I said, I can't say too much. But if she was murdered, who do you think would be most likely to want her dead? Who had the most to gain?" Sven presses.

"Spoken like a true detective. Well that's a hard one, it could be one of many: Bernard the CEO, I reckoned he fancied her, then there was Stephanie, the second-in-command in HR who was meant to get the job but then Bernard employed Cat at the last minute. Then there was that creep of a guy who is now heading up the Science, or should I say SHIT unit, Alex – he's been a bit too close and personal with her. Oh god, I don't know, it's making my head hurt just thinking about it. But you know in my job I get around the floors a lot. I may not be noticed a lot, but I observe and hear titbits as I do the rounds," Lloyd hints.

"Now, now, Lloyd, you're being a tease," Sven laughs. "Okay, let me see… apart from your rounds on the various floors, aren't you downstairs in the basement, near the tunnels between Parliament and BS? You must see a lot of the characters coming and going between the buildings."

"Like you wouldn't believe, Sven, you see all sorts of liaisons and rendezvous down there. Did you know my office has a one-way glass window which looks out into the tunnel?" Lloyd takes a sip of his cocktail.

"Why would you have a one-way window from your office into the tunnel?" Sven asks.

"Some 'best practice' initiative by the last HR manager before Cat," explains Lloyd. "They reviewed the natural lighting for all offices in the BS Ministry and decided that all offices had to have at least one window. I had some noddy put a window in, so we get the so-called 'natural light' from the tunnel. The funny thing is we can see out but the foot traffic walking through can't see us. I see all sorts; in fact, I could write a book about it."

"Well that's exciting, but that may be career limiting if you were to write a book about all the secret liaisons you've witnessed down there," Sven comments. "Secret affairs down in the basement? I thought that was reserved for the stationery cupboard upstairs, for the security and receptionist young folk?"

"No, I don't mean them – they're small fry. I mean people much higher up the chain getting up to all sorts. I wish I had a camera installed in the tunnel so I could record all the goings-on," Lloyd says.

"Excuse me a minute," says Sven as she orders a couple of cosmopolitans from Zac and processes what she has just heard. "Could camera footage down there shed some light on Cat's demise?"

"Absolutely, but there aren't any cameras, are there?" Lloyd replies. "Oh, the things I've seen."

Sven wonders if Lewis, the BS Head of Security, had a camera installed to cut down staff numbers needed on his security team. "Great talking to you Lloyd, we should catch up after I've had a drink with Freya."

*****

"Finally found you!" Sven says, meeting Freya at the bottom of the stairs. "Here's your drink. Now where shall we talk?"

"The restaurant has emptied out; most people are either in the courtyard or on the rooftop dancing to the music," Freya answers, motioning towards a far table. "Let's sit over here away from the noise. How are you feeling,

Sven?" she asks as they sit down.

"A little tired, but my mind is doing overtime after the last couple of conversations," Sven replies. "I think I may have a new angle on Cat's death."

"Are you still doing my job, Sven?" Charlie asks, coming up behind them to take a seat at their table.

"Hey Charlie!" Freya greets him. "How is the police party going?"

"They're starting to wind up, as we have a bit more on tomorrow," Charlie replies. "Rex is ordering the taxis now."

"Babe, did you check the BS security camera footage yesterday?" Sven asks.

"No doll, we didn't have time as the Commissioner was pushing us hard for a result," Charlie answers, "but I did check the camera room briefly with… what's his name… Lewis."

"Did you notice if they had a camera in the basement tunnel?" asks Sven.

"Come to think of it, they did. Why do you ask?" Charlie enquires.

"Well, Lloyd, our Latin dance instructor and BS mail man has a one-way window from his mail room into the tunnel and reckons he's seen all sorts of goings-on," replies Sven, "and he is hinting that Cat was murdered."

"Wasn't that reported as an overdose on the news?" Freya asks.

"Yes, it was, but I've had my doubts," Charlie replies, taking his phone out of his suit jacket pocket. "Damn, I guess I'd better get that footage before it gets wiped. Sometimes this police work lark just takes over your life. Excuse me, girls."

Charlie walks away from the table, referring to his notebook for a mobile number, tapping out a text message: 'Lewis, we need to see the camera footage at the BS first thing tomorrow, make sure nothing is deleted until we get there'. Then thinking again, sends another: 'Marama cuz, do us a favour, can you send me the tox-screen results from yesterday'.

Chapter 26

Case Closed and Swedish Synchronicity

"Wasn't that just the best party?" Carmen enthuses over breakfast in the restaurant, where everyone has gathered. "I've still got that remake of 'Strawberry Letter 23' going through my mind."

"I bet you're proud of your 'Lloyd the Latin Lover' getting everyone up on the dance floor last night," teases Freya, causing Carmen to blush a little as she nods.

"That's the secret to a good party," Sven comments.

"Oh? What's the secret, Sven?" asks Zac.

"Someone who is courageous enough to instigate the dancing, and to encourage everyone to give it a go," Sven answers, "because once you're on the dance floor, it's so much easier to stay up grooving and having fun."

"So, you saw through my cunning plan. Once you get a couple up, it's much easier to convince others to join them,"

Lloyd laughs, adding admiringly, "but the real secret is the music – just who were those DJs? They sure know how to read a crowd."

"A couple of my gym buddies, Isaia and Paulo," replies Zac. "They were looking for somewhere to try out their new dance mixes they've been working on."

"Could you ask them who the artist was that covered 'Strawberry Letter 23'?" asks Carmen.

"Sure, I'll text Paulo now," replies Zac, pulling his phone out of his pocket.

"I'm sure it's Tevin someone… damn, I can't remember the surname," laments Charlie. Just then his phone beeps. "Excuse me, I've just got to check this… ah… Rex, check out these results."

Rex leans over Charlie's phone. "Damn, those opiate levels don't look right to me, they're off the charts!"

"You're right, that's not prescription," Charlie comments. He looks apologetically at Sven. "Sorry babe, looks like I'm going back to the BS Ministry, Cat's investigation is about to be reopened."

"Man, I believe today will be busier than yesterday," sighs Rex. He gets out of his chair and puts his suit jacket on before taking his last mouthful of coffee. "Compliments to Micco once again, Freya. Can we have our rooms again tonight?"

"Sure, we aren't booked out yet," Freya replies.

"I knew it wasn't accidental," Lloyd remarks. "In fact, I think I might know who is involved."

Everyone turns to look at Lloyd.

"What do you mean?" asks Carmen.

"Did you see something?" demands Sven.

"Well, out with it man," Charlie says. "If you know

something we can use to find the killer, we need it quickly before they can dispose of the evidence.”

Embarrassed, Lloyd hangs his head. “I should have said something earlier, but I didn’t know it would be hushed up. Okay, have a look at Bernard’s wife, Margaret.”

“What!” Sven and Freya say in unison.

“I’ve seen both Margaret and Cat in the tunnel, very chummy to start with a few weeks back, but last week it got nasty,” Lloyd spills. “They both had a stand-up argument, Margaret slapped Cat across the face and then I saw Cat run back to the BS.”

“Thanks Lloyd,” Charlie says. “Write down your mobile number for me and give it to Rex, and perhaps stay close to Portobello, as I’ll need an official statement at some stage today. Excuse me, I need to make a call…” He turns away as he answers his phone. “Marama, Charlie here, cuz. Look, do us a favour and check the body for puncture marks. Cheers cuz…” He rings off and turns to Rex. “Got that number, Rex? Come on, let’s go.”

The table is quiet, everyone reflecting, as the police detectives leave the building. Freya is the first one to break the silence. “Never a dull moment at the Portobello!”

*****

“Thanks for showing us around, Freya,” the curly-haired woman says. “You have such an amazing place.”

“I’m sure Bronnie and I can speak on behalf of the others in the coven, we will be back,” the long-haired woman says enthusiastically.

“You will all be most welcome,” Freya replies, “and if the turret and rooftop are booked, you can always use the courtyard and garden."

"I think the courtyard garden option may be best, I was out here the night of the shake with Tommy, while we waited for Gary. What do you think, Toni?" Bronnie asks her colleague.

"I agree, closer to Papatūānuku, or Mother Earth, Bronnie, but let's check with the coven," Toni replies. "Can we pencil-book the next full moon, Freya?"

"Absolutely, Toni. I'll mark the diary now," Freya smiles, shaking each of their hands. "Thanks for coming and we look forward to seeing the whole grou... coven soon."

As Toni and Bronnie leave Portobello, Zac approaches Freya with the booking diary. "Did I hear that right, Fin? A witches' coven booked for the next full moon?"

"Yes you did, Zac," Freya answers. "Bronnie was here the night of the shake with her son Tommy and came back today with her priestess to check the place out for their monthly gatherings – 'Sabbats' I think they're called."

"I thought I recognised her, they didn't look like witches," says Zac conservatively.

"How exactly do you expect witches to look, doofus? Black pointy hats with black cats on their shoulders whizzing through the sky on broomsticks?" Freya teases.

"Well that's the way they're portrayed," Zac says defensively.

"Hmm, my dear, witches are everyday folk like you and me. How do you know that Sven and I aren't witches and belong to our own coven?" asks Freya.

"Ha ha, good one Fin," Zac laughs.

Sven sneaks up behind Zac and suddenly pokes him in each kidney, giving him a huge fright.

"Are you a disbeliever of my sister's religion?" Sven mocks. "Shall I put a hex on him, Freya?"

"What do you think us girls get up to on our 'girlie weekends', Zac?" Freya asks with a straight face.

"W-w-what?" Zac stammers disbelievingly.

The girls burst into laughter. "Oh, we got you there, doofus!" Freya laughs.

*****

"Well would you look at that, Lloyd wasn't kidding," Rex says, bent over the video screen. "Lewis, can you wind that one back and get a copy of that sequence on the external hard drive? Thanks."

Charlie has already dialled his phone. "Inspector Burns… yes, we have the video tape being downloaded as I speak… as we suspected, it's very damning… yes, we will need search warrants for the office, house and their bach in Peka Peka… Rex is texting the addresses through right now… thank you Sir."

As Charlie disconnects the call, Rex whistles, "Wow, this is going to be huge. Bloody Thomas was right."

"I know bro," Charlie agrees. "We just need to find the connection between the Commissioner and Mrs Johnson."

"Hopefully the search warrants will turn something up," Rex replies, "but I'll contact Patel about the interviews, he's got an amazing memory, that will save us a bit of time reading the interview transcripts."

"Lewis, do you know if Chris from IT is at work today?" Charlie asks.

"Yes, he is. The IT team are working hard to get the servers sorted so the rest of the staff can work from home until the building gets the all-clear," Lewis replies. "Only essential staff are allowed onsite at the moment. I can phone him if you like."

"Yes thanks, I've got a little job for him," Charlie replies with a twinkle in his eye.

*****

"Sven! Sven! Where are you?" Freya calls urgently as she rushes to her friend's room.

"Up here on the roof, Freya," Sven answers from the stairs. "What's the panic?"

"It's Flat White! I've got an email from her!" Freya bursts out.

"Is she okay? Where is she? Oh Freya!" Sven bursts into tears as she rushes down to Freya on the landing.

Freya hugs her friend. "It's alright Sven, she's okay. Here, let's sit in your room and I'll read her email out to you."

Wiping her eyes, Sven apologises. "Wow, sorry Freya, I don't know where that came from."

"Who's not being real now, girl?" Freya replies. "We've both been really worried and we've just parked our feelings until we heard some news. Some personal coach-cum-counsellor I know taught me that. Now wipe your eyes and listen up…"

Dear F and S,

You will never guess what I ended up doing. I walked out of my new job and was gone by 10am after that middle manager bitch tried bullying me. I was on the train to Petone and had seen Leo for a reading. Before I knew it

I was heading to the airport and on a plane to Auckland. You know I always carry my trusty passport, and I treated myself to a new suitcase and clothes at the airport. I just got the basics, nothing flash, and I am now sitting in my hotel room in Kathmandu, my first night. I met this amazing steward on the plane – charming, good looking, but GAY. Isn't that always the way? Anyhow, he upgraded me from Premium Economy to First Class. Long story short. I have many questions and I'm not even sure you'll get this.

1.   What's the story with the earthquake? Are you guys okay? Are you alive? If so, where are you and who are you with?

2.   The Kiwi Con – I saw her parked up at the railway station on Monday morning then on the news last night, or whatever day it was (I'm confused with the time difference). I heard there was a murder. Cathryn Tennyson? Is this true? Who murdered her?

3.   I've met up with Jack. It hasn't gone at all well. As the saying goes, 'I'm in Kathmandu, what to do?' He's building and doing repairs and maintenance over in the mountains near Pokhara. Remember that place, Sven? Didn't it rock? Anyhow, he doesn't want me.

4.   Please write, I am lonely, I am homesick, and I think I have made a complete fool of myself. I've just revealed to him I want children but can't, and I have PTSD, and I did it all without alcohol! Not a single drop! I nearly drank the plane dry, but not the hotel's mini bar.

OK babes, I am soo jetlagged, so I am crashing. Please please write or text ASAP. I MISS YOU GUYS. Love your high maintenance homesick trinity gal on the other side of the world, xoxo

"Wow, 'Kathmandu what to do' no less," Sven marvels. "Those texts kinda make a bit of sense now – she must have heard about the earthquake before she boarded her flight."

"Yes, unbelievable," Freya comments. "She can't be roughing it; that just wouldn't be her style. But in the middle of the winter? Oh my god, what a time to be over there in the mountains, but I know it will be beautiful. She finally saw the light and followed old lover boy Jack over there."

"Yes, I reckon that last big deep and meaningful we had at Waitarere Beach, and at Waiheke really paid off. She has finally followed her heart," Sven replies wistfully.

The girls sit down and write one back.

Dear Flat White, you dark horse!

The Himalayas, how exotic! What about our New Year's Eve plans? We were going to have them over here. How can we do that now with you gone? You deserter, you piker...

No, just joking, this is fabulous news that you have followed your heart. We are both writing this.

We are all okay over here, Sven took a bump to her head in the quake, but Charlie got her help and she is recovering here. Yes, Charlie is back on the scene! Wellington is starting to calm down a little since the big shake up. Everyone we know is okay – well, relatively okay. I think some people are quite traumatised by it all. You were so lucky to miss this one. A little bit of damage here, nothing serious. Everyone is either working from home or just taking their holidays earlier. A lot of people have got as far away from Wellington as possible and headed up north to warmer climes and less shaky ground.

Yes, it was Cat who was found dead on the Kiwi Con on Monday morning, a suspected overdose, but now not so sure. Charlie has reopened Cat's investigation, hence why Charlie is back on the scene...

Sven and Charlie after all these years apart are finally working things out and it looks pretty solid from my perspective. (Freya commenting) and Sven agrees, Pokhara rocks – see if you can find that little bar we danced in.

And Freya finally kissed Zac, it's great to see young love (Sven commenting).

Anyhow, what are you doing for New Year's Eve? Let us know! Wish we could be with you. Remember that New Year's Eve we had once up in Sweden, out in the archipelago – wasn't it great? Zooming around in the snow on those cute little sleighs.

OK, well we are signing off now. Charlie and Sven are staying here at Portobello with Zac and me, and business has taken off big-time since the quake, but it will quieten once everyone goes away as planned on holiday. You know how Wellington and the CBD dies over Christmas and New Year's with all the public servants away.

Now kia kaha girl, stay strong and be straight with Jack, you know honesty is the only way to his heart.

Take care and keep us posted on where you are going for Christmas and New Year's and we will have some bubbles and a Wellington Pilsner for you down here.

Take care, Love F and S xxx

"Wow, who would have thought when we were sitting there at Waitarere Beach only a few days ago we would have got our men," Sven remarks.

"I know, right?" agrees Freya. "Let's keep our fingers crossed for Clara and Jack."

*****

"Well here you go, Sergeant Rogers," Bernard says as he opens the front door to the bach. "I knew there was something going on, but I honestly didn't know what."

"Thank you, Sir," Charlie says. "Look, don't be so hard on yourself, often it's the spouse who's the last to know."

"But with Cathryn?" Bernard shakes his head. "I had her in my office consoling her over some drama… I suppose it's just desserts, as I cheated on Margaret in Sweden."

"Okay, officers, you know the drill." Charlie directs his staff inside to conduct the search, and then offers to drop Bernard's keys back to his office.

"Thank you, Sergeant Rogers, I'd appreciate that. I've commandeered the office next to Security on the ground floor," Bernard replies. As he walks back to his car in a daze, his phone rings. Charlie looks back to see Bernard take the call, and hears him say, "Bernard speaking… yes Dimitri…"

Charlie says under his breath, 'He mahi kai takata, he mahi kai hōaka.'

"What's that, bro?" asks Rex.

"It's an old Ngāi Tahu whakataukī. Translated it means, 'It is work that consumes people, as greenstone consumes sandstone'," Charlie explains.

"That's a good one mate, very fitting. Now shall we get on with this?"

"FIND!" a voice calls from inside. The two friends race towards the calling officer. "FIND!"

"Where..." Charlie asks as he and Rex enter the bedroom, to find Constable Patel standing over a black leather shoulder bag, his disposable gloved hand pointing inside. "Right, what have we got here?"

"Careful Sarge, there could be sharps in there, I spotted a syringe," Constable Patel explains.

"Great work Patel," Rex congratulates the constable, slapping him on the shoulder.

Charlie carefully empties the contents of the shoulder bag onto the floor. "Can we get this lot bagged up and to the lab for fingerprint and DNA analysis a-sap? Patel, I'll get you to take your car there directly and ask for Marama Mason, she's heading the forensics on this one for us."

"Sure thing, Sarge," Constable Patel replies.

Rex is frantically writing in the evidence log. "Syringe, with needle attached, bottle of morphine... is there a batch number on the bottle, Charlie?"

Charlie replies, "Yeah, SFX29555G78. Got that?"

Rex tears off the sheet from the evidence log. "Right Patel, all lights and bells, go like the wind man so we can make that arrest stick today!"

"Roger that!" Constable Patel beams as he takes the evidence sheet and bagged items and runs from the room.

Standing up, Charlie comments to his partner, "Right, let's see what else we can find, but I believe that's the key."

"Shall I phone Burns and give him the good news?" Rex asks.

"Go for your life, Rex," Charlie smiles. "I think we might be having another beer or two tonight."

"Just as well we booked another night, eh?" Rex smiles as he reaches for his phone.

*****

Zac looks at the online bookings for accommodation. "Yes, looks like we're going to be pretty quiet as I'd suspected."

"Early days, Zac. You never know, we might be one of the few 'earthquake-proof' hotels over the holidays," Freya replies positively.

"You could well be right," Zac agrees. "Have you heard from Dimitri? I'm just thinking about your contract and making those payments."

"I sent him a text and he replied saying he'd call in to discuss the project," Freya replies, looking at her watch. "Oh geez, he must be just about here, I'll check how Micco is for some baking."

Walking out to the coffee caravan, Freya sees Dimitri and Micco having a great laugh.

"Hey Boss, what are you doing out here?" Freya asks. "I was expecting you inside."

"Ah, there you are Freya," Dimitri answers. "I was just ordering the best coffee in Wellington from the capital's most excellent barista! I was wondering where Micco had gone."

"Guvnor, you didn't tell me you worked for this gregarious Greek gentleman," says Micco.

"Oh, I can just see you two getting up to all sorts of mischief!" Freya laughs, sitting down at a nearby table, indicating to Dimitri to join her. "Now Dimitri, what did you want to catch up about? Did that last proposal make sense?"

"Funny you should ask – I've just heard back from the Minister that he would like us to go full speed ahead. Just where did you get that mad idea?" Dimitri takes the offered seat.

"Finland and Norway – they're streets ahead of the world in trying new education practices, with Sweden coming close behind. I heard the concept when we were working over there a couple of years back," Freya replies.

"I thought as much. The Minister is adamant that he wants us to improve New Zealand's OECD PISA rankings. For him it means a promotion within cabinet, so he's prepared to fund a short-term study." Pausing, Dimitri looks Freya in the eye. "I can't trust just anyone with this project, I need someone who knows the countries involved and has established connections, and I only know one person who fits that bill."

"Thanks for the offer Dimitri, but I've just got Portobello up and running," Freya explains. "It's very tempting, but I've got mortgage payments to meet and…" Freya looks towards Zac as he walks out to the courtyard.

"Ah, young love, eh?" Dimitri observes. "Zac, come over here young man, you need to hear this and talk some sense into your girlfriend."

"Dimitri! This is not the dark ages. I don't need my 'man' to make my decisions," Freya scolds.

"My bad!" Dimitri says, throwing his hands up. "Let me try again. Zac, please take a seat, I have an offer for both of you."

"You have my attention, Dimitri," Zac says, taking a seat next to Freya, instinctively taking her hand in his.

"Okay Zac, Freya, I'm going to pull out all the stops on this, but first a question," Dimitri says. "Do you have someone who can run Portobello on your behalf for four to six weeks?"

All business, Zac asks immediately, "What dates are we talking here, Dimitri?"

"Well, the Scandi school term starts around the seventh of January, so I'm guessing a bit of a holiday, travel time, and three to four weeks' project work – perhaps New Year's to the first week in February?"

"Okay, and what are you offering?" Zac fires back quickly.

"All reasonable costs paid for the two of you, flights, accommodation, transport, food, a new laptop and smart phone, and a sizable bonus on completion," Dimitri answers just as quickly. He writes a figure on a piece of paper, folds it and hands it to Freya.

"Wow, you've thought of everything," Freya says, shaking her head. "That's one very attractive offer. Any catches?"

"Just one. Our Minister is keen for some inter-ministry oversight, you would have a staff member from the BS Ministry as an observer," Dimitri answers. "But before I phone the BS DCE to go any further, I need to know if you're keen. As I said, I wouldn't trust just anyone for this project."

"How soon do you need an answer?" Freya asks.

"Today would be good, as I don't know how long the BS will take to make their decision, and you will need to start booking flights and accommodation soon," Dimitri replies.

"Give us a moment please, Dimitri," Freya says, standing. "Zac, can we talk?"

"Sure thing, sugar plum," says Zac, winking as he follows Freya towards the club house.

Once they have some distance, Freya turns to Zac. "Oh,

now I'm torn babe. I know I want to stay here and make Portobello the success I know it can be. But…"

"…but this is a once-in-a-lifetime offer, Fin," Zac finishes for her. "Look, I know Mum is keen to help out, but I'd need to check if six weeks is okay."

"It's a big ask for Zita," Freya says.

"Well, maybe not. If she can have Harry here, and maybe if Micco and Simon help a bit… just thinking out loud here, Fin…" Zac trails off, his mind clearly ticking over. "How much is the bonus?"

Unfolding the paper that Dimitri had written on, Freya glances at the figure, her face going white. "You're shitting me… this would almost pay the mortgage off!"

Looking at the figure, Zac whistles. "Well I guess I'd better phone Mum. You can't turn that down."

*****

"Thank you again for your co-operation, Mr Johnson," Rex says, handing the bach keys back to Bernard.

"It's Bernard, please. Look detectives, after Cat's overdose and then the earthquake, I'm a bit lost. Can you tell me what happens now?"

"Do you mind if I take a seat?" Charlie asks, before explaining. "This is strictly off the record, and if I was in your position, I would want someone to tell it to me straight."

"Yes, yes, please take a seat." Bernard waves at the chairs.

"Are you sure about this, Charlie?" Rex asks, then thinking on his feet, "Ah, I'll leave the room. What I don't hear I can't be asked about."

Once the door closes, Charlie begins, "Well Bernard, I'm only telling you this as Samantha Svensson talks so fondly of you."

"Thank you, Charlie, please go on," Bernard says.

"Okay, it's not looking good. Are you sure you had no idea that Margaret and Cat were involved in some way together?" Charlie asks.

"Ah… no. I've been a bit distracted with my own… ah… dalliance," Bernard blushes, before continuing, "although I did wonder why Cathryn insisted on meeting after hours at our place so often recently. I just assumed it was all work-related."

"So, it is possible that Cathryn and Margaret were having an affair?" Charlie asks.

"Well, I suppose it is possible, especially after seeing the footage that you asked Lewis to find," Bernard concedes.

"With the forensic evidence starting to stack up against Margaret being involved with Cathryn's death, we will have to bring Margaret in for questioning at the very least, but I would expect an arrest soon after," Charlie explains. "Do you know where she is now?"

"Margaret is at work. Like me, she has a new ground-floor office since the earthquake – hers is one of the meeting rooms next to reception," Bernard answers.

Charlie's phone beeps. "Excuse me, Bernard," he says as he scans the text. 'Cuz, puncture mark on the upper left arm consistent with a downward thrust, and the morphine batches match, need fingerprints and DNA. MM'.

"I guess I should see a divorce lawyer," Bernard says.

Standing, Charlie says, "That would be a good move, Bernard. Sorry, but our next stop is Margaret's office."

"Before you go, do you know where Samantha is?"

Bernard asks.

"Ah, yes, she's staying at the Portobello in Jackson Street, Petone," Charlie replies.

"Thanks Charlie, and thanks for your frankness. It's about time Margaret and I started living our own separate lives." Bernard stands and shakes Charlie's hand.

*****

Freya is beside herself; she can't believe she has just scored this fabulous project working in Scandinavia.

"Are you sure, Mum? It will be at least six weeks," Zac explains into the phone. "Thanks, you're the best! Okay, we'll start planning the dates."

"She said yes!" Zac shouts excitedly, picking Freya up and swinging her around.

"Oh Zac, you said you wanted to go to Scandi, and now I get to show you around," says Freya, overcome with happiness.

"I've checked and we're pretty much empty after tomorrow night, which is great as it'll give us time to catch up on finishing stuff around here," says Zac. "We can get some menus sorted, finish our interior renovations, tidy up the garden and maybe set up the club house and turret for back-up accommodation. It's amazing what you learn while on the job. I just saw where we could make a few more improvements after having all those guests here."

"Yep, ditto," replies Freya. "Now, time to check out your cold weather clothes as it's the middle of winter over there, and that includes your sexy thermals!"

"Now that's something I'd like to see you in," Zac laughs.

*****

"Rex and Patel, I want a thorough search of her office; hopefully you'll find something that she hasn't been able to retrieve since the quake. O'Malley and Moreau, you're with me, Chris, stay behind the officers," Charlie directs. The officers gather beside him as he strides towards the office entrance, while Chris the BS IT contractor follows.

"What are we doing, Sarge?" O'Malley asks.

"Tackling the target, O'Malley," replies Charlie. "Make sure you have the search warrant to hand."

As the officers enter the building, Charlie sees Margaret sitting at a table in the meeting room. "In here," he says to the others. Margaret looks up from her laptop as Charlie opens the door. "Margaret Johnson, please stand and keep your hands where we can see them…"

"What is the meaning of this! You can't barge in here!" Margaret cries indignantly.

"Margaret Johnson, you are under arrest for the murder of Cathryn Tennyson, anything you say can and will be used in a court of law. Moreau, cuff her," Charlie finishes.

"You are making a big mistake, young man. Just wait until the Commissioner hears of this," Margaret threatens. "You will all get the sack for this!"

"Moreau, O'Malley, put her in the van while we conduct the search," Charlie says, pointedly ignoring her threats as he picks up her laptop. "Chris, can you get this one open?"

"You can't look at my laptop! It's a breach of privacy!" Margaret calls as she is led from the building.

"This search warrant says I can," Charlie smiles, then turning to Chris, "Can you get in?"

"Too easy. She wasn't able to lock the screen," Chris replies, plugging in an external hard drive. "Shall I start on the deleted emails?"

Charlie's police radio beeps, then Rex's voice crackles, "We've found an interesting diary, Charlie, I'll see you in five."

"Bingo! A stack of deleted emails from Cat!" Chris says.

"Chris, can you check if there's any correspondence with the Police Commissioner?" Charlie asks.

"Yep, give me a sec… Ah, there they are… nothing stays deleted if you know where to look," says Chris triumphantly.

"Fantastic!" grins Charlie.

Rex enters the office holding the diary. "Check this out, Clara was right – you can just make out the pencil impression on the page."

"Today is just getting better and better," Charlie replies.

*****

As Sven looks up from her laptop, deep in thought, her gaze settles on the new arrivals walking into Portobello. Recognising her friends, she calls out, "*Hej* Bernard! *Hej* Katarina! *Kom hit!* Over here!"

Greeting each other with European kisses on each cheek, they take a seat around the table. "So what's with this rushed meeting?" asks Sven.

"Ah, straight to business, very Kiwi, *älskling,*" Katarina replies.

"Look Samantha, I know what we told you a couple of days back; this is very delicate, especially at the moment,"

Bernard starts.

As Sven reads both her friends' body language, slowly the penny drops. She listens intently.

"What with Margaret being arrested for Cat's murder, we just have to get real," Bernard continues. "I guess what I'm trying to say is that Katarina and I haven't stopped seeing each other."

"Sven, you know how much I love this man," Katarina adds.

"Whoa, back up the bus, has Margaret been arrested?" Sven asks.

"Yes, it's all been a bit of a blur this morning. I've been working with Charlie and Rex, and the Minister has been in my ear, and Dimitri…" explains Bernard.

"Dimitri from the Education Ministry?" Sven asks.

"Yes, that's the other thing I want to talk to you about," Bernard says. "Sorry, I'm a bit jumbled today."

"Okay, let me get this straight. Margaret has been arrested for Cat's murder, right?" Sven clarifies.

"Yes," they both answer.

"And you two lovebirds are still together?" Sven adds.

"Yes," they chorus.

"I knew it! Congratulations you two! So what happens now? And what's this about Dimitri?"

"Did I hear my boss's name?" asks Freya as she comes down the stairs into the room. "Oh, hi Bernard and Katarina."

"*Hej* Freya," says Katarina.

"Hi Freya," replies Bernard, "I'm about to make your friend here an offer, come join us." Then he turns back to Sven. "Our Minister wants us to send a BS representative with the Education Ministry's project investigator to

Scandinavia, who I believe is young Freya here. I would like you to be that BS representative, Sven. Of course all expenses would be covered by the BS."

"Are you serious, Bernard?" Sven asks.

"Would I kid around on this? Well, what do you say, Sven?" he asks expectantly.

Sven shakes her head. "Damn, Leo was right; he said I'd be back in Europe soon. I never believed him."

"Sven, you and me back in Scandi!" Freya says excitedly, "Mazarin and kanelbulle here we come!"

"Will the budget extend to a plus one, Bernard?" Sven asks.

"I'll see what I can do for the flights, but in principle, your plus one can be covered for food and accommodation," Bernard smiles.

"Then count me in!" whoops Sven.

"I think that calls for a celebration. Bubbles or coffee, team?" Freya asks, then adds, "We only need Flat White to make up the whole gang."

*****

The End
Ka Kite Anō

You are cordially invited to join our regular newsletter to learn more about the author's upcoming releases, entertaining blog posts, competitions, giveaways and much, much more at:

www.bachdoctorpress.com

or follow us on our Facebook page:

Hinemura Ellison and Ted Hughes

GLOSSARY

Acronyms

JAFA	Just another Fucking Aucklander
OE	Overseas Experience
DQ	Drama Queen
OSH	Occupational Safety & Health
BS	Big Super Ministry
JAB	Judiciary Advisory Board
WTF	What the Fuck
FFS	For Fuck Sake
HSP	Highly Sensitive Person
BIC	Kiwi brand of lighter (back in the day)
OECD	Organisation for Economic Co-Operation and Development
PISA	Programme for International Student Assessment
DCE	Departmental Chief Executive

Phrases and words

Shebang	And all that 'stuff'
Tosser	Jerk, loser
Palaver	And all that 'stuff'
Plonker	Jerk, idiot
Frog and Toad	Up the road
Gassing away	Talking away
Sheeple	A group of unaware people
Handbags at Dawn	Fight, scrap
Little Possie	Little place, area
Red/Yellow stickering	Condemning a building unsafe due to an

	earthquake and engineer's report
Perving	Looking at
Empath	Sensitive, intuitive person
Theosophy	A society dedicated to universal brotherhood of humanity, based on both eastern and western philosophies and science
Bubbles	Sparkling wine or Champagne
Noddy	An idiotic person
Hori	An offensive derogatory term for someone of Māori descent.
Remuera Tractor	Range Rover

Māori Dictionary

Waka	Mode of transport, boat, car
Hīkoi	Journey
Māori	NZ indigenous people
Hui	Meeting, get-together
Te Reo	The Māori language
Marae	Meeting place
Te Ao Māori	The Māori world
Whakapapa	Family
Tupuna/Tipuna	Ancestors
Rongoā	Māori medicine
Whare	House
Tohunga	A skilled practitioner
Rangatiratanga	Authority, sovereignty
Aotearoa	New Zealand
Maunga	Mountain
Awa	River
Moana	Ocean, Lake
Tōku Ingoa	My name is
Pepeha	Greeting, where you are from
Tangata Whenua	People of the land
Tūrangawaewae	Where you are from
Whānau	Family
Matariki	Māori New Year

Ata Mārie	Good Morning
Mōrena	Good Morning
Ka Kite Anō	See you again
Papatūānuku	Earth Mother
Whakataukī	A wise proverb or saying

Swedish Dictionary

Alskling	Darling
Scandi	Scandinavian
Skål	Cheers
Hej	Hello
Kom Hit	Come here
Mazarin	Swedish pastry
Kanelbulle	Swedish pastry

Samoan Dictionary

Seki a	Sweet as
O ā mai 'oe?	How are you?
fa'afetai	Thank you
manuia	Cheers
palagi	A European person
Talofa Lava	Hello
toe feiloa'i	See you later

Main Characters

Freya (Isobel Nilson)
a.k.a. Fin — The heroine, first bestie of the Trinity

Sarah Nilson	Freya's mother
Wolfe Nilson	Freya's grandfather
Lois Nilson	Freya's grandmother

Nils Nilson	Freya's father
Samantha Ann Svensson a.k.a. Sven	Second bestie of the Trinity
Clara James a.k.a. Flat White	Third bestie of the Trinity
Zachary Tyler MacLean-Smith	Freya's old school friend
Zita MacLean-Smith	Zac's mother, Freya's godmother
Harry	Zita's dog
Marty MacLean-Smith	Zac's father
Simon Brown	Conservative bank manager
Mr Tombe	Lawyer from Smith, Smyth & Tombe
Charlie Rogers	Detective Sergeant
Rex Croft	Detective
Marama Mason	Charlie's cousin and forensic officer
Micco	Turkish coffee caravan entrepreneur
Leo	Palmist
Evelyn	Numerologist
Timmy	Leo's Border Collie dog
Dimitri	Freya's boss at Ed House
Martin Jacobsen	High Court Judge
Donald Church	Property developer
Judge Chute	High Court Judge
Malcolm Prendergast QC	From Russell, Whitaker & Prendergast
Thomas Harris	The Choir Boys' Gang
Damien Bradshaw	The Choir Boys' Gang
Jack	Clara's absent boyfriend
Bernard Johnson	DCE, Sven's boss at BS Ministry
Margaret Johnson	Bernard's wife also a DCE
Claudia	Clara's work colleague
Cathryn Tennyson (Cat)	BS HR Director
Lewis	BS Security
Chris	BS IT contractor
Carmen	BS Senior HR Advisor
Lloyd	BS Mailman
Nigel	BS Recruiting Manager
Ernest	Nigel's Boyfriend

Isaia	Zac's gym buddy & DJ
Moana	Isaia's wife
Talia	Isaia's daughter
Loto	Isais's son
Sefina	Isaia's aunt
Paulo	Zac's gym buddy & DJ